DEAD OR DISAPPEARED

A Jack McQueen Novel

David P. Fraser

Ascent Aspirations Publishing

Cover Art by Patricia Carroll (www.patriciacarroll.ca)

ISBN 978-0-9878357-8-9 (paperback)
1. Abduction—Fiction. 2. Detective Investigation—Fiction.
3. Identity—Fiction. 4. Memory Loss—Fiction.
5. Childhood Trauma—Fiction. 6. Drug Trafficking—Fiction.
7. Human Trafficking—Fiction. 8. British Columbia—Fiction. I Title.

Library and Archives Canada Cataloguing in Publication

Title: Dead or disappeared / David P. Fraser.
Names: Fraser, David, - author.
Description: First edition.
Identifiers: Canadiana (print) 20230586759 | Canadiana (ebook)
20230588115 | ISBN 9780987835789
(softcover) | ISBN 9780987835796 (ebook)
Subjects: LCGFT: Detective and mystery fiction. | LCGFT: Novels.
Classification: LCC PS8611.R38 D43 2023 | DDC C813/.6—dc23

For Patricia who inspires me with love, music, and art.

DEAD OR DISAPPEARED

CHAPTER 1

My face hit the pavement outside Brogans. I hadn't seen it coming. All I could do after that was lie stuffed in the trunk of a blue Honda Civic. I smelled used crankcase oil and blood from my scraped face. I heard the hum of fast tires. Freeway. Faint murmurs of conversation from the car's interior.

I wriggled around and, ignoring the pain thumping on my face, tried to kick out the taillight assembly but hit mostly metal. So much for getting a view of where I was going. Think, Jack, think. Who were these guys? Who had I pissed off? Couldn't be anyone I was after since work had been slow. After the kick, my knee told me I needed a few more shots of Scotch, but the trunk was devoid of amenities.

I heard the tires slow down. The car went up a ramp and stopped. If this were a TV show, I'd come out feet first, send those two goons hurtling across space with one kick, spring out of the trunk, dive across the concrete, avoid a spray of bullets, grab a gun that had come loose from goon number one's jacket and start shooting. Yeah, that's what I'd do. Right.

I stayed still and reflected on my earlier encounter with Chief at Brogans. Did these clowns have anything to do with him and his problem?

Brogans was a near-authentic old-time bar in Vancouver. Dark, jazz-smokey, and quiet. A place where I could drink in peace and scratch a brooding itch that never left me. I came here to think and make notes to myself on my phone. At Birken Psychiatric Hospital they'd had me use a cheap recorder to capture my feelings as raw material. I was fragmented glass, twitchy, nursing a beer and single malt in a corner when I noticed a tall First Nations guy come in. I knew him. Chief. Why was he here on the mainland at Brogans? He walked up, scraped out a chair beside me, and fell into it like a bag of rocks. How did he know to find me here? I hadn't seen him in years, and never in Vancouver.

"Jack. I hardly recognized you."

I swallowed a mouth full of pale ale and gave him my poker face. It was strange that he'd found me here. I played along. "Thanks. Do I look that bad?"

"Well, it's been a long time." He slouched in the too-small chair. He wore greyed-out jeans that had once been black with a blue flannelette shirt, and a yellow baseball cap turned a little to the side. I knew him from the Island when I worked for the force, Royal Canadian Mounted Police, RCMP. He wasn't in charge of the Snuneymuxw council, but everyone called him Chief because he had such lofty ideas, had a lot of pride in his heritage, had a big ego, and threw his weight around like he was the boss.

"Sure has," I said. "How many years?"

"At least three."

"Do they still call you Chief?" I motioned to the waitress and pointed at our drinks.

Chief laughed. "I am the chief. Someone's got to do it."

He had the skills. I looked around the room and sure enough, he had an entourage. Two guys lurked close to the door. One was short and stocky but all wire and muscle. The other looked like Chief Bromden from *One Flew Over the Cuckoo's Nest*. He was an immovable object, but he didn't have that far-off psych-ward look. Sharp-eyed, lot goin' on there. I looked back at Chief who sat across from me.

"So, you are the Chief? And you got your own band, raking in government handouts for sitting back and basking in the sun." I knew that would get him going. He looked at me, trying to decide whether I really meant it. "Just kidding," I said. The Scotch and beer chasers arrived. "You're not dropping in here for a social call," I said. "Your muscle at the door tell me that."

"Cheers," he said.

We touched glasses, gunned the shots, and followed them with long draughts of beer. I motioned for more shots. I remembered Chief in the old days. If he showed up at my door and I had a six-pack in the fridge, he'd stay until they were gone. If I were unlucky enough to have a twenty-four of beer, he'd stay till every drop was gone and I poured him onto the front porch full of tears, laughter, and sad stories.

"Remember that rattlesnake tail you hung around your neck when we went camping in the BC interior?"

"You remember that?"

"Thought you were really brave, biting off that rattle." Chief shrugged off the compliment. I looked him straight in the eyes. "Chief, what do you want so badly that you needed to track me down?"

"I need your help. I hear you keep yourself busy helping people find their lost ones."

"I keep busy." I wondered if he'd heard about my stint in Birken Psychiatric Hospital. I booked myself in three months ago, on my therapist's advice. Washington state; east of the Cascades, west of Spokane. Anger management and treatment for my addictions: alcohol and missing people. They told me there was some post-traumatic element mixed in with everything that went down. They got me making personal notes and speaking into the recorder. Memory flashes, jumbled words, and phrases. The process turned into a habit. I didn't share that stuff. Too personal. And who would understand?

"I need you to find some people for me," Chief said. "This is important, close to the heart."

I waited for it.

"My two nieces are gone. My sister, Louie, called me up and told me they left the Island on their own. I thought she was holding something back, but I didn't ask. But I knew it was the father. The girls are fourteen. Twins."

It had been a few years, but everyone remembers twins, Iona and Skye. I knew them before they were teenagers. Kids with laughter and constant smiles, ran around the reserve as if every day was a holiday. Their father was never around, but Chief doted on them. I looked him square in the eye. He'd aged a bit. The outdoors and the drink.

"Shit Chief, you must be worried. Is Louie in a panic? How long have they been gone?"

"Three weeks."

Not a good sign. "Police?" I asked.

He shook his head. That told me more than he really wanted to. We sipped Scotch and washed it down with beer. "Do you know if they are in the city, on the Island, or in the interior?"

I needed details.

Chief grunted. "Once their mom told me they'd gone, I came over to the mainland. It wasn't hard to find them. It was then Louie who told me their father had come back to the reserve. She couldn't control what he did with her or the girls. I figured those girls had enough of daddy messing with them and took off. So rather than take them back, I found them a place to stay, an upstairs bedroom in a small house owned by a widow in the west end. Nicer than their place on Vancouver Island. I paid the rent and made sure they went to school. Someone had to look out for them on the side. They didn't know I was having them watched. Then they disappeared."

"Disappeared?"

"One day it was all routine: school, back to the house, homework, you know. A roam around the neighborhood at night, hanging out as kids do. They had a friend, a girl who took them places. Don't ask me who she is. But one Friday afternoon they didn't come home. I had that short wiry guy at the door watching them," Chief motioned toward the entrance with his head. "But he didn't see them leave the school. Then I had people from the reserve looking for them without success, then I heard you were back in town."

"Chief. Three weeks is a long time. Sexual abuse is serious. And you've got to suspect the father. You should have gone to the police at the beginning. They have many ways to find people. Did you think that maybe the kids knew they were being watched and wanted out? Lots of kids run away and for various reasons."

"No. Someone grabbed them or got them to leave that school and disappear. Fuck the police. You think they're going to bother looking for runaway First Nations kids?"

I knew the police could have helped but I wasn't going to argue with him. Then again so many teenagers run away from home, it would hardly be news for very long.

"What makes you sure someone grabbed them?"

"My first thought was their father but then my gut started telling me they got into trouble with people far worse than him."

I could see his frustration. He couldn't find them on his own. He couldn't locate their father and he suspected something sinister had happened to them, something he wouldn't let his mind express.

"Do you know the exact date Iona and Skye left the reserve?

"It was in early May. I found them and convinced them to get back to school. They attended J.S. Henderson Secondary School until the end of June, then after the summer went back to school. I thought life for them was going well."

"What did mom think about them being off the reserve and in Vancouver? I assume you stayed in contact with her."

"I did. She was worried of course but I assured her that they were better off with my guys watching them than back on the reserve."

"Really." They're only fourteen for Christ's sake. "Did your sister report them missing at the Shaplow RCMP detachment?"

"No, Louie contacted me because she knew I'd do something to help her. She knew the police would push an amber alert to the media and post it on their RCMP website. The story would run on the news for a few days then what happened to the kids would disappear from the headlines. We don't have much faith in that, what with the missing and murdered indigenous women."

I understood the suspicion First Nations had of the police. I dealt with their hesitancy to talk to us when I was on the force.

"Do you fear they are in danger?"

"If someone grabbed them, yes, but they could be hiding," he said.

"From you?"

"I'm not sure."

"From whom, then, the father? You said he was messing with them."

"We don't talk about that stuff."

"Look Chief if you want me to help you find your nieces, you've got to give me something better than that." I thought of Jessica, my daughter, and how young kids are so vulnerable. I thought of my lost childhood I was still piecing together.

"Fuck," I said. "The father was physically and sexually abusing these kids. And he beat up and forced himself on their mother. I had my suspicions about him when I worked the force, but no one ever said anything."

"Yes. He's a big man and he's violent."

"Isn't that reason enough to go to the police here in Vancouver? Especially after three weeks."

Sweat ran down the side of Chief's face. He ran his fingers over the beer glass.

"I thought I'd find them on my own. I told Louie when they disappeared that I'd handle it, that I could keep the father away from them. I had my guys to help me, and she accepted that."

I could see his point about the police and believed he had good intentions, knowing about the trust issues regarding law enforcement. He wouldn't be here if he had other options. I leaned forward, close to his face, the booze fumes a bond between us. "Okay," I said. "Names. Details."

He pulled an inch-thick manila envelope from his jacket. "It's all in there. They might be in the city. They might be long gone. Keep this quiet. No police. It's not worth it getting them involved. The money is in that envelope."

I glanced at the package and looked up. Poker-faced. Didn't want to seem too eager.

"You need it, Jack."

I hesitated. Chief put the envelope in my hand and looked right through me. "Please get them back."

"What else other than money is in the envelope?"

"The girls' photographs, typed notes, the West-end address where they stayed before they disappeared, school letterhead, a phone number, and an address we traced when we kept an eye on them over the summer."

"When did you put this together?" I said.

"Last night. I finally realized I'd fucked up. I need your help."

Three weeks. Usually, if things were going to go well, there was realistic hope in twenty-four hours.

Chief finished his pale ale and downed his single malt. He stood up. I felt compelled to stand, too. He grabbed me around the shoulders and hugged me close and hard. I tensed a bit, then relaxed a bit. I'm not the guy-hugging type, but I fell into it. The tension in his shoulders reached in and hit me hard. Louie must be sick with worry. Chief had let her down and that ill-judged failure must be gut-wrenching for him. Even with my probing interrogation, I didn't have all the information. "Find them, Jack."

He turned and walked past the bar and out the door, his muscle trailing behind. The big man was the last one through, blocking the sunlight. I had a memory flash from the reserve when I knew the nieces. He was a strong silent young man then who rarely spoke but watched over everyone. Then the door swung shut and they were gone. When Chief put that package together, he must have had eyes on me, tracking my every move.

I heard a shoe scrape on grit and a key in the trunk lock. I lay still. They wanted me for something, or I'd be dead. The trunk lid yawned open. Dim incandescent light filtered down from a solitary bulb that hung from a ceiling. I heard, "Get out."

I rolled one leg over, then the other stood up and backed against the car. My knee was raging. Two shaved heads, black leather jackets worn and frayed—Value Village racks—black jeans, T-shirts, skull-and-teeth tattoos peeking out above the collars, silver ear-studs. I glanced back at the Civic, Wreck 'em-Race tired, a patchwork of Bondo and undercoat. I glanced at the plate and saw 976 Y. The rest was covered with duct tape. I looked toward the two leather jackets, wanting to call them Hans One and Hans Two. They had the same clothes, ink, and bling but one was scarred, one more stocky. They were almost identical, each of them no more than twenty years old.

We waited in a surreal tableau. We were in a parking garage, except the only thing parked was us, and a few scattered wrecks gutted for parts. Subsidized housing. A black Escalade came up a ramp at the far end. I caught 233 A on the plate before it passed me and came to a stopped.

A driver got out wearing a black suit and tie, chauffeur's cap, and white shirt. One Hans motioned with his head for me to get in. The driver opened the front-seat passenger door and waited. I moved to the open door and looked inside. I smelled cigar smoke on the upholstery blended with aftershave. With the smells, I felt dark anxiety I knew I should know from my past. Another vague memory buried. I got in and closed the door.

An altered voice came from the back seat, speaking through an intercom. "Be patient, Jack."

I turned my head, but the interior behind my seat was shielded by black-tinted glass. I tried to be polite. "Tell me what you want from me," I said. "Or fuck off."

"I told you, be patient."

I couldn't see the face, but there was something familiar about the voice, even with the distortion.

The driver put the car in gear, and we were gone. The two hired-for-the-day errand boys were left with their beat-up Civic and a few dollars for rough-up and delivery. But I wouldn't forget them like my therapist said I should. I never forget guys like that. For me that was a problem.

I focused with my head turned toward the glass partition. I couldn't see any details through the tinted glass. This guy was deliberate. From the voice cadence, I imagined an expensive suit, a designer label, and a tanned complexion.

"So, Jack," he said. "How's business? Are you still pretending to be an investigator, spying on adulterers, providing muscle for celebrities, and searching for all the stray kids in this city?"

I started thinking of him as Voice.

"You know, off and on," I said. "You find a few. Some never turn up."

I thought about Rory Kimball. Three years old. Gone missing from the mall while his mom tried on earrings and sampled make-up, her mind on how beautiful she looked in the mirror. That was a while back, but when kids go missing for more than two days, odds are they stay missing or are found dead.

I paid attention. We cut off Granville, headed south, turned at 41st Avenue West, and headed to Southwest Marine Drive. I liked this area; beaches, parks, trails through the woods, families out on Sundays, rain, or shine, to feed the ducks. Something sad in that. A pastime to lift you from a brooding that dwelled deep inside. Pacific Spirit Regional Park looked the same as when I was younger, but the bush was overgrown, a haven now for rag folks, demented shoeshine-polish drinkers, and crackheads.

The driver turned left onto Old Marine Drive and stopped at Beach Trail Seven, the car's nose facing the ocean.

"I need you to drop what you were asked to do at Brogans," Voice said. "This is important."

I waited for it.

"Forget about who you're looking for right now."

I faced forward and looked at the ocean. I wanted to know how this prick knew my business. "How long have you been watching me?"

"Don't ask."

"Or what?"

Voice laughed. It was a sad laugh with a sharp edge. I wanted to say, "Fuck you", but waited.

Voice tapped on the glass and spoke to the driver. "Give it to him."

The driver produced a folded package from his breast pocket. "Something to make you swallow," Voice said. "Keep quiet, Jack. Don't disappoint me. I'll check up on you from time to time."

I heard the door beside me open. The driver motioned to me, and I stepped out.

"You get home safe now," said Voice, and the door closed behind me. The Escalade spit gravel as it left. What was it about these teenage girls that were so dangerous to him? It wasn't a coincidence Voice abducted me. I sensed I knew him. He too had tracked me and was watching Chief as he moved about the city.

My Westie was still parked in the alley outside Brogans, and it would be hard to find a cab from here. I trudged back along Old Marine Drive. I passed the remnants of a gull in the grass beside me. An explosion of feathers. Its body was gone; a detached wing tinged red with blood. A hawk, I thought. A decisive death and I could imagine the strike. The swiftness. The shock. From my pocket, I pulled the recorder out, pressed the button, and spoke my thoughts into the microphone.

I am back in memory.

> Feathers in my hair. Green feathers and sequins on yellow leotards. Cigar smoke. Aftershave. A smooth hand takes me by the wrist. I dance on top of someone else's leather shoes. His huge feet lift my legs, one by one with every step he makes.

I made it out to S. W. Marine, where civilization buzzed with traffic. I peered into the envelope. I was holding a chunk of cash, maybe five-large. Enough to last a while. It had been a long sad walk up from the shore, past unconscious meth addicts, and sleeping bag ladies among the shrubbery. I was still thinking about the scattered gull feathers and the man holding the dancing boy.

I hailed a cab. Inside, I scanned through Chief's envelope. I couldn't focus. I'd look at the details later.

The Westie was where I left it. I was tempted to step back into the bar, but climbed into the van, put the envelopes in my black duffle where I stored a flashlight, binoculars, and other investigative gear along with extra clothes, my latex resistance bands, and two palm-sized, dollar-store notebooks for case details. I tilted the rear-view mirror down and looked at my face. A landscape of scrapes, bruises, and dried blood. Then I headed out toward Mark's marina where he owned and operated a ship-repair business near the City of Delta.

It was dark but not late in the evening when I got there. The marina sat beside the Fraser River and its muddy flow. A ten-foot chain-link fence topped with razor wire surrounded the compound—Mark's gated community, such as it was. I unlocked the gate, drove in, locked up, and opened the shipping container I'd called home since I came back from Birken.

From Birken two months ago I caught the train to Seattle, then a transfer to Vancouver. Mark waited to gather me up. An old friend who'd do a little of this and that, when I had an investigation on the go.

Mark had been in my life for quite a while. No connection to the RCMP or the military. He was a guy who stuck with me. We used to fish, and harvest oysters on Vancouver Island's west coast. He was an American citizen who drifted across the border after the Gulf War and decided to stay in Canada. Mark's wife at the time had a furniture finishing business called Strippers and he did the heavy lifting. I met Mark when Del, my ex, was in a renovation phase and needed a table and chairs refinished. Mark and I had stuck, even though nothing else had for him or me in our marriages.

The container had plywood walls, a single bed, Sally-Ann's desk, a wooden chair, and an overstuffed recliner. I poured the last shot from a heel of Scotch. It burned but told me I was home for now. The night was early, and I didn't want to disturb Mark. I dumped the contents of Chief's envelope onto the desk.

I didn't want to think linearly. I wanted to get a feel for things. The twins' photo: they looked like they could pass for seventeen or older, but I knew they were only fourteen years old, identical, with dark hair, and androgynous. Their heads were close together, arms around each other's shoulders. Couldn't tell if their eyes were brown or blue. Two other photos showed them separately. Younger. Maybe grade school. Taken on photo day, all smiles on the same backdrop. I stared at those two photos closely. I remembered how Jessica looked the same. Something about a happy smile. No hidden agendas. No secrets making them cry at night. Seeing the younger pictures took me back to working on the RCMP force, thinking about how I'd made it a point to cruise the First Nations reserve that was located on the Georgia Strait in Shaplow. I got to know the kids. These twins were a hit. Smart. Athletic. Everyone liked them.

There were other pictures, deeper in the pile, along with a typed sheet of paper with their names: Iona Stewart, age 14, black hair, brown eyes, 5' 5". Nil on illness and deformities or mental health conditions. Skye Stewart. Identical information. The address showed Cougar Creek Road, Shaplow Lake, BC. Shaplow Lake where I grew up. Where I worked on the force. I thought of Chief. He got to me. I thought I'd left the Island forever, and this assignment might drag me back. I looked at the puzzle pieces on the table. They were abstract art.

Then I looked up to my notice board attached to the wall. Gone-missing posters, snapshots, newspaper clippings, memorabilia, anything that struck a chord—old family photos, cards, and typed-up quotes. Stuff I couldn't get rid of. But what I saw there was only the tip. The rest was back on Vancouver Island with the buried boy.

At Birken, they'd worked on my memories about that buried boy. Therapy to curb the anger and unlock the root causes. Right. They put me in a fridge. Let my blood slow down. Floated me in a warm saltwater tank, with no light until my mind slowed down. Did it work? Fuck no. Got me recording. Dreams. Memories. Scant stuff. How I wanted to kick the shit out of those orderlies who were 'just doing their jobs.' Right. Sadists.

I put on a CD. Georgette Frye sang about how she'd rather go blind than see her man walk away. Maybe these girls weren't abducted, weren't locked up somewhere, turning tricks in a cellar. Maybe they were on the lam. A hunch as I looked at the pictures. They were twins, identical but different in the photographs—one with long black hair, the other with a tomboy brush cut, confident and macho. I had their west-end home address, two journals, a letterhead note from a school, a scrap of paper with a phone number, a business card from a tattoo parlor, and a mystery address at 349 Anderson. No newspaper clippings. No surprise there. Missing kids happened all the time. If the kids were little, the media took notice. But runaways and street people were the disappeared that no one cared about.

I looked over all the stuff, read the note, looked at the pictures, and scanned the journals until I developed a sense for these teenagers. As Georgette wound up her CD, my gut told me these two weren't in the city anymore. I'd check these leads and gather more data before I decided where to look for them. I wondered if the Chief had followed up on this stuff, gone back to the home address in the west end that he'd arranged for the girls so they could be safe and go to school. The other address was a mystery he hadn't mentioned. I'd find out soon enough. I looked at the other envelope, from the Escalade encounter. I leafed through the bills. It was enough to keep me in juice for a while, pay Stacie what I owed her, and send some work Mark's way. I scribbled the partial plate numbers and letters for the Escalade and the Civic on a notepad and ripped the paper out, walked out of the container, and hammered on the door of Mark's trailer.

Mark opened the door. He stepped back and studied my face. In the overhead light, I knew I looked awful.

"You look like crap," Mark said.

Mark wore a gray-white T-shirt that fit him so tight it had to be uncomfortable. He'd let himself go since his army days, but he worked hard repairing boats, so there was linebacker muscle beneath the flab. I wouldn't want to mess with him.

I stepped in while he returned to his recliner.

"You should see the other guy," I said. "I'm too old for this. I don't bounce back like I used to."

I was not too old, but I was tired of the abuse my body had taken over the years. At five-ten, I wasn't exactly cut out for roughing it, but I was solid. Kept myself fit. I had that rugged look some ladies told me they liked.

"You look like you're working on a case," Mark said. "I can always tell. Spit it out."

I gave him the details from my meeting with Chief at Brogans, my abduction, and the warning to drop the case. Mark listened until I finished. I expected him to jump in with probing questions, but he went in another direction as if he didn't want to get involved in my detective problems.

"She called for you last night," Mark said.

"Really?"

She was my ex-wife, and the mother of my teenage daughter, Jessica.

"Del didn't say what she wanted. She was angry you weren't here and said you never answered your cell."

"My cell! Where was it? Fuck. I was supposed to pick up Jessica. Tuesdays. Jazz-dance classes. Forgot. I was detained."

"You're going to fuck it up," Mark said. "You won't even be allowed to see her. If you jerk Del around when it comes to custody, the court won't see you as reliable."

He was right. All my life, I'd tried to cram as much as possible into too little time.

"I need you to do something for me," I said. "I have two partial plates: 233 A on a black Escalade, and 976 Y on a blue beat-up Honda Civic. They were involved in the rough-up I had today."

I reached into my pocket, and I dropped some cash that was in Chief's envelope on the coffee table. "Will you find out who owns those vehicles?"

"No sweat."

"I'll be gone early in the morning. If Del calls again, tell her I lost my cell. Tell her I'm sorry. No. Don't tell her anything. You haven't seen me in days, and you're worried about me."

"Oh yeah, that'll work."

I closed the screen door and stepped out into the moist delta air. I needed to sleep and be alone. But before I slept, I listened to bits and pieces on my recorder. One image took me back to Vancouver Island and the buried boy. A sad horn played a quiet riff inside me. The kind that can cut through a person's ribs and leave him exposed, without the bleeding.

CHAPTER 2

I woke early and I forced myself to do two sets of pushups. It always served to settle my mind and kept me from falling apart. The repetitions put me in a calm state. When I was done, I recorded what came to me.

> "Out of darkness, where lichen live on stones, shards of glass,
> a night train comes through the fog."

I went out to the Westie, with its front bumper nosed against the chain-link fence. My cell was on the floor on the passenger side. I checked messages. Del had left a few abusive words. Six calls. Escalating. Stacie, too, had left a few frantic messages. I rang Stacie. I knew my family was more critical, but I couldn't deal with Del right now. I couldn't eat humble pie. Work was work. Stacie employed me, as a bodyguard for clients and for investigative work off and on for her business, Triple AAA Security & Consulting. As well, Stacie and I worked together when I had my own cases.

"Hi Stacie, it's me."

"Where have you been?"

"I know, I know. Del called, didn't she?"

"Only about a dozen times. Didn't you remember? No, don't answer that. You forgot. One of these days, Mr. McQueen, you will lose everything."

"Thanks for putting up with this," I said. "I have a client. I need you to do a few things."

"You haven't paid me in weeks."

"I can pay you today. I'll slip by in an hour." I hung up before she could wade into me about money or my family.

Stacie and I had a strange relationship. Sure, I worked for her company. But for my own investigative work, to my mind at least, I saw her as a personal assistant who worked only for me. I knew she had a thriving business, and really didn't need me bothering her with my stuff, since half the time I couldn't pay her and the other half I was late with the money. I really didn't know why she put up with me, but she did.

An hour later, after stopping in a Staples and photocopying everything in Chief's envelope, I pulled up to Stacie's small bungalow on a quiet tree-lined street in East Hastings. A sign beside her driveway said Triple AAA Security & Consulting. I walked past the sign and down the driveway to the back entrance and stepped up onto the glassed-in porch. I peered through the antique French doors and saw her at her desk. She waved me in. "Well, Mr. Jack McQueen, what cougar dragged you into my neighborhood? And what did you do to your face?"

"Don't ask. Nice to see you, too, Stacie."

"Don't nice-to-see-you-Stacie me. You haven't paid me for your last job. I'm not even sure how you feed yourself."

I dropped an envelope with some cash on her desk. "That should turn you back into Stacie Sunshine."

She thumbed through the bills and put the money in her top right desk drawer. "It's more than you owe me. I'm worried about your face."

"Don't be. Scrapes and bruises. Looks better today than yesterday."

She had a warm thin smile on her face, and the light from the side window caught her cute but not necessarily beautiful face. She was a small young woman, not yet thirty, with a tight frame that she kept in shape with yoga and kickboxing, though in denim and a loose-checked shirt, it wasn't obvious. I sank into a soft chair and set Chief's package on the glass coffee table. Stacie remained at her desk.

"I have work for you," I said.

"When I saw the extra, I was afraid of that."

I stood up and I gave her an envelope with the photocopies of everything Chief had given me. "I need some research to go along with my legwork," I said.

"Well, I'm glad to hear you'll do the legwork after that last job. I may be fit, but I will not do that shit for you anymore."

It sounded like she'd rehearsed her lines. "No more shit," I said. "I'm a little short on leads for this one. I need you to follow up on some data. It might turn up nothing, but I want the larger picture."

"Shoot." She leaned back in her chair and rolled a pencil between her fingers.

I told her about Chief and how we were close once and showed her what I had. I said I'd start with the school, J.S. Henderson Secondary School, the tattoo lead, Lobelia's Lair, and the addresses, 349 Anderson and the west end address, where Chief had arranged for the girls to safely stay. See if I could flush out some detail. "Can you search the usual records?" I asked. "Civil and criminal court, police reports—"

"Spare me the details. I know what I'm doing." Stacie scrutinized me with a long stare, then leaned forward on her elbows.

"Right. The usual records."

"So, this is what's kept you from picking up your daughter for jazz-dance class," she said. "And kept you from answering your voice mail and assuring Adele you were still alive enough to be your child's father?"

Stacie used Adele rather than Del because it was more formal. Distant.

"Take it easy," I said. "Is there someone in your life now?"

"Don't change the subject."

Stacie sometimes played for the other team, and I knew she knew I knew. I wasn't sure what her current relationship status was, but she tended to get cranky when things didn't go well. "It's a long story," I said. "I forgot. Maybe you'd forget too if someone roughed you up and stuffed you in a car trunk."

"You got stuffed in a car trunk? I wish I'd seen that."

"Messed up my schedule, believe me."

"Maybe, but I'd have found a way to pick her up."

I knew she was right about staying involved in Jessica's life—but given the circumstances, I could not have done that. "Got to go," I said. "You're right. I'll do better. I'll call you."

As I went out the door she shouted, "Better call Adele first and find a way to talk to Jessica. Get back in the moment. Grow up. Start being a real dad."

I had it coming, but I didn't show her she'd hit a nerve. Instead, I gave her a wave on the way out. Perhaps it would never be any different in my life. I breathed in, closed my eyes, and let the air out. Then thumbed the recorder.

> "A real dad, sweet rye whiskey sting, mouth against my ear
> bare feet perched on scuffed boots, dancing in a kitchen
> his body bouncing off the walls."

CHAPTER 3

I drove to J.S. Henderson Secondary School. From its location, I realized it was a factory farm for inner-city adolescents, an old, imposing brick building with wide stone steps and impressive wood doors with brass footplates. The building's two towers reflected its prominent position in a bygone era where education was valued, and teachers respected.

I'd always seen high schools as places of incarceration, holding cells for most. And, for a few aspiring souls, labyrinths to be negotiated on the way to freedom and—perhaps—better things. This place, though not a prison, still fit the bill.

I was greeted by two security guards and a metal detector. I was asked about my appointment. I'd phoned the school from the van and set a meeting with a vice-principal named Sanderson. Once I had my visitor's badge, I was told to turn right and enter the third door on the right. There I met an office counter staff member, who directed me to wait outside V.P. Sanderson's office on a hard-backed orange plastic chair that no one would ever steal.

I waited, feeling somehow sheepish as if I were in trouble and had to get my story straight before I saw him. Not too long into my ordeal, a truculent female student opened the door and stomped past in gothic attire, smacking black bubble gum. She looked at me like I was in the wrong place. I was beginning to think I was. Then Sanderson came out. "Mr. McQueen?"

I stood up and shook his hand. On the phone, I told him I was connected to the police. I flashed the ID I used for investigations. He ushered me into a tiny six-by-eight office with a window that looked out on the corner store across the street. I sat in another hard plastic chair, while he settled in behind his desk, on a typical padded swivel chair with armrests and a tilt-back. Ah, the power seat. Though I knew just how limited that power was for those in middle management, at the beck and call from above and below. I was surprised at how young he was. He couldn't have taught for more than five years, and now he oversaw discipline and all the odd jobs no one wanted.

I opened a folder with the official VPD crest stamped on the outside and took out the three photos I had. "We're looking for two teenagers, twins, Iona, and Skye Stewart. We believe they attend or did attend Henderson." I placed the pictures on his desk blotter, neat and squared and facing him. School officials tended to be suspicious and protective of their students, especially minors, so I waited patiently for the inevitable question.

"Why are you looking for these girls? Are they in trouble with the law?"

"They're missing. Are they still on the register here?"

"Let's see," Sanderson said. He swiveled his chair left to line up with his computer. He was checking the database, but I got the feeling he already knew these kids. He typed and then hit a single key like it was punctuation. "They're in the system," he said, "but they're no longer active."

"Last known address?" I asked. I knew this address from Chief's material, but maybe the school had a different one.

"I'm not sure we're at liberty to give that out."

"I respect that," I said, "but this is an official police investigation, and we need that data to help them."

"Help them? In what way?"

Sanderson thought a bit. He looked unsure. I assumed he wanted me out of his office so he could get back to the real vice principal's work: suspending kids, cracking down on poor attendance, and riding herd on the ten percent who didn't fit.

"They are missing," I said. "I don't have to tell you the odds of successfully finding kids who've been missing for more than two days."

Sanderson started to sweat at his temple. The room wasn't hot, and he seemed uncomfortable that the kids had been missing. Was it because he hadn't been doing his job looking after absentee students and was worried this would come to light?

He wrote an address down on a school notepad and passed the sheet to me. It was the same west-end address I already had from Chief's package.

"I hope that helps, detective."

"Thanks. This address, we've already got. Are there any other addresses linked to these kids?"

"That's it." He stood signaling I should be leaving."

"Can you tell me about these kids? Something that might help us find them: friends' names, behavior, interests?"

Sanderson took a deep breath and blew the air out through his nose. "The record shows they were in the tenth grade when they left. They were here for two grades, the end of grade nine and the beginning of grade ten. They kept to themselves and weren't too popular."

"No friends, then?"

"Not that I know of, but being the V.P., I didn't have too much contact. Not as much as their teachers. If anything, they got bullied. I remember now I had to discipline some boys for calling them dykes when they arrived."

"I guess they didn't play on any school teams?"

"I could look at the last yearbook, but I'm pretty sure they'll only have their class photos and individual form photos." He took a yearbook from a shelf and leafed through the activity pages. "There is nothing here."

I took a deep breath. "May I borrow a yearbook? I'll give you a receipt and return it once we're done with the investigation."

He paused. I thought he was about to say no, but then he said, "Sure, since it is official police business." He handed me the book. His hands were sweating. There was something more he wasn't telling me.

"Would it be too much to ask if I could have their timetables for last year and this year?"

He hesitated. "I can print out this year's, but I'd need to dig into paper records for last year, and frankly—"

"That would be great," I said. "I think that's all I need." I knew I'd pushed it almost too far, so I pulled a receipt book from my folder and wrote one out for the yearbook.

Sanderson printed the timetables and remained standing as they shot out of the machine. The cue that I had all I was going to get from him.

"Thank you for your help, Mr. Sanderson," I said. "I'll be in touch when I return the yearbook."

He ushered me from the office, and I walked past the orange plastic chairs, each occupied by a glum male student with pent-up nervous anger in his eyes. I passed the guards and the metal detector and walked out onto the street. Kids were everywhere. They sat on the steps and on the grass, leaned against the wrought-iron fence, and grouped in clusters outside the variety store across the street. Mostly guys with blue jeans hanging off their asses. No belts, and gym shorts underneath so their butt cheeks didn't show. They looked like inmates in an exercise yard. I made a mental note to come back to the variety store after I checked out the class pictures and timetables. Maybe I'd recognize some kid who took the same classes and was interested in talking.

The attendance pattern didn't jibe with Chief's story. I figured the vice-principal didn't know these kids were having difficulties, or he knew a lot more than he let on. The fact that the girls had arrived at the end of grade nine, was why their pictures weren't in the yearbook. They attended 'til June, then came back in the fall—and disappeared. They would have had all summer to get into trouble, maybe something they couldn't shake off once school started up again.

It seemed like when someone disappeared these days, no one followed up. Certainly not a vice principal, who was too busy handing out late slips and detentions. So where were they all summer? Chief didn't mention that. And what about his continuous surveillance? Then—three weeks ago—they disappeared. I thought of Voice. Again, what was it about these girls that could be so dangerous to him that he'd give me juice to call off the search?

Before getting into the Westie, I pulled out the photo of the girls and wandered around the front of the school asking random students if they knew them. Very few were even interested in looking at the photo. I came up empty.

CHAPTER 4

I headed the Westie further east to the address for the tattoo parlor. It was still morning when I pulled into the alley behind Lobelia's Lair. When I entered, a small mechanical bell rang above my head. I thought back to the corner store in my youth, with its comic books and ten-cent sodas, and how the owner would roust us out if we hung around reading at the back without buying.

Lobelia's Lair was long and narrow, the walls lined with tattoo posters. A girl sat at a back counter, flipping through a magazine. She didn't look up when I got there, so I glanced down at the page: a photo of a shaved pussy with two red hearts on either side of the cleft. "I wonder if you can help me here?" I asked.

She looked up. She was in her late twenties. Long tousled hair and thick eyelashes. On her breast below her neckline was a small feather tattoo with blackbirds breaking into the air. She had a thin white scar across her left wrist. "Depends," she said.

"You own this place?"

"Yeah. I'm Lobelia. Who's asking?"

"I'm Jack. I'm looking for someone. Two girls."

"Many people are looking for someone. It seems they never do find them."

"There's truth in that," I said.

I put the twins' photo on the counter and looked at the two hearts on the smooth pudendum. Those tattoos must have been put there with a great deal of pain. Lobelia saw me looking at the photograph.

"Oh, that. Hey, I don't do that stuff. I'm an artist. I create. I do all my own stuff. Not that stuff. If someone wants that, I send them down the street."

I pointed to the photo. "Do you know these girls? They're missing. Many people are worried about them. They want them home safe."

She focused on the picture. "It's hard to say. Many girls come through here."

I looked around; the place was empty.

"Okay, maybe not so many people come in here now, but I had a good business. Still do, you know. Who has the cash these days?"

"Okay, have you seen them?"

She took a long look. I watched her thinking. "Not really."

"Take another look," I said.

"You're not police, not working for them?"

"Hell no. Hard to trust the police these days, don't you think?"

I said that because it was what she wanted to hear. But I half believed it myself.

"Not sure if I've seen them. Do you want to look at my work?"

I went with it, since I knew she'd seen them, and I hadn't created any trust yet. She grabbed a huge binder and put it on the counter, facing me. Then she opened it and flipped the pages. "Did this for a guy who was into dragons and lizards and stuff. All original art by moi. Finally covered his whole body, you know under the collar and cuffs. Paid me enough to keep going. And this is my First Nations stuff. When someone comes in and wants something special, it sets off the creative juices and I go on a jag designing ideas that go way beyond. I'm part Salish, quarter, my grandmother, so I got roots."

I looked through the album with her and concluded that Lobelia was one talented woman. In different circumstances, she'd be a Georgia O'Keefe or an Emily Carr. "Your work is beautiful," I meant it.

She smiled. Were compliments rare for her? She looked back at the photo on the counter. "So, you're not a cop? Are you trying to help these kids?"

"It's what I do. Find missing people. The family's worried sick. I know them too. Damn right, I'm trying to help find these kids."

"Where are they from?"

"They're not city kids. They're from the Island. Reserve kids."

"Rez kids, huh," Lobelia said. She glanced at the picture again.

"I know you've seen them, right?"

She hesitated. "Yeah, I've seen them. One has a tattoo. One I did. A gorgeous dolphin. I put it curling over her ankle bone on her right foot."

"How long ago?"

"Oh, must have been three, four months."

"Have you seen them since?"

"Two days ago. They swung by, but they didn't buy any more tattoos. I was surprised. I thought the other one would get the same, being twins and then both would keep coming back, adding on when they could afford it."

"What can you tell me about them?"

"Well, they had these overnight trail backpacks, like they were going into the woods for a long time."

"How did they look, the kids I mean?"

"Identical, but they were different in a way one looked more like a boy but wasn't. They were in a hurry. Had that frantic look people get when they are late for an appointment and must get going."

"Anything else?"

"That's it."

"Why did they come into your store that day if they were in a hurry?" I asked.

"I wondered about that too. I had the sense that someone might be following them, and they came into the store to get away. But before I knew it, they said goodbye and were gone."

"Really." I picked up the photo and said, "Thanks, Lobelia. Don't stop doing your art, no matter what."

When I got to the door, Lobelia called out. I saw her shake her hair a bit and raise a hand. "Come back some time. I'll give you a great tattoo."

"Thanks. I might do that."

I'd got lucky. Three weeks missing narrowed down to two days ago and they were alive.

Back in the Westie, I phoned a number from a scrap of paper in Chief's envelope. I let it ring. No one picked up. I made another call. "Hey, Becky. It's Jack. I need a favor."

I sensed some hesitation, but she'd done work for me before. I didn't think she'd hold onto a grudge for the brief fling we had before I left the force. It happened over booze, after all, and no one could cast blame when both were into it. She asked me what I wanted. Her voice was clipped.

I gave her the number I'd just called. "I need an address… Good. Call me back. Thanks."

Becky was a former Vancouver PD officer retired early, then headed up an insurance company fraud squad for a few years before working for herself. She was tech-savvy. I was not. She could get what I wanted.

I spent some time asking around Lobelia's neighborhood, going into a few run-down convenience stores and pawnshops. No success. It seemed no one's memory except for Lobelia's stretched back farther than a day.

Becky called with the address. "That was quick," I said.

"Got to go." The line went dead

CHAPTER 5

I stood on the stone front porch of a stucco house, 394 Anderson in Oakridge. The girls' address was written on a scrap of paper from Chief's envelope. Same address the school had. I glanced at the dying sun and shivered in the chill coast air. I readied the girls' photos and an official-looking badge and rang the doorbell. Four rings later, a guy opened the door. He wore saggy black track pants, a T-shirt that said Bahama Mama's. He looked like he'd been sleeping.

I flashed the badge. "I'm working with Van PD. Are you the owner of this house?"

"What's this about?"

"A routine investigation. Do you own this house?"

"I'm renting it. Why, is there a problem?"

"We're looking for two missing people." I showed him the photos. "Do you know these girls?"

He stepped back, jerked his head up, and looked me in the eye. "What is this?"

"I'm looking for these kids."

"That's the second time today. I don't usually answer the door. Two guys came this afternoon. Man, I work nights."

"I'm sorry Mr... this is important," I said.

He didn't take my hint for his name.

"I don't know these kids. Told 'em the same. I don't know 'em and I ain't seen 'em. Nothing to do with me."

"Did you get the two guys' names from this afternoon?"

"Oh yeah, as if."

"What did they look like, then?"

"Man, I gotta get back to sleep."

"Help me out here. This is important. Could save some lives."

"Okay, okay. They were big guys. One had a suit, but he looked uncomfortable in it like he was a wrestler or something. It seemed he would be more relaxed in tights."

"The other guy?"

"Not as big but tall. He had on palazzo pants, wore gold chains, had a heavy watch, and rings on each hand. Like out of Ali Baba. He flexed his hands like he would punch me."

"Did you talk long?"

"No, two minutes. I told them the same as you, didn't know nothing and then they drove off."

"What did they drive off in?"

"What do I know about cars? It was an expensive black SUV."

Seemed like a guy who would know cars. Didn't all guys know cars? I started to wonder about his story.

"No chance you caught their plate number?"

"Didn't think."

"You're sure you don't know these girls?"

"Honest."

I sensed I had to keep this guy talking or he'd slam the door. "What's your name? For the record."

"Mike."

"Got a last name, Mike?"

"Burns."

"Have you lived here long, Mike?"

"No, my girlfriend and I rented it for a year since she got transferred here. I'm tagging along."

I decided we were done. "Thanks, Mr. Burns. You've been helpful. Oh, by the way, what's your girlfriend's name, and where's her new job?"

Mike hesitated for a moment, then said, "Laura Wells. She works for Hoskins Pharmaceuticals. Don't ask me where that is. We just got here."

He was hiding something. I could get Mark to cross-reference who Mike and his girlfriend were and see if they were legit. I turned to go, and he reached out with his left hand and grabbed my shoulder. I tensed. "Is there a reward? If you find them, I mean."

"There might be," I said. I stepped down the stairs. "Thanks again."

"If there is, let them know I helped you."

"Oh, Mike. One more thing. Where do you work these days?"

"A bit of this and a bit of that. You know. I'm in between something steady."

"Thanks, Mike."

I heard the door close as I headed down the steps.

I climbed into the Westie, turned the key, and punched the CD player. I drove off to Nora Jones' "Come Away with Me". I drove two blocks, pulled over onto the shoulder, stopped, and turned off the engine. I phoned Mark. "I need you to do more investigating," I said. "Find information on Mike Burns and Laura Wells currently living at 394 Anderson. Laura Wells apparently works for Hoskins Pharmaceuticals."

"I'll do my best. Will I see you tonight?"

"Maybe, but somehow, I don't think so. I have damage control to deal with." He knew what I meant and wasn't surprised that I hadn't dealt with it yet.

I drove across 41st, a straight road toward the west side, an active real estate area in the city. Prices were out of sight. Whole neighborhoods had changed because of the influx of international money and speculative greed. The area was a sharp contrast to the lower east side, where Lobelia worked ink magic and the urban poor found refuge from the mainstream expensive housing.

The address Becky matched to the phone number from Chief's envelope— 3360 West 32nd Avenue—was close to the university, and the park where Voice dropped me off the day before. I knew about these homes. Mansions sold for millions. Smaller middle-class structures were gobbled up by speculators, some left derelict until they were bulldozed for future monster homes. As I pulled up to the address, the old song "Trash is Cash," by a Nairobi hip-hop group came to mind. The house lurked in the dark, surrounded by overgrown foliage. The place looked abandoned. I waited in the van for about half an hour, watching. Nothing happened. A few dogs barked in the distance. No one drove by. No one walked by. I felt suddenly tired. This sad place took me back to Vancouver Island.

> I see three kids on a logging road, black outlines holding hands
> as they recede in the distance. Darkness closes in, and there are
> childhood thoughts of bears lurking in the shadows, and cougars
> waiting in low-limbed trees.

In the Westie van, I drifted off into sleepy memory and woke up to darkness. My thumb flicked on the recorder.

> "Before morning, it will rain, no time to think of bears

I flicked off the recorder, grabbed a flashlight from my duffle, got out of the van, and walked across the street to the house.

CHAPTER 6

Outside the house, at 3360 West 32nd Avenue, nothing moved. I stood at the front door, which was set back on a veranda that had been ridden hard, left wet, and never saw a tender hand. A rough mat runner supported an entire ecosystem beneath my feet. After I searched for a doorbell without success, I knocked on the paint-peeled door. It swung open with the impact. Not a good sign. Neither was the odor that poured out at me.

I covered my nose and listened to the silence, then stepped inside. I let my eyes gather up what little light hung in the darkness. Stairs led upward from the door. A room on either side and a hall in the middle that led to what I assumed was a kitchen. I stepped to the left and felt my feet leave the carpet runner. The floor was hardwood, the old kind, laid in long narrow strips that you could sand down after years of use, traffic wear, dents, and piss marks from dying cats.

My eyes adjusted and I made out living room furniture, a small couch, and a La-Z-Boy chair arranged around a box television. A cheap lamp stood on an end table. I moved toward it. Hoped it worked. Felt frustrated in all this dark. I stepped closer and something caught my foot and spilled me across the end table where I clutched the lamp to keep it from smashing on the floor. I felt around for the switch. Didn't expect it to work but the light came on. I wasn't prepared.

Two bodies lay on the floor between the couch and the La-Z-Boy. Both male. They were lined up straight as arrows: feet toward the door, legs together, arms crossed like they were already in their coffins. A neat bullet hole in each forehead. Blood had pooled and dried around each head. The bodies did not exhibit rigor. There were also bullet holes in their hands and feet. Ritual? Torture? A signature?

I was two or three days behind whoever killed these guys. The dried blood, the absence of rigor, and their skin temperatures the same as the room gave me not a coroner's accuracy but a layman's guess. Did I leave now, forget I saw this? Or phone 911 and hang around to be interrogated? Did I wipe the lamp, the end table, and the door, or search their pockets and check the rest of the house? Part of me wanted to get the hell out, even forget hunting for the twins, and give Voice his money back. That's what Stacie would whisper in my ear. And what Del would say more harshly. But should I listen?

I rummaged through the pockets for wallets and extracted driver's licenses. No cash. I wiped down the lamp and the end table. I'd pushed the door with my knuckles, so I didn't worry about that. In the room to the right, I saw a dining room table. It was covered with plastic bags and brown paper wrappers and was dusted with powder. I picked up the powder with a wetted finger and rubbed the substance along my gum line. I felt the numbing. Cocaine. Yep. I went back to the lamp and held both licenses to the light. The names were Russian. I switched the lamp off, then turned on my flashlight and explored the rest of the house.

The entire house had been ransacked. The kitchen was a wash of broken dishes and strewn cutlery. Upstairs, the two bedrooms had been tossed. I looked through the debris with the lights on. A photo of the twins was in a cracked frame. I slipped it out from behind the glass. It looked more recent than the one I had. One twin looked like a guy now; the way the hair was cut, a shirt, not a blouse.

I remembered that kid in a cowboy shirt. She had a six-shooter cap gun when she was five. Firing off caps downtown while shopping with her mom. A sadness fell on me as I thought about that.

In the bathroom sink, I found a used toothpaste tube, a throw-away razor blade, and a cracked bar of soap. I decided to leave. I killed the lights and left in the van. The old VW engine was too loud in the stillness.

At the first convenience store with a pay phone outside—a rare breed since the world had gone cellular—I phoned 911 and reported a break-in. With staff shortages, the authorities might check on the place sometime tomorrow. They'd find the front door wide open. I needed to switch gears. I pointed the van to what had once been my home: Riverside Drive, North Van.

CHAPTER 7

I parked on Riverside Drive, steps from Del's door. I waited in the van building up my courage to face her wrath. A few cars passed by, and one stopped behind me. I finally got out and walked toward Del's house. I didn't see it coming. A Taser hit as if a concrete block smashed into my back. I went down on the sidewalk beside the van. A boot caught me under my chin, but I lashed out with my right foot and nailed a dark figure square on the ankle. I followed with my left foot and nailed his knee. He staggered sideways in his black leather jacket. The Taser was now in the gutter. I was up but felt groggy. We grappled beside a low brick wall, rose bushes neatly pruned, hedges trimmed and squared. I heard a car door slam, and another figure lunged at me. I twisted, used my hip to throw him, and followed that by smashing his face against Del's front wall. But that cost me. I saw a wire come across my throat from behind. I threw my arm up. He had me, a garrote, my arm stuffed up under the wire to prevent its tightening action on my neck.

The night was red. I gasped for breath. There was no control, only panic; blind, teeth-grinding, visions-of-the-void panic. The wire was tight and getting tighter. I felt the searing pain in my forearm, where the wire began to cut into my shirt. There were few options and little time. I stomped down hard on his foot with my heel. Caught his temple with my left elbow. The wire slackened. I pounded with my elbow until I was loose enough to twist, lunge and crack his nose with my forehead. He dropped like a stone.

Lights flicked on in nearby houses. I turned as a fist grazed the side of my head. Face-in-the-wall was back. Blood from my forearm ran into my hand. I drove my open palm toward his face as he began to charge forward, but the blow's slippery contact rushed past his chin. His full momentum hit me low and flipped me backward, over the three-foot wall and into the rose bushes. I got ready for what was coming, but suddenly he was gone. I heard two car doors thud shut, followed by screeching rubber. I caught a partial plate: 233 A. Black Escalade. I remembered Voice saying he'd check up on me. This was a tad extreme. Why bother attacking if they weren't about to finish what they started?

I trudged up to the house and knocked softly on Del's door. It opened a crack, and Del's eye peered out. I was afraid to face her, but now I had nowhere else to go, and I was too tired to argue with myself.

"Oh God, Jack," Del said as she opened the door a crack.

I wanted to be polite and say something simple like, "Can I come in? Can I lie down on the carpet for a moment?" Or something deeper: "Del, can you save me?" But I couldn't speak. She opened the door wider, and I lost my balance, as my knees buckled like a rusted chassis on a hoist. I tumbled inside with a half-twist, my face scraping across her waist. She caught me at the last second, and we both slumped to the floor. I was the Prodigal Ex-Husband, and the lost lover finally returned. Del pulled me into the hall, closed the front door, and turned the deadbolt. She sat me down in a comfortable chair in the living room.

"Christ, Jack, what have you done to yourself this time?"

I still couldn't speak. She brought a glass of water and a small plastic tub with warm water and soap. I let her clean me up until I could think straight. "Thank you," I said.

I didn't tell her that this mess I was in, happened right outside her door. Why scare her? Why let her accuse me of bringing my world into hers and threatening her and Jessica? The cut on my arm was superficial, not deep enough to damage muscle or ligaments.

"How do you manage to keep doing this?"

"I had nowhere else to go."

"Did you plan this, Jack, or was it spontaneous?"

I wasn't sure what she meant. Was this residual abuse, pent-up from when I'd forgotten to pick up Jessica? "Can I have something stronger?" I asked and pointed to the water glass. She brought me a Scotch. Neat.

"You've always been out to destroy the love in me," Del said. I looked at her and took a sip. The Scotch burned down my throat and settled in my empty stomach, like a warm peach left in the summer sun.

"And you do it so well," she said. "Never here when expected. And you always turn up like this. Battered. I'm not sure what breaks my heart more, the unexpected or the battered."

She was angry but full of tears she couldn't or wouldn't let go. "I'm on a case," I said.

"I'm happy for you, but why do these cases have to end up on my doorstep late at night? I hate the way you always manage to hack your way in and out of my life. Little by little, Jack, you're using me up. I'm almost empty."

I looked at her and saw the woman, but also the girl I fell in love with. "I'm trying to find two missing girls. Twins. I'm trying to save them."

After a pause, she said, "Have you ever thought about finding yourself, saving yourself, for God's sake!"

"I thought this one would be simple, but now it's complicated, and I seem to be in the way."

"Who did this to you?"

She meant the face scrapes from two days ago, and the near-death experience outside her door that left me with an arm that should have stitches. I didn't want to tell her about anything, but she was waiting. She still looked good; filled out pajamas and robe in all the right places.

"Stop looking at me that way," she said. "What's wrong?"

"No, no. You look good, soccer-mom good."

Del looked at me as if to say, was that the best I could do? "Yeah, sure," she said. "But Jessica takes jazz dancing. Or have you forgotten that! She missed the class. I had to stop everything and pick her up at school after she called me to say you were a no-show. By then it was too late to get her there."

"I'm sorry. I was beaten up bad, thrown in a car trunk, driven halfway across town, and left stranded."

"But you still forgot, right?"

I thought about it. "Yes, I did forget."

"I really don't know what to do with you. I don't need you anymore, but Jessica does, and you don't seem to care."

"I care. I really do, but I get caught up."

"Well, you'd better get uncaught up, because things are about to change. You've taken the better part of me, and I need to move on. So does Jessica."

"What do you mean, Adele?" I used her full name when I felt something grave about to descend. I loved Del, but Adele the lawyer, the power broker in a suit, was a different character. She was the one who gave me all the trouble.

I heard soft footsteps coming downstairs. Jessica was in her pajamas, sleepy-eyed, clutching a turquoise satin ribbon that was once a part of her "blanky." I remembered the various blankets, all the same, three-by-two feet with turquoise satin trim. And I remembered how each one wore away to small satin strips that she clutched while sleeping. Now even as a teenager, she clung to that last satin strip for comfort.

"Daddy," she said. "You're here. Oh, Daddy." She hugged me and nestled in on my lap. She was twelve, almost a teenager. Not much younger than the twins. "Are you staying?" she asked.

I looked at Del.

"Just 'til morning," she said. "Daddy will take you to school tomorrow." A smile spread across Del's face. A smile was good. I felt Jessica's warmth melt into me, her face snuggled in my chest.

"What happened to your arm? Your face?" Jessica asked.

"I ran across a road and tripped."

"Never heard of crosswalks, Daddy?"

Before I could make the explanation more complicated, Del said, "Up to bed with you, now."

Jessica gave me a kiss on the cheek and went upstairs. Del brought me a pillow and a blanket and pointed to the couch.

"I've got a big case starting tomorrow, and I must leave early. Get Jessica to school by 8:30. Can I trust you to do that? She'll get you up with her alarm." Del switched off the light and left me in the dark. I sipped the last of the Scotch.

Del spoke from the stair landing. "You know, it's really strange, but I can't get over you."

Before I could sleep, I slipped out the front door. I walked down the front path to the sidewalk then came in again and turned the deadbolt.

The next morning, I thought about Del's last words. It was strange, but I really couldn't get over what happened to me. I couldn't get over love, couldn't get over hate. Not that I hated Del; I knew I still loved her, though we were bad business together, too caught up in ourselves to let go and help each other survive.

I took Jessica to school in the Westie. I couldn't help but think of the twins' school pictures. Maybe they got dropped off like this. Maybe someone watched them, grabbed them coming or going from Henderson. If that happened to the twins, it could happen to any kid. Even my kid.

"Thanks, Daddy," Jessica said. "I like the noisy car."

"Sorry I forgot to pick you up the other day."

"That's okay." She released her seatbelt, gave me a kiss, and stepped from the car. "I wish you could be around more, Jack."

I noticed the daddy-to-Jack switch. What was coming? "I really do," she said. "Mom wants to take me to Seattle with her, and I'll miss my friends. I'll miss you. But I could live with you instead."

"What!"

"I'm going to be late. Think it over. I won't be any trouble."

She scampered off so I couldn't say anything. I watched her climb the school steps with her purple backpack. Del wanted to take her to Seattle. Jessica wanted to stay with me. All this was coming about because of my inability to be a real dad. I felt like I'd been tasered.

CHAPTER 8

I was still reeling from Jessica's comment when I pulled up before the West End address given to me by Chief and Vice Principal Sanderson. The twins had stayed there at the start of summer, living with a widow. I got out of the van, walked up to the door, and knocked.

A short round woman, maybe sixty-five, cute as a stubby boat came to the door with a smile, as if she expected a package. She was disappointed.

"Hello, ma'am. I'm Jack McQueen." I flipped out the standard credentials, then stuffed them back in my pocket. Then I showed her the girls' photo. "I'm doing a routine investigation on these two girls who rented a room from you a few months ago."

"Oh my," she said. "Are they in trouble?"

Everyone thought the worst. Must be the news. All the tragedy was delivered, deadpan, so we always expect bad things and become numb to them. The news needed a few happy dog stories. Border collie leaps out of the burning building and saves a kitten.

"No, no," I said. "We need to locate them. Let their mom know they're okay."

"Well, they were so nice. They were no trouble. Stayed in their room most nights after school. I baked them cookies in case they got hungry in the evenings. We drank tea. They told me all about Vancouver Island. I have never been there, but I've always wanted to find a nice B&B with a beach."

"What happened that they left? Weren't they going to school?"

"They were until the end of their semester. But when summer came, they went out all over Vancouver. They went back to school in the fall. One day I went shopping, and when I got back, they were gone. Didn't leave me in the lurch since the rent was paid, but they could have told me they were going." She wasn't angry; more disappointed.

"Do you know why they left?"

"It was the panel van that kept coming by, and they'd go out there in front like it was an ice cream truck. And then as I said, one day they were gone."

"What color was the van? License plate? Did you see the make and model?"

"Oh my, I don't know about cars. I know it was white, but it had mud on it, like they never washed it. I always looked out the window, so all I saw was the side."

"Did you see the make?"

"Oh, I couldn't tell you."

"Was there anything printed on the van?"

"No. It was a dirty white van. I'm so sorry. I know this must be important."

"When did you see this van?"

"It must have been early September. The rose of Sharon was in full bloom then." She wrung her hands on her apron like she was squeezing out tears. "I knew the two guys in that van were bad. Older. They had scruffy faces like they forgot to shave. There were other guys that came and took them with them. Those guys were younger, maybe twenty-one or so. They were too old for these girls. I saw a change in them over the summer and sensed they were getting into trouble."

"Mrs. . . ."

"Mrs. Milroy. I'm a widow. By renting rooms I make do. I do miss the twins since they helped me in the garden, and always tidied up when I baked, but they didn't have time to help me much as the summer wore on. I think the bad company affected their behavior."

"You've been a great help," I said. "Thank you, Mrs. Milroy." I turned to go, and she said, "Wait a minute, son."

She retreated into the house, leaving me on the porch. I felt like a paper boy, waiting for an old lady to shuffle back to the kitchen for a tip. Not a quarter, but a fresh-baked cookie.

When she returned, she said, "They left this," and handed me a photo of the twins thrusting their right arms into the air. They wore matching shell bracelets, strung together with nylon fishing lines.

Back in the van, I called Mark. I reminded him to investigate those partial plates again: 233 A and 976 Y for the Honda Civic and the Escalade.

CHAPTER 9

An hour later I entered Lee's Variety store across from Henderson Secondary School to check out the layout: video games and candy at the front, close to the till; coolers at the back; two rows for staples in the middle and a magazine rack across from the counter. Lee's Variety was crowded with kids, most of them up front. High-school kids leaned over the gamers' shoulders, bumped up against each other to watch these wannabes rack up their scores. I could see it was an addiction. I jotted down details in a pocket-sized notebook. Some kids came and went, crossing traffic like immortals, defying death to get back to class. Others lingered, drawn by the video game graphics and the sound. I saw them as empty fish reeled in, while the store's owner, without remorse, suffered them to spend money and waste time.

I sat in the Westie, five yards from the store. I watched the faces move behind the front window and studied the kids who came out. I had the yearbook open on the steering wheel, trying to spot faces from Iona and Skye's class. Guys and girls smoked, chewed gum, and tossed wrappers on a bungalow's front hedge next door. Who bought a house beside a variety store, across from a high school? What motivated them? Economics? Proximity to bus lines? Voyeurism? I imagined a parted curtain and a lone eye that watched a young girl's breasts in the late spring's heat. Then at the store's front door, I spotted a girl's face from the yearbook.

Two other girls and a guy had her cornered against the hedge. The guy stood with his hands in his low-slung pockets, holding up his pants, crotch seam around his knees. The two girls pushed her shoulders with their open palms. She pushed back, but with no conviction. The two girls stepped close, mouths flapping and fingers pointing. They started hitting her with their fists.

I stepped from the van and moved toward them. "Leave her alone," I said.

Hands-in-his-pockets turned and said, "Who the fuck are you, her dad? Stay outta this."

The two girls were too absorbed in pounding on their victim to notice.

"Where do you come off givin' me the eye?" one said to the girl.

"I saw you," the other one said. "Standoff my man, bitch. He's mine."

I moved in closer and flashed my official-looking badge. "Now get back to class."

I figured they might take me for a cop, or a school official. It worked. I didn't get any "Fuck you's." But the victim made a break for it, down the street. I told the bullies again to get back to class, then ran after the girl. It took two blocks to catch up with her at a bus stop. She turned and leaned up against the shelter. "Fuck off, man. Leave me alone. I didn't do anything. Who the hell are you?"

She was about fifteen, in jeans, two fleece layers, and a knitted wool hat. Each earlobe sported a silver stud. Another stud centered on her lower lip. Despite the mutilation, she was an attractive kid.

I was dressed in the extra clothes I carried in the van: blue jeans and a checkered work shirt. I knew I didn't look too official. "I need some help," I said.

"Yeah right, like all the other perverts around here. Leave me alone."

"I'm looking for two girls you know. They need help." I showed her a photo of the twins.

"I don't know them." She didn't even look at the picture.

"Look, I'm a private investigator. This is what I do. I try to find people who may be in some danger or trouble. I'm not going to hurt you. I need to find them before someone gets killed." That last word got to her. It was a little extreme.

"Killed!" She looked at the picture. "Who wants to kill Iona and her sister?"

"So, you do know them. Where can I find them?"

"Yeah, they're friends, or at least I thought so until they left suddenly."

"Left suddenly?"

"They didn't even say what was wrong."

"Did they tell you where they were going?"

"Nope. And that really pissed me off because I thought we were close."

"Did they ever mention any favorite places?"

She thought for a moment. Her eyes looked up to the right. "They loved the Island. They talked about it all the time."

"Vancouver Island?"

"Yeah, a place called Shaplow Lake where they grew up."

"Do you think they went there?"

"You know, if I think about it, that must be where they went."

I thought of the tattoo parlor. "Did either of them have a tattoo?"

"Iona did. A small dolphin on her ankle. I used to like tracing the outline with my finger." She stopped and swallowed hard to fight back tears.

She really was close. Closer than she was about to tell me. I could see the twins now with their trail backpacks, waiting for the ferry to take them home to the Big Island. My Big Island, too. "So, what was that about back there?"

"Oh, that? One bitch thinks I'm looking at her man like I want to steal him from her. They're all so fuckin' paranoid. Oh, 'you gave me the eye' and all that. Like they've got nothing better to do."

"So why don't you tell someone at the school?"

"Yeah, right. They will do nothing and if they do, it gets worse for me later, so why bother. I can handle it. They don't scare me."

I believed her. "Do you know if the twins were mixed up in anything?" If someone was making them do things?"

"I really don't know. They kept to themselves."

"Any change in their behavior before you lost track of them?"

"Come to think of it, the last time I saw them, they acted weird."

"How so?"

"They were in a hurry. They looked a little scared like they'd seen a ghost."

"Did you ask them about it?"

"You know I wanted to, but they were in a hurry. They didn't even say goodbye that day."

"How long ago?"

She mused a bit, then said, "Three days ago, I guess."

"Thanks for talking to me," I said. "It's been helpful." I paused and turned away, then turned back again. "If I find them, can I call you?"

Her face lit up for a moment. "Yeah, why not." She fumbled for a scrap of paper and wrote her number on it. "I'm Geena."

I felt her hand when she passed me the paper. It was stone-winter cold and too rough for a fifteen-year-old. I dug out a card with my number. Handed it to her. "In case you remember anything else."

I knew Geena probably had a phone number for the twins, but I was the one who wanted to be able to contact Geena especially if I found them.

I walked back to the van and phoned Stacie. No answer. I phoned Mark. No answer.

I thumbed the recorder.

"Somewhere in the distance a sad dog barks.

CHAPTER 10

By the time I drove across town and headed out toward the delta and Mark's marina, it was dark. The river and its braided outlets to the sea made this place flat and fertile. But even so, agriculture was a shadow of its former self, with falling wholesale prices, less initiative, and cheap trailer homes spreading outward from the city.

I pulled down a dirt lane and passed abandoned greenhouses with smashed panes. A tractor rusted beside a barn with missing wood siding; no doubt torn off for reclaimed lumber or firewood.

I arrived at the marina's front gates, but it wasn't gated so much as smashed, as if someone had driven through the gate with a heavy truck or a front-end loader. The gate's two buckled jaws gaped open. The chain was snapped and lay like a ribbed snake without its skin.

I pulled into the yard and stopped beside Mark's trailer. The outside light was on over the door. The screen door and the main door were open. My cargo container doors were ajar. I picked up a small pipe. I'd kept my handgun licenses but seldom carried a weapon unless I did security work for Stacie's company.

The steel pipe felt cold in my hand. I stayed in the shadows outside Mark's trailer. I didn't want to go inside. I didn't want to find Mark neat and tidy on the carpet beside an empty beer bottle and his paperbacks.

My first step onto the porch was a mistake. I heard gravel squeeze between my sole and the faded wood. Then I heard a gunshot and a dull thud on the cargo container's side panel. I froze. Mark's voice came from inside the trailer. "Come into the light, then don't fucking move."

"It's Jack," I said and stepped into the light.

"You bastard," Mark said. "What have you got me into?"

"Can I come in?"

"Are you alone?"

"Of course, I'm alone."

"Just checking. Yeah."

I stepped inside.

"Close the door."

I closed the door.

"Put on the counter lights. They're not too bright."

I flicked the switch. He sat in his heavy-padded chair with an MP-443 Grach, standard Russian military sidearm in his hand. A fifteen-shot magazine and a half-empty bottle of Laphroaig sat on the coffee table. He must have thought he was going out and planned to do it in style. The place was a mess. Tornado in one window and out another. Mark saw me look around. "Your container's trashed, too."

"Fuck."

Mark placed the gun on the chair's right arm, muzzle aimed at the door. I expected him to do a quick grab just for practice, like a gunslinger in the movies. Barney Fife came to mind; Mark wasn't goofy, just a bit shaky with guns. It had been a while since he'd been in the service.

I sat in another chair. I plucked a sort-of clean glass from the coffee table. "Do you mind?" I motioned toward the Laphroaig.

Mark poured us each half a glass.

"Where'd you get the MP-443?"

"Is that what it is? It belongs to one of the assholes who tossed this place."

"Oh, he just left it?"

"Don't be a smart-ass."

I sipped the Scotch. "Are you going to tell me what happened?"

Mark nodded. "I'm on the *Albatross*, the big schooner. It was this afternoon, and I was scraping down her upper deck.

"Well, I heard this crash, metal hitting metal and I looked up and there's a three-quarter-ton truck with a wide box that's plowed right through the gate. I knew it wasn't an accident. You don't pile on through a chain link gate by accident. So, I got scared. Two beefy guys got out of the truck like a mini-swat team. I stayed low and watched them. One's got a gun out and the other has an aluminum practice bat. I can't imagine why they'd be looking for me, so I figure it's you and some crap you're involved in. I stayed put, thinking they'd look around, find nothing and leave. But they trashed the place and found your container, shot off the lock. I think they took your computer. The guy with the bat took it to the truck."

"Fuck," I said. "I knew I shouldn't have let Stacie talk me into that computer. More stuff to worry about. Nothing worthwhile on it, but I guess they didn't know that."

"Hey, focus. I stayed low but must have moved my foot and made a noise on the loose-scraped paint on the deck because the other guy who was milling around down near your container looked up at the Albatross. He shouted something and came running for the ladder leaning against the bow. I popped up. A press of air pass by my head. I almost crapped myself. Then I heard a gunshot.

Fuck, Jack, I had to do something. I ran to the bow, still bent low below the gunnel. The only chance I figured I had was the loose anchor and its chain.

"I grabbed the sucker. I could hear footsteps coming up the ladder, no puffing so I knew he was coming fast and fit. I clutched the anchor in my arms and held it against my gut. Fuck it was heavy. Sitting here now I couldn't lift it, but in the heat of that moment, I did. I lined up where I knew the ladder was and dropped it. I saw a gun fly in the air as the anchor hit his face. The chain followed. The guy fell backward. His hands clutched that anchor, his face pressed up against it as he fell.

"It happened so quickly. I simply reacted. I scrambled down the ladder. Picked up the gun. Took one look at him and I knew he was dead. I've never killed anyone, Jack, not even in the service. I felt sick, but I didn't have time to be sick. There was the other guy. I looked around the Albatross' bow and there he was, running toward the trailer with his bat, so I fired the gun at him. Missed at first and he turned and ran back toward the truck. I fired again. I think I winged him because his one leg caved over, and he hobbled getting back to the truck. Next thing I knew, he was out the gate and gone."

Mark paused. He was exhausted. We both took a large gulp of Scotch.

"Say something, Jack."

"What do you want me to say? It's going to be alright in the morning?"

"They were after you, right?"

"Mark, they probably got the wrong address." I laughed until there were tears in my eyes. Not funny.

At that point, Mark let his head slump, elbows on his knees, and started to cry.

It was two in the morning, dark with no moon. Clouds crept along the coast and blocked the stars. Mark and I were beside the river. "Are you sure about this, Mark?"

"It's the only way," he said.

I wasn't usually in favor of screwing with police but reporting this body could lead to unwanted, violent retaliation, not to mention grief for those girls. I'd checked the dead man's pockets. Yuri Dostonovich on the license, forty-three. Yuri was about to take his last swim.

I recognized the surname. I told Mark the guy was Russian but didn't tell him about the two guys who were popped on West 32nd. Or that their IDs were also Russian. Or that the MP-433 was a Russian military-issue sidearm.

We both wore gloves. Mark leaned across Yuri's smashed face and slipped the plastic sheet beneath his head. I put the MP-443 in the Russian's pants pocket. We rolled him up with two five-foot lengths of #18 rebar. The body looked like a grotesque cocoon. I wrapped wire around the feet, waist, and head.

By the time we got the package into the herring skiff moored beside the trailer, I was sweating. I saw Mark had spent all the adrenaline he had. He was finished. But he fired up the engine and took the tiller. Then we headed out into the channel. The running lights were off, and we edged out into the fog that hung low on the water. Mark cut the engine, and we rolled the body into the current, held it while I stabbed the plastic with a screwdriver, then let it go. It disappeared in seconds.

"Give me your gloves," I said. In each glove, I put a fist-sized stone and dropped them into the water. With the motor turned off, the current had taken us downriver. Mark started the engine and steered us back to the boatyard. Neither of us said a word.

CHAPTER 11

The next morning from a chair in Mark's trailer, I watched the sun come up. The Scotch bottle was empty, and my head felt like a rugby team had used it for drop-kick practice. Mark floundered on a mattress beyond his open door. I had a tattered threadbare blanket draped over my shoulders. The weather had changed. Clouds were rolling in, and the air was dense and chilled.

I started drip coffee, made noise, looked in the fridge, and remembered I'd not eaten since yesterday morning and barely had any sleep in three days. The fridge was bare. I banged a few cupboard doors and found nothing. It made me feel empty. I thought about the body at the river's bottom and got a quick flash of dead boys beneath a lake.

Mark lumbered out into the main room. I poured him a coffee. "Plates?" I asked.

"In the cupboard."

"No, license plates?"

"Forgot to tell you." Mark went over to his desk, waded through the debris, and came up with a printed list on thin yellow paper. "There are hundreds of Escalades registered on the Island. The Civic is registered to a Sammy Lumbar, thirty-five, 2213 272 Street south of Aldergrove in the township of Langley." Mark went to the bathroom and threw up. Not easy to kill a man, even in self-defense.

When he came out, I said. "Drink warm water. If you barf again, you'll have something to throw up." I paused. "Tell me about the Escalade 233 A plate?"

"I narrowed down the registration to a Nicholas Calvino on Vancouver Island." Mark scanned down the list again. "That guy we dumped in the river was Russian. I have a Russian name on my list. 347 AWP. Registered to an Anton Tarasov, Campbell River."

Tarasov. Another Russian connection. I kept quiet.

Mark wiped his eyes and breathed hard. "Any of this connected with the guys who came here?"

"I know this Calvino," I said. "When I worked undercover on the Island, he was known to the police. His name came up when we worked on the disappearances of kids and young women. But we never got a connection though."

"I started digging," Mark said. "He's employed by Strang Corp. Owned by Otto Strang. Strang has waterfront, big acreage on Vancouver Island."

I remembered the mansion. Mark's word "digging" triggered a memory flash.

> A man stands a short distance from me, wearing a tailored black suit. A red rose in his lapel. I walk down in dim light in a long tunnel. I'm not alone; somewhere children are laughing. Others are crying.

"Where did you go?" Mark said.

I didn't answer but I asked, "What's Otto Strang into now?"

"He's Strang Corp's CEO. Subsidiaries, lumber, mining, oil, and gas, importing and exporting. He even owns a helicopter, and flies back and forth from the Island to the mainland, where he has a few addresses. Not Russian, right? Old family on the coast for generations and has many connections."

> I have a memory flash. I smell the Escalade's interior. The aftershave and cigars. And I see this same man in the black suit with a thick cigar.

I knew about the Strang family. Big house on a hill, but my memory was blocked. Same, problem after the shooting. Everything from before I left the Island as a kid was shadowy too.

> But inside that Escalade, its odor draws me to the black-suited man with the cigar, and now he's surrounded by little kids.

"Are you okay?" Mark said.

The memories wouldn't sort themselves out today. "Yeah, I'm fine. Looks like I'm going to the Island, even if it's the last thing I want to do. Can you keep working on this for me?"

"Can you assure me those guys aren't coming back? Russians, right?"

"Yeah, those guys are Russians. That doesn't mean they're all Russian. We have many gangs in Vancouver. There are over a hundred and fifty gangs in BC. In Vancouver, we got Asian, Punjabi, and Eastern European. Home-grown neighborhood gangs named after telephone prefixes, a UN gang that's ethnically inclusive, and there's always Hell's Angels, right? Russians aren't that big a deal. You don't want to come with me, do you? For your own protection?"

I hoped the twins hadn't fallen prey to these bastards. And I'd already brought Jessica and Del into this.

"Hell no, smart-ass. I can handle myself. I've got too much to do around here. And you need to get the fuck away, then maybe these guys, whatever group they're in, will follow you and leave me alone.

I heard tires on the gravel. "Are you expecting anyone?"

Mark looked like he was ready to barf again. I peered out the small window over the kitchen counter.

"Fuck," I said, "a black and white and a plain Crown Victoria."

Four cops; two in suits, two in uniform. The latter stayed with the cruisers as the suits approached the trailer.

"Sit tight; I'll talk," I said. I swung the door open and stood in the doorway, leaving Mark in the darkened trailer. I recognized the lead suit, from my Island time with the force. Reynolds. He recognized me too. Was he in Vancouver PD now and not working for the RCMP?

"Jack McQueen," Reynolds said. "Funny how you keep turning up with your nose in shit."

The other suit was tall and nondescript. He smiled like he'd swallowed a cream cake that was still stuck in his cheeks. Reynolds was hard-nosed, lean, wired muscle. His suit hung on him like wet laundry. He had the crumpled look as if he'd never gone near an iron and didn't bother with dry cleaners. "Well, Reynolds, someone's got to do the work and keep the taxpayers from thinking their money's being wasted."

"You were always such a smart-ass. I see that hasn't changed. We've got a problem, Jack. You were where you weren't supposed to be."

I'd worked only one investigation with Reynolds. Wasn't exactly high profile. Tommy Turd. The guy would do B&Es. Had a trademark. Always left a dump in the toilet. After working with Reynolds on that one, I lost whatever little respect I'd had for him. No sense of humor. He bagged shit and submitted it for evidence, long before DNA testing was serious. As if a detachment budget could afford tests on a simple B&E. Fuck. "And where was that?" I asked.

"Don't get cute. Why don't you tell me where you were two nights ago?"

"Visiting my wife and my daughter. Is there a crime against that?"

"Del might think so, seeing how she threw you out a while ago."

I took a deep breath. Counted. Followed my therapy. Then I cut to his chase since the only connection he could possibly have on me was 3360 West 32nd and the two dead guys. The house on West 32nd must have been under surveillance and they got the Westie plate number. "I stopped by a house on West 32nd a little before I saw Del. You might be interested. I discovered two guys who'd been dead for a while with neat little slug tattoos on their heads, an empty house, and no welcome mat. Have you heard about it?"

"We've got you on a surveillance photograph entering the premises at 9:07 p.m. Got your van parked outside for a good fifteen minutes, enough time to pop two dealers. So why don't you tell us about it? Are you involved with this stash house?"

I had trouble treating Reynolds seriously. "Do you have video footage of me entering the house?"

"No. We have a grainy photo of you and your license plate," Reynolds said. "That is enough to identify you as being there and to find your registered address."

"What's to tell? Didn't know it was a drug stash. Went in there, opened the door, and found them. I looked the place over and got out. Forensics will tell you that those guys had been dead long before 9:07 p.m."

"The only reason I might believe you is that once you were one of us. Why were you there?"

"So, Reynolds, are you still bagging shit?" I asked.

Cream Cake Cheeks gave Reynolds a weird look. Maybe I'd struck a chord.

Reynolds let my comment slide. "Give me a good reason why you were there. See if I believe you."

I figured it wouldn't hurt, to tell the truth. After all, that shit was bagged with Tommy Turd, Reynolds did make the collar. I told them about the missing twins, and the West 32nd address lead I was about to follow up on. Then I asked, "Who are those guys?" Did you see two young girls go into that house?"

"That's our business and I'm asking the questions."

"Well, that's it." I kept standing on the porch, blocking the door. No sense in letting them see inside, or they'd know something happened at the trailer and my container.

"Who busted down the gate?" Reynolds asked.

"Delivery truck. Put it in reverse, hit the pedal hard instead of the brake."

"Should report that. For insurance."

I sensed Reynolds believed me about the missing twins but knew I was lying about the gate. He turned to his partner, and they walked away.

When the uniforms were back in their cruisers and Reynolds' silent partner was settled in the passenger seat, Reynolds called out, "Don't leave the city, Jack. You are under investigation. Oh, and Murphy says hello. She's up the ranks now on the Island."

"Right." What a load of crap. Murphy didn't even know I was alive. She had her career and didn't need a fuck-up like me to mess with it. "So, Reynolds, you still RCMP, or have you jumped ship to Van PD?"

"RCMP, if you must know asshole. This is a CFSEU-BC operation."

I turned toward the trailer. The Combined Forces Special Enforcement Unit – British Columbia. That mouthful sounded like it carried too much weight for an anti-gang agency. The police cars' tires skidded on the gravel as they left. In the bathroom Mark was barfing.

I called Becky and asked her to check on the Sammy Lumbar registered address for the Honda Civic to see if Sammy was still living there. In ten minutes, she got back to me and left a message. Sammy Lumbar was no longer living there despite the registration address for his license plate. So, I'd forget about driving all the way out to Aldergrove.

Mark came out of the bathroom and went into his bedroom and closed the door. I felt guilty I'd dragged him into my investigation.

CHAPTER 12

A few minutes later I went back to the cargo container. There was a small safe bolted to the back wall and disguised by a screwed-on plywood cover that blended in. I was surprised the Russians had missed this. Perhaps they were in too much of a hurry. I opened it, took out a gun box, and opened that. Inside: a holstered, Glock 22 Gen4 with the extra fifteen-shot magazine, and a Beretta Px4 Storm Compact 9mm pistol with a nylon ankle holster. I attached the Glock in its holster onto my belt at my back and beneath my shirt, then in the Westie's glovebox I locked the box with the Beretta.

When I had left the force, I was required to turn in my guns, the regular issue sidearm, and my undercover snub-nosed revolver. Later I applied for carry permits for the Glock, and the Beretta when I linked up with Stacie Machado and her security company that did protection work, and security surveillance, among other things. That was my main employment, but I did my own investigations too, and Stacie helped me out. She paid me for my work and billed me for the technical work she did for me. If not for the security job and my past service with the armed forces and RCMP, there was no way I'd have carry permits for the guns I had now.

I stopped by Mark's trailer to let him know I was heading over to Stacie's office and planned to talk to Del.

"What did the cops want?" Mark asked.

"They tracked me here from a house they had under surveillance."

"Russians?"

"No. I followed a lead on the case, and they got my license plate." I lied because I didn't want to give Mark any more information than he needed to know.

On my way over to Stacie's office, my cell went off. I thought it was Stacie who hadn't picked up on my calls and messages, but it wasn't her. I pulled over and stopped the van. It was Jessica.

"Jack."

She called me Jack sometimes, instead of Daddy, and had since she was little, back on the Island. It seemed as if she called me Jack, I was her friend and not the father who had to love and cuddle her.

"Hi," she continued. "Where are you?"

"On the way to Stacie's office. What's up?"

"You must talk to mom. I don't want to go. She's making me and it's too far away. I'll lose all my friends and I'm going to die if you can't change her mind. Anyway, I'm running away, so you must talk to her."

"Jessica, slow down. Is this about Seattle?"

"Yes. She's really doing it. She packed stuff and threw out old clothes. She wants me to organize my room, and my stuff. She even told the school we're leaving."

"Where are you?" This wasn't happening. Del said she thought she needed to move on, and so did Jessica. She didn't say anything about this.

"I'm home. It's the teachers' professional development day."

"Is mom home?"

"No. She's at work."

I looked at the clock on the dash: 4:30. By the time I drove to Del's place, she'd be home. "Okay, I'm coming over," I said. "We can all talk about it."

"Thanks. See you soon." I heard her panic subside. Her voice sounded grown-up.

I phoned Stacie. After six rings, her voicemail picked up. "Stacie. We need to talk. I'm off to Del's to sort something out. Call me. I'll drop by later."

I drove toward Del's. The weather had cleared, and the sun glinted off the windshield like ripples on water. I got a quick flash.

The August summer light reflects on Shaplow lake. Peter on the dock trails his toes in the water. I sit beside him. We wear faded red swim shorts and watch Kat lean against the wake on one ski behind Tyler's cedar strip motorboat. The thirty-horsepower motor has decided to work, and the three of us, and Tyler are water skiing. Peter and I wait for our turns as our sister leans back and sends a rooster spray toward us.

She wears the same faded red swim shorts. Our father got them at a sale. I can see the small buds of her breasts as she passes. The boat circles one more time. Kat drops the line five feet from the dock and slowly sinks to a stop. Peter dives in. He's identical, her twin, without the developing buds. He swims under the water and comes up beside her and they touch, arms holding each other, and he kisses her on the cheek. She kisses him back. Now it's his turn on the lake, and then it will be mine. I watch Kat and Peter and know that no matter what happens next in our lives, I must keep them safe.

Keep them safe. Light winks on and off on the water. The man. The tuxedo-man. The carousel. Kat's budding breasts, the frightened horses, and the smell of aftershave.

I stopped the van on the curve of the cul-de-sac and turned off the ignition. Jessica sat on the stone bench at the door to the house. She was slumped down, her gaze on the ground. I watched for her to look up as I climbed out, but she didn't. I walked up the path and sat beside her. "I see mom's not home?"

Jessica continued to look at the ground.

"I guess we wait. But I've got to see Stacie. She's not answering her phone."

"Take me with you now, before mom gets here. I'll run in and throw my stuff in a bag"

"I can't. Your mom has custody."

"Won't, you mean. I'll die in Seattle. Please, Jack, please for once do what I want."

"I can't."

Del's silver Jaguar pulled up the drive. I felt midgets tie knots in my stomach. I heard Jessica murmur softly, "We had our chance, and you blew it." She was being unreasonable. We needed to discuss this, not run away. Jessica was no longer the little girl I thought she was.

Del reached over to the passenger seat, grabbed something, and got out. She wore a navy-blue suit, skirt, white blouse, and jacket. She carried her black leather briefcase in her right hand. She was professional and hotter than a pistol.

Del didn't miss a beat. "I'm doing this for us, for me, for Jessica, and for you," she said. "I can't keep letting you and all the garbage that trails your flat-foot heels into our lives. One day we're going to pay, and sure as a fistfight with some low life, it will happen if we stay."

I didn't say anything. I heard Jessica get up and move toward the door.

"Thanks," Jessica said. "I knew you wouldn't stick up for me." She slammed the front door on her way into the house.

Del moved closer and looked me straight in the eye. I felt woozy like I'd been slipped a mickey, but it was my heart racing and my mind falling into a deep well of sadness.

"You know, I'm right." She reached into her briefcase and pulled out a document. I knew what it was. Technically, she couldn't leave the city without it, and being a lawyer, she was all wrapped up in the law, however weak enforcement might be these days.

"I'll fight you on this."

"Don't even try," she said.

"I'm not signing it. Jessica wants to stay. She has her friends."

"You haven't even looked at it." Del shoved the papers closer. "We're not going across the country, and you'll have visiting rights."

"I don't want visiting rights. I want my daughter. I want you around, not hell-and-gone to Seattle."

"Jack be reasonable. You're dangerous for us. Think about Jessica and me. We're not safe. I can feel it."

Del grazed the papers against my arm.

I touched the document, brushed my fingers against her hand, and felt something I'd missed for a long time. I went to a place where a naked foot slides across a lover's ankle late at night.

She handed me a pen. I stared at it. Looked at the blank line for name and date. Thought about the ugliness that had slithered into my life in the last few days. And they were too close to it.

Del stepped back. All I saw was the concrete bench where Jessica had been a moment before. I couldn't bring myself to say anything.

"Jack."

"I know."

I scrawled my signature, illegibly. Filled in the date, stood up straight, and handed the document to her.

We stood beside each other for a moment. "Do you want to come in for coffee?"

"Thanks, but I must be somewhere. Another time."

"Alright then." She kissed me on the cheek, held me longer than I thought she would, then pulled away.

CHAPTER 13

On my way over to Stacie's, I grabbed a cheeseburger and fries at Burger King. Not sure the quick stop really helped. She still hadn't called me. I parked in front of her house, walked past the AAA Security & Consulting sign, and went down the driveway, as I'd done so many times before. I stepped up onto the deck. The office porch was dark. I tried the door. It was locked. I pressed the code into the keypad, entered and punched in the code to prevent the alarm activation. Her office was the way it always was with a clean desk and tidy folders for each project.

I stepped into the main hall and listened. I heard movement, like a shoe sole sliding across the floor. "Stacie? It's Jack. Are you okay?

I listened again and heard the same foot shuffle, along with a mewling sound. Not quite a whimper. I stepped into the great room. I saw Stacie, her back against an oak veneer counter, knees tucked up to her chin, arms wrapped around her knees, head down. She was barefoot in black leotards and a white cotton blouse. I looked around. A small marble pedestal table was on its side. Papers and letters were on the floor. There was broken glass. I thought Russians, then Voice. But how? "Stacie, talk to me. What happened here?"

Head still down, she croaked out softly, "It's my business. You don't need to know."

"Were they Russian?"

Stacie laughed, part tears, her face pressed into her knees. I wasn't making a joke; Russians had come into my life like a tired cliché.

I got down on my hands and knees and leaned against the kitchen drawers beside her. "I can wait. I've got all night. Do you have anything to drink?"

She pointed. Her arm looked bruised. Dark blood flecks stained her blouse. I got up, opened the indicated cupboard, and poured two Johnny Walkers. I gave her one and sat down on the floor again. I drank while I waited. When I got up and poured a second, Stacie raised her head and sipped her drink. "Fucking bitch!" she yelled.

Her words told me this could not have been a regular. Rather, someone, she picked up between serial monogamous relationships. "I could rip the cunt's heart out."

"Stacie, my tender ears."

"Shut up, stupid." She paused. "How could I be so dumb on the rebound? Went down to Coppers Bar. Tonight, was butch-bar night. I should have known, and me trolling bait. I should have known better. Why did I let her talk me into bringing her home?"

I kept quiet and listened. Felt like I was in the wrong dressing room.

"It could have been a good night, but things got out of hand," she said. "She wanted it rough and took it. Fisted me and I'm so sore and numb I'm afraid to move."

When she finished her Scotch, she leaned her head on my shoulder. I touched her hair, felt her tears through my shirt. Her whole body trembled beyond her control.

"I have nowhere else to be," I said. "If I did, I'd still be here."

She murmured something that drifted away, curled closer, and nuzzled her face into my chest.

"Sleep now," I said.

Sometime later, birds irritated me into knowing it was morning. I was still on the floor, laid out flat. Stacie was wrapped around me, sleeping. I slipped away from her and searched the fridge. I found some eggs and turkey bacon, put on a coffee maker, and started breakfast. I heard Stacie moving. The smells must have awakened her. "Hey, sunshine. I'm making breakfast."

"Oh fuck. You're still here? Thought I dreamed you came over. Forget anything I said. Mind if I take a shower first?"

"Go ahead. I'll wait to start the eggs."

While we ate, Stacie said nothing. She kept her head down, but I sensed she felt a lot better than last night, so I didn't push it. "About those girls," she said.

I nodded. She got up and brought her laptop over. "They're off the grid. Runaways. The parents are on Vancouver Island, not together. The father is Ian Stewart. Hasn't been around much. Could be anywhere. Their mother lives on a reserve near Shaplow Lake. Louise Stewart. Married name. Goes by Louie. No credit cards, old credit card debt. Seems the twins did go to high school. I hacked the records." She looked up at me. "You'll want to see this." She hit a key on the laptop and swung the screen around so I could see it. "Tell me if you recognize anyone."

There they were, walking down the gangway to the ferry at Horseshoe Bay, packs on their backs, ratty baseball caps shading their eyes.

"When was this taken?"

"Three days ago."

"How did you get this?"

"Oh, please, Jack. That's what I do."

"I had a hunch they were off the mainland, but this confirms it."

"Did you patch it up with Del and Jessica?"

"Couldn't be much worse. They're going to Seattle. I signed the custody amendment so she could take Jessica. She didn't want to go. I'm not surprised."

"I told you, Jack. But you wouldn't listen. You are addicted to spending time on anything but them."

I wanted to admit that even with good intentions, I wasn't the best daddy material. But I kept that to myself. "Will I make more coffee?" I said.

"That's your answer to everything, a cup of coffee, a glass of Scotch, some insane quest to save lost souls and endangered prey?"

I poured the coffee and kept silent. I handed a mug to Stacie, and she said, "I'm going with you."

"Right."

"I mean it. The security contracts and ongoing bodyguard work operate on their own. My accountant can handle it. You're the only other client I have right now. I can't stand this mess. Psychologically after last night, I can't stay here, and you need me."

I thought of the two Russians with the neat round holes in their foreheads, the one weighted down in the river, the guys who'd nearly killed me outside Del's house, the traces of drugs on the dining room table at 3360 West 32nd. "Look. Stacie. These twins are mixed up with drugs and gang members and maybe someone else I don't trust. Nothing good can come of this. I know how gangsters and drug dealers operate. They are predators who don't befriend young girls."

"You weren't kidding about Russians? And who's this someone?"

"I don't know," I said. "These kids are into something that's not going to end well."

"All the more reason for me to help you."

"And get yourself killed. No, Stacie."

"I can take care of myself."

I looked around the room, at all the clutter from a violent night. "Sure, you can."

"I'm going and you can't stop me."

CHAPTER 14

That afternoon I stood on the ferry's passenger deck. Stacie slept below, in the Westie. The ship passed a long-humped island that was all rock. A beacon flashed intermittently on each. And then Vancouver Island loomed into view. I saw its sedimentary, steep-sided rocky slopes, and darker jammed juts of exposed basalt—different formations that drifted together and slammed each other in a perpetual creep, as the Island itself shifted northwest in the Pacific. New-growth fir softened the exposed rock. Arbutus trees and Garry oak thrived in the dry meadows high above the sea.

We'd caught the last ferry to Vancouver Island for a while. Times were tight. The ferry service had been cut back to once a week until further notice. This ferry was half full. Only people who already lived on the Island, and a few souls wanting to escape from somewhere or someone were on-board.

It would be a different story on the return trip from Nanaimo. More demand for people to get back to the mainland. As the channel narrowed, the terminal came into view with its waiting vehicles, windshields glinting in the sun. Foot passengers funneled into a line outside the main doors. This wasn't going to be pretty. When the intercom came on and announced the arrival, I made my way downstairs to the Westie and slid in beside Stacie. She was still asleep. Trauma often required such escape. She stirred on hearing me get in. "It's been almost three years," I said.

"Huh?"

I didn't answer her but babbled in my head. Thought I'd left this place for good. Once I left the force, we moved over to the mainland. Del went over for work most weeks anyway. I did PI work for myself and Stacie. But things weren't going well with Del, so I moved out. Stayed with Mark. Then Del and Jessica talked me into Birken Psychiatric Hospital. Rehab. Anger Management.

"So, we're here?" Stacie asked dozy from her sleep.

I didn't tell her that while I walked down below through the cars, I'd seen a black Escalade with the 347 AWP plate, or that there was a white van behind us with a bullet hole in the driver's door.

I drove off the ramp and looked toward the line-up area. A police presence was assisting the ferry workers with the car lanes. Frustrated foot passengers looked angry as more police monitored the walk-on line. I wanted to stop and witness the consequences that the cutbacks on ferry sailings had caused, but we were in the steady stream of disembarking traffic, which pushed us onto the streets leading to the city's core.

That's when I heard it, cloth rustling behind me, like a small animal rummaging. The hair on my neck bristled. I thought about the gun. I was ready to whirl around and shoot when Jessica's head popped up, her face in the mirror. I was stunned. I kept driving in the traffic, from which there was no escape. "Hi Jack," my daughter said.

Stacie's eyes met mine. My eyelids dipped, and I shook my head. "Fuck, Jessica! What are you thinking?"

"Daddy don't be mad at me. I'm not going to Seattle."

"So, stowing away in my car's a solution? How'd you get back there anyway?"

"Simple. I knew you were going to Stacie's office, so I got up early but pretended to be asleep. Then I waited for mom to go to work and took a taxi over to Stacie's."

Smart devious little monkey. "And getting in the van?"

"C'mon, it's a Volkswagen." Jessica held a fist in the air and made a pounding motion. "If you keep punching at the triangular side window where that latch slides over, the latch jiggles loose. Bingo you're in. Then I crawled under this blanket."

She'd make a good burglar. I drove into downtown Nanaimo. Found a guesthouse, The Purple Frog. Checked us in. I tried to call Del from the lobby on my cell, but I got no answer or an opportunity to leave voice mail. I called on the office landline and got the same response. I had to get Jessica back to her mother. Back to safety. I turned to Stacie. "Stay with her. I know someone who might help us." I left the lobby, turned right, and walked down Commercial Street to the Queen's Hotel.

CHAPTER 15

Queen's Hotel. Hookers leaned against a concrete pole. The wind was picking up, and I sensed rain coming. Coffee cups and food wrappers slid along the road as the hookers waited. Maybe for the last bus. Or one more trick in the alley beside the hotel. Or a savior who'd never come to take them from this sad light.

Nanaimo, born out of coal and timber a century ago, had evolved into a struggling tourist town. But even with evolution and good intentions, it had sunk down closer to its frontier roots. The bookstores, art galleries, and trendy bars had disappeared, leaving secondhand clothing stores, tattoo joints, the Queen's Hotel, Cove Arms, and a few diners with cracked, upholstered stools. Here at night, hookers worked the streets.

I had a fondness for hookers, not to use them but rather to show kindness. Buy them a drink or a coffee to get them through another hour. I paid them for their time. They helped me now and then, providing information from the street. I wondered if Bella was still at the Queen's, running her girls out the back. I wasn't disappointed. I lingered at the door and saw her tapping beer behind the bar. I slipped into a booth in the corner, near the back, and let her find me.

She looked over six feet tall in high heels. She had long legs, ample breasts, and a smile that still worked, though time had worn the freshness from her lips. She came over and spoke in a quiet voice. "What the fuck brings you here, Jack?" She didn't wait for an answer. "Thought you left this God-forgotten Island when you fucked-up so bad?"

"Great to see you, too, Bella. I can see those hips are working fine. You've got your cheerful smile, and everything else is packed in tight."

"Sure, don't kid me. What you see is life support. If I didn't have young blood to help me out, I'd probably be sleeping below the underpass, scrounging every day, nattering to myself through knitted mittens from the lost and found," she laughed.

"No pensions for you gals, huh? I need your help," I said. I kept my voice low, even though there were only a few people in the bar. "Now, you are not too busy."

"Fucking ferries. Not sure if there's enough trade left to get off in town."

I caught her pun and smiled. "I'm looking for two girls. Twins."

"Thought they drummed you out. Made you turn in your badge."

"They did, Bella, they did. I work for myself. Over two years now."

"Aren't we all when it comes down to it? We're all alone, you know."

I felt the sadness in her words.

She slid into the seat across from me and made a motion with her hand. A tall slim guy went behind the bar. He had his pants cinched up high around his waist. His cigarette trailed smoke, and he sported a three-day grizzled look. Seemed like everything was going south here, even the smoking ban. I showed Bella the girls' photo.

"What do you want these twins for?"

"Have you seen them?"

"Maybe I have, maybe I haven't."

"Why so coy?"

"You aren't the first to come by asking, that's all."

"What did he look like?"

"One young guy. Shaved head. Stud in his ear. Scruffy. He was talking to an employee here. She told me. I personally didn't get a look at him."

"Was there another guy? Looked the same?"

"Not that I know of," Bella said.

"These girls have been here, right? I haven't got time to fuck around with twenty questions."

"What do you want them for?"

I told her about Chief. I mentioned Voice. I told her about the money and how I took it because I needed it and because I really didn't have a choice. I told her about the backpacks and the cocaine, my vague suspicions about Russians, and the video that showed the girls boarding the ferry three days ago.

"So, what are you going to do if you find them?"

"I will listen to their story and keep them safe."

"Jack, do you realize that's what got you so fucked-up last time? Don't you know that's always been your problem since you were a kid? You couldn't let it go. How long have they been missing?"

I tried to piece together how she knew about me as a kid.

"Based on what Chief told me, they've been missing from the house he set them up in for three weeks. But what's considered missing? No one has reported them. The school they went to hasn't followed up on anything. One friend I interviewed was concerned, but family services doesn't know or care. A tattoo parlor owner said she gave one of them a small tat. The only people who seem interested in them are Chief and Voice, and Voice worries me."

"Sounds like a case of flight to me," Bella said.

Since she was keeping me in suspense, I wanted to accuse her of having them out back, of grooming them. But I couldn't bring myself to believe she'd do that.

"One had a tattoo, small dolphin, ankle, right foot," I said.

"I know," she said.

I smiled at her. She was holding out like she didn't trust me. But I knew she had a soft spot for girls in trouble.

"Kept them out back for a while," she said. "Gave them food. Tried to talk to them, but they didn't talk much. Got the sense they were originally from up Island. They mentioned Shaplow Lake. That's why I was cautious with your history back there. I arranged for them to get a ride to Shaplow Reserve. One of the girls stayed with them outside until the car came and picked them up."

"What car picked them up?"

"I made a call. Asked someone I trusted. I believe he drives a beat-up red '93 Tempo, but he could have had something else."

"What about this guy? Can I talk to him?"

"I haven't seen him in a while. I know he's not in town, now. He doesn't have a cell, but if he turns up, I'll ask him."

I tried not to sigh. I wasn't getting lucky here. "What about the girl who saw them leave? She's here, right? Can you get her to tell me what she saw when they were picked up?"

"She's out back. I'll ask her."

Bella got up and turned. I watched her high heels move across the floor. I couldn't help sizing her up again. Life support? She was like a vintage collectible Mustang. All mint condition as far as I was concerned. She came back in a few minutes. "The girls were picked up by a Blue Honda. Two guys in front and the girls in the back."

"Was it a beat-up Honda Civic?"

"Yeah, my girl said it looked like a wreck."

Either Bella's friend had traded in his Tempo and got a Civic, or the twins got picked up by Hans One and Two.

"They got into the wrong car. Not your friend's Tempo or whatever," I said. "I know that Civic and the guys who picked them up work for Nicholas Calvino and Otto Strang."

Bella's face betrayed her anguish.

"Bella. It's not your fault. These guys must have been looking for them. Waiting around for an opportunity if they showed their faces."

"I assumed my guy had picked them up and delivered them to Shaplow as planned."

"How many days ago?"

"Two nights ago," she said.

"You've got some friend. The guys who worked for Calvino beat him to the pick-up because they were watching for them to show up on the street. Your friend if he showed up late, didn't even bother to tell you that they weren't out there waiting." I took a deep breath. Tried to stay calm. I changed the subject. "What do you know about me as a kid?"

"Only what was in the papers at the time. Then when you fucked up on the force, it seemed to make more sense."

I wanted to sit and talk to her. Tell her I couldn't remember much. Flashes mostly. Tell her how Birken seemed to make it worse. But I knew she didn't have the time, and I was not ready yet. I left her with a kiss on both cheeks since I knew she liked that. I gave her my card, with Stacie's email on it. I wrote my cell number on the back and gave her money for her time. As I headed out the door she said, "It's not the same up there. The new players are as dangerous as the one that has run things all along. Be careful."

I knew she meant it.

When I got back to The Purple Frog, I found Stacie and Jessica asleep in single beds. I spoke low into the recorder.

> "Lesions with no starting point for narrative, no details, no
> voice, cuts beneath uneven skin, open mouths that cannot speak."

I stripped down to my boxers and a T-shirt and lay in the dark on the other bed.

> I see my father, sleeves rolled up at the elbows, red baseball cap
> askew, its brim smudged with grease, cigarette in the crook of
> his ear. He grips the truck's steering wheel like a man desperate
> to hold onto things. I watch the spaces in the forest open and
> close, listen to the gravel, see those cracked dirt-lined hands
> that so frequently lashed out at us, and could swing an axe deep
> into the heart of a log, cut meat like a surgeon with a skinning
> knife, and chop beef, lamb, and chicken with a cleaver.

Another time I see him and we're doing stuff.

> "Don't add too much water," he says. We're mixing cement and
> fitting rocks together to make a wall.

> Another time he says, "Hold your right hand near the head. Let
> it slide back as you bring the axe down."

> "Axe work clearing brush beneath the sun. His sweat
> and muscle, we're together, me a part of what he dreams."

"Axe work clearing brush beneath the sun.
His sweat and muscle, we're together, me a
part of what he dreams."

CHAPTER 16

In the morning I bought Scotch, six beers, and breakfast provisions—bacon and eggs, bread, butter, jam, red peppers, and cheddar cheese. Then we headed north in the VW Westie to Shaplow Lake and the homestead.

A low-pressure cell came in, curled the air counterclockwise, and sent a brisk south-easterly across Vancouver Island, bringing rain. Summer had disappeared.

I'd tried to speak to Jessica, but she remained sheepishly silent. I tried to call Del on the cell, but again the ringtone finished without an opportunity to leave a message.

I looked at Stacie and said, "Damn connections. Can you contact her on the computer?"

"I can't find an open Wi-Fi connection," she said. "I'll text her to let her know Jessica is with us. When my phone gets a connection, my computer will send it."

It would be a little while before I felt Adele's unleashed wrath. I was in an impossible place. Couldn't leave Jessica safely anywhere and couldn't send her back. And where we were going, I had every reason to believe we would not be safe. I drove to the nearest gas station and filled up the tank and two ten-gallon containers. I strapped the jerry cans in the luggage hollow on the roof. With the cutbacks on ferry sailings, there would be gasoline shortages and I didn't want to run out.

One main highway snaked up and down the Island, and a few roads led to the west coast. The rest were logging roads that led into the mountains. Shaplow Lake was three-quarters up from Nanaimo, in the shadow of mountains that were bent and scraped up from sea-floor lava long ago. I'd already told Stacie about the Escalade, the white panel van, and the blue Civic that took the twins away. Hans One and Hans Two were working for Voice when they roughed me up. Were they still working for him?

"Jack, are you still mad at me?" Jessica asked.

I looked in the rearview mirror and saw one bunny slipper sticking out from her knapsack. Jessica looked sad. At times she was so grown-up, and at others, she was still a little girl. "I'm disappointed and worried," I said. "How do you think your mother feels? She's probably worried sick. You didn't leave a note, did you? Don't answer that. When your mother knows you're with me, she'll go ballistic."

"Maybe she'll understand," Stacie said.

"Yeah, maybe." I could imagine Del devising ways to disembowel me and watch me bleed out.

The rain grew more intense as we headed north. We had the highway to ourselves. No trucks were coming over from the mainland and nothing was heading south to catch a ferry. The water slapped hard, and the underpowered wipers had trouble keeping up. We rode in silence. Stacie tried to get a satellite Wi-Fi signal without success, and Jessica was in a cuddle with her blanket. I focused on the road. Three ravens duked it out over a soggy pizza box and a crust on the roadside, and my mind went back to Shaplow Lake.

My father keeps a raven in a chain link cage in the barn. He loves this bird more than Kat and Peter or me. We sleep beside the raven at night in our own cage.

One day when our parents are shopping in town, I open the cage and take the raven out. I paint the bird yellow and green and when he is dry, I take him from the barn to see if he can fly. Kat and Peter follow me.

"Let's set him free," Kat says.

"Let's hurry before they come back," Peter says.

Their coming back is never good. They always look for an argument with us. We never can make them happy or do the right thing or be good kids after they come back from town.

My dog, Max, sees the raven on my arm and barks at us from the yard.

I release the raven into the air. He goes up about four feet but drops back to the ground and watches us. Max stops barking and lays down in the yard beside the barn. He stares at the raven. As I suspected the raven cannot fly.

But a flock of ravens gathers in a nearby Arbutus tree. I realize we've made a big mistake and I move toward the raven to gather him and put him back into his cage. Then as a flock, the ravens descend from the tree, toward us, cawing like one entity, a fist of malice, some twisted retribution from the sky. On mass, they hammer into us and the painted raven. Their sheer collective weight knocks us to the ground. Beaks crash against my neck and head. Kat and Peter fall. Their arms flail at the birds. The painted raven is prey among beak slashes and beating wings. Max retreats to the barn door. He curls into a small, dark, indistinguishable shape.

My father's truck comes down the drive. Two doors slam. Our parents have been drinking and are argumentative. Painted feathers are spread across the baked dirt. The raven's head lies limp and severed from its body. Kat and Peter start to cry. My father moves toward me. I am sad for the raven and want to cry with Kat and Peter, but I don't. I stand up to meet my father. His hot hand slaps me across the face and knocks me down. He hits Kat and Peter too.

"What the fuck were you thinking?" my father says.

I get up and try to tackle him, but he slaps me back, hard enough to keep me on the ground. "Idiots. Fucking idiots."

My father continues to beat Kat and Peter, then he drags them into the barn. I get up and follow. Max barks from the shade as the barn door opens.

My father's face is purple. "You should know better."

He cracks me across the forehead with a wooden stool. I go down and stay down. I see my mother by the fence, watching him. She looks calm like she always does. Locked up inside a stone. Max barks again. My father sets the stool down and sits on it. Max comes up to him, a little cautious, and puts his head between my father's legs. My father shakes his neck, takes the fur firmly in his beefy hands, and wrenches it from side to side, near to choking Max. Max lashes out, teeth ravaging my father's hand.

"It's your fault," I shout. "You're too rough with him."

My father turns and I know by his eyes that something has shifted into a dark corner of his brain. He picks up the stool and lifts it high in the air above his head, then swings it down upon Max's head, once, twice, three times. Max's legs splay out like a busted table, and his eyes glaze. He shakes and pees on the ground. My father steps back and watches his terror, looks at his own blood trailing down his fingers, takes a breath and moves closer to the dog, raises the stool once again, and continues over and over and over. Max stops moving. Blood runs from his mouth onto the ground.

"Fucking dog," my father says and turns to me.

I run and run and run.

CHAPTER 17

Shaplow Lake was almost a full gas tank away, so halfway up I pulled off the main highway onto the old highway that ran along the coast and stopped for gas.

"I can only give you half a tank," the guy at the pump said. "I'm running low and have to share it around."

Usually, folks would pump the gas themselves, but with the ferry cutbacks, gas stations were rationing. "That's all I need," I said to the guy. I gave him cash and drove off. I gazed into the dense forest beside the highway, and I was back in memory again.

We have been abandoned so deep in the forest that we are not expected to survive. We need to find our way home. I see the words on paper in our lunch boxes: "You're on your own." And I remember. A bushtit flits among the leaves from the ground to perch and down again, as if he knows he needs to wake me early. I wake Kat and Peter from their sleep; they're nested together like spoons. They jerk awake like I caught them in a net and hauled them to the surface where they can breathe. We haven't spoken since we read the notes. All night we've huddled close and slept.

With nothing to eat but the stones in our lunch buckets, I tell them, "Take out the smoothest stone and suck on it."

We test the stones in our palms. Pop the best into our mouths, let the weight balance on our tongues and feel the coolness join the warm saliva that rushes in. Kat and Peter trust me here, and in this way, we have our breakfast before we start the day.

I lead the way, but there is no path, and the ground dips and sways beneath my feet. We walk through bracken and sword fern, with salal slapping against our legs. What's hard is knowing where the ground is firm. We step over huge trunks blown down by the wind, some rotting and nursing young fir, and cedar. My foot sinks down and locks itself in a cross-hatched thicket that trips me.

Kat and Peter, being smaller, struggle on all fours, creeping along and reaching out to be pulled up. I look for breaks where the blow-down is less thick, and the undergrowth is stunted by the lack of light under a heavy canopy. I look for notches on the trees, or colored plastic tape tied to limbs, but see none and realize we're too deep in this wooded prison to find a logging spur anytime soon. But I can't give up; I need to keep Kat and Peter focused and not afraid. I find them branches they can use as hiking poles and turn it all into a game. When they complain of hunger, we suck our stones.

I wondered now where I'd learned about stone-sucking.

The rain had lightened up, and I could see the mountain spine that stretched the length of Vancouver Island. Eighteen miles on the eastern side formed the lowland coast, the sea on one side and the rising slopes on the other—mountains as high as six thousand feet. There was nothing benignly rounded about these peaks, which had remained above the mile-thick ice sheets that came down from the north more than ten thousand years ago.

On the range's west side, few roads cut through a great temperate rainforest, where more than three hundred inches of rain fell every year. On the east side, half the year was drought, but for snowmelt and a few remaining glaciers. The rains came in fall and winter, with storms even the mountains could not hold back.

A strong wind cleared out the clouds, leaving only low shore mist and fog coming from the water. It would burn off a few miles inland, as the land rose to meet the mountains. Shaplow Lake, the town, was not much to talk about: gas station, a few cafes, a bar, The Duke Hotel, a general store, small farms surrounding the lake, and a log-sorting dump in a bay leading out to the strait. The lake was recreation only; part park, part privately owned. At least a hundred acres belonged to the Strang estate, with its ten-thousand-foot shoreline.

We had another hour or so to go, driving up the only coastal road. Stacie tried to pick up Wi-Fi again. I tried to speed dial Del's number but got no answer or voice mail. She was going to kill me. She wouldn't believe I tried and tried to reach her.

We drove some more, and suddenly my phone buzzed. All that time I couldn't get through to Del, and now I got a call.

"Jack. Jack, I finally got you," Mark said. "Did you have it turned off? I've been trying you since last night. All hell's broken loose. Adele's been calling me, asking me where you are. Jessica's gone missing. The cops are looking for her everywhere. Your wife must have some pull because no one looks for anyone anymore."

"Got it," I said. "She's with me. Long story but she stowed away in the van when I came over to the Island."

"Well, the cops came. They know you're there."

"Are you okay?" I asked. "No more Russians?"

"I'm over it. I've done some more research. Remember that address Chief gave you. You talked to Mike Burns who answered the door and said he and Laura Wells had just moved in and that she worked at Hoskins. Turns out that the house is owned by Otto Strang. It's a safe house. Laura doesn't work at Hoskins, and both have large rap sheets. Possession, child abduction, B and E, aggravated assault, you-name-it. I think they work for someone much bigger. I'll let you figure it out."

I clicked off. While I was talking, Stacie got through on the internet.

"They've got an APB out for Jessica," Stacie said, "that says the abductor is armed and dangerous. Approach with caution."

"What's an APB?" Jessica asked.

"All-points bulletin," I said. "Your mom went to the police, and now I'm in trouble."

"I can't go to Seattle. Mom is serious."

"Yeah, I know she is. And I'm thinking now, her decision is right."

"Do you know a Staff Sergeant Brigit Murphy?" Stacie asked.

"Yeah, why?"

"A media release from Vancouver Island RCMP, Staff Sergeant Murphy says, 'Police suspect: Abducted child Jessica McQueen presumed to be on Vancouver Island with her father, Jack McQueen'. Goes on to say call the police and not approach the child or father."

"Really."

I started to go back and reminisce about Murphy and how we were partners once. My God, she'd done well for herself. She had risen to staff sergeant.

I tried Del's number again. It buzzed, then voicemail clicked on. "I've been trying for days," I said. "Nothing got through until now. Believe me. Jessica's safe. She stowed away in the van. Don't worry."

CHAPTER 18

We left the coastal highway. Finding the farm was easy as if I'd come this way before. Which I knew I had, first in my childhood and then when Murphy and I combed the landscape and wracked our brains to find out why so many had gone missing. Why so many families had been left with no answers and a bag of tears? I remembered bits. Some clearly: what Murphy and I did, what happened to us all when we were children. Then there were huge black holes as if I'd been emptied out and left with half-memories that were dark and out of focus.

I stopped the van by the farmhouse. I rummaged in my duffle and retrieved a flashlight. I left the engine running and told Stacie to stay with Jessica and lock the doors, then walked on alone.

The homestead was a backdrop, a curtain in the fog that the Westie's headlights couldn't penetrate. Behind those walls, I knew, lay the answers I'd tucked into my mind's dusty crevices. The porch sagged, and grass and vines protruded through cedar planks slippery with mold where the dampness stayed hidden in the shade. The steps were bent and protested under my weight. The screen door still slammed, and the lock mechanism failed to meet its partner in the jamb. The front door was heavy oak. I used my key, and it opened with a push and a whine.

The moment I stepped through the farmhouse door and scuffed my feet across the wooden boards worn by grit, I knew the place had been wrong for my parents. Wrong for Kat and Peter. Wrong for me. My memory was foggy about how this place belonged to me. But I did recall that I was the oldest child and that my parents did not have a will, but I was deemed to be the closest living relative.

The power had been off at the breaker for years, and no one had been inside since the day Kat and Peter, and I were forced to leave. Sheets covered the furniture, and dust covered the sheets. My flashlight scanned the mantle, and I saw the two oil lamps we used when storms knocked out the power lines. I never was interested in the place, but I kept it, thinking one day it might help me recapture my memories. I paid the basic electric bill when I hooked up with Del after we were together on the Island. Still, the property remained vacant.

Standing there in the dark I see my parents, their first arrival, as in a movie. Three kids press their noses on the rolled-up windows and make moisture smudges like dogs curious to escape. My mother smiles, standing in the sun beside the '53 Chevy, a tired old truck from the beginning.

I can see my father as he glances back at her before stepping into the hall. As I stand here in the present, I can sense her sadness too. Not so much in her eyes, but rather a heaviness of the body, as if the world hung stones on her and forced her to walk for miles with no destination.

The farmhouse had windows, but there was no light inside. There never was. Dead flies lay on their backs upon the windowsills, and an opaque layer of dust and old cooking oil coated the glass. The place was tidy. Everything was in its place.

I knew this homestead was all wrong, now as then. As if it harbored a future of misery. But I also knew it was the end of the runway that was our life back then. All the rooms were small, with a living room with a fireplace, and a kitchen with a walk-in pantry. One downstairs bedroom and one bath, another two bedrooms upstairs. And a low-ceilinged basement. I didn't need to investigate; I remembered. I checked each room; the place was empty. I went downstairs and turned on the power.

I went into the kitchen. This was where my mother always cleaned like there were stains on everything. It kept her busy. Numb. I couldn't remember anyone ever hugging her. In memory, I smelled the blood that had pooled beneath the kitchen table. I lingered for a moment or two until I remembered that Stacie and Jessica were waiting in the van. I stepped outside and waved them in.

CHAPTER 19

I took my duffel bag from the Westie and retrieved my Glock 22. I left the Beretta locked in the glove box. I was home now, but I didn't think of it that way. There was too much I couldn't forget. Couldn't remember.

Back in the house, Jessica snuggled in a sofa chair beside a raging fire reading a YA paperback. Her slippers flopped back and forth like two furry animals. Stacie was on the sofa, busy on her laptop, doing research. I sat on the sofa at the far end. The room was like a sauna. Stacie had stripped down her upper body to a black tank top. Looking at the muscles in her arms and shoulders, I wondered how that pick-up bitch got the drop on her. I looked toward Jessica. "Let's try again to contact your mom."

"You've got to be kidding," she said.

"No, I mean it. We both must face the music." I rang the number. Five rings and I was about to click off.

"Jack?" Del said.

I heard anxiety rather than anger. I knew the anger would come later. "She's safe," I said. "She's with me and Stacie."

"Stacie?"

"It's a long story."

"Where are you?"

"We're at the homestead. If the ferries were running, I would have taken her straight back. She smuggled herself into the back and popped up when we got on the Island. You know she doesn't want to go to Seattle."

"So, what are you going to do? You could have flown back with her on a small charter plane. Island Air. She can't stay over there. I don't care what you say, she's not safe. I've got the police looking for you."

"I know. I'll contact the police."

"Do that," she said.

"As far as Island Air is concerned, with the ferry cutbacks to once a week, air seats are fully booked."

"Right. But I don't believe you even checked, did you?

"You got me there. Here's Jessica."

I handed the cell to Jessica, who looked worried.

"Hi, mom." Jessica got up and went to an upstairs bedroom to talk. I was happy to let her sort it out with her mother. I swung around to Stacie.

"Where do we go from here?" she asked.

Did she mean with Jessica, the twins, or her own life? She still had that fear in her eyes, like a dog that had shut down. No fight. No flight. I figured I should leave it alone and distract her with work. I went to the kitchen, got the Scotch and two glasses. I set the glasses on the coffee table and poured the whiskey. I handed her a glass. "What have we got?" I said.

I'd come this far, and what with Jessica here and an APB, the Escalade and the beat-up Civic, my old home turf that I'd been running away from for years, the Strang estate, Murphy, and the Russians, I was starting to shut down a bit myself. I took my first sip of Scotch and felt it burn its way down. The confusion felt a little clearer, but I knew it was the drink and not reality.

"There are a few directions we could take," Stacie said. "Locate that blue Civic. See if we can find their mom. We should call the police."

"I'll do it. Give me time. Tomorrow."

"I'll look for local video footage I can hack," she said. "Do a search for this Anton Tarasov. Did you know him when you were on the force?"

"No. Never heard of him. This Russian involvement seems new for here."

"Who is he?"

"Another Russian I think is connected."

Stacie jiggled her glass. I poured her another Scotch and topped mine up. I took the recorder from my pocket.

"What's on that anyway?" Stacie said.

"Nothing."

"At times you seem a tad consumed with recording stuff."

"You really want to know?"

"Are you writing your last will and testament?"

"Right. Like the Old Testament. Genesis. The origin of things."

"You're many things, but religious you're not," Stacie said. She flung her head back and was about to laugh.

"How about an eye for an eye?"

"Come on. What have you been saying into that thing?"

"It's stuff. An attempt to get the flashes down. Phrases jump into my head. They saunter in and if I don't record them, they saunter out again."

"Let me hear it."

I took a sip from my glass and handed her the recorder. She clicked it on and listened. Then she fast-forwarded, listened, and fast-forwarded again. She picked another spot and listened some more. "You could write this down. It's powerful stuff." Her eyes were animated.

"I knew I shouldn't have let you listen."

"No. No. It's a surprise."

She handed the recorder back.

"Surprise. Right. That's why no one knows about it."

"It's really good," she said. Her words came from a place deep inside her. She held out her glass again and I topped it up. I felt like I'd had my ribs cracked open and my heart exposed. I brushed her arm as I drew away to place the bottle on the table. I felt her emotion. A longing for something terribly missing from her soul. I couldn't blame her for showing emotion toward me, after what she'd been through. It was that coming-out-of-shock reaction when the hormones try to get the body back in balance. Stacie shut her computer down. "I can't do this now. I'll return to it in the morning."

She slid closer to me on the couch. Drank her Scotch and poured another. We drank a few more. Sooner than usual the buzz hit me.

"Hold me, Jack."

I leaned back. Stacie curled her head into my chest. I stroked her neck and kissed the hair on her head. "Stacie—"

"Don't speak."

She turned her head and kissed me on the lips, lingered, then kissed me harder. She pressed her tight body close, and I wrapped my arms around her. For a long time, we were on the couch, finishing our drinks before I said, "We have to sleep."

I leaned back so there was space between us. I was attracted to her. I felt the tension and the spark, but I was hesitant. Not for wanting her, but for fear that we could lose what we had. Friendship could be broken. Stacie took my hand and we both stood up. "Don't leave me," she said.

She led me to the downstairs bedroom. Before I knew it, we were in bed together, me in my boxers and Stacie naked. "Stacie," I said. Caution in my voice.

"Shush. Don't leave me."

I didn't. I held her and we fell asleep.

I woke in dark, alone. I heard Stacie in another room, tapping on her computer. I rustled around in the sheets.

"You might want to look at this," she said.

My head hurt from the Scotch. I thought of Jessica. Was she up? How long had I been in bed by myself? I was still in my boxers. I shuffled into my jeans and pulled on a T-shirt and a quilted plaid shirt. With the fire down to coals, the farmhouse was cold. Stacie was at the kitchen table, fully dressed in black tights and thick fleece. She looked like she'd been working out. I started to make a comment about last night.

"No, Jack. Relax. Last night? You held me and we went to sleep."

That was an answer. "What have you been doing and for how long?" I asked.

"I went for a jog to clear my head. There was a break in the rain and the moon was out. Besides, who can sleep with all the toilet noises coming from your mouth when you're asleep."

"Charming. And I thought I was helping."

"You were and I appreciate it. Believe me, Jack, I really do."

"What have you got?"

"Well, this island isn't as backward as it looks. I searched for links where I could hack into video surveillance. Highway turnoffs."

"Stacie, don't keep me in suspense."

"Look at this," she said.

I came over behind her, resisting the impulse to put a hand on her shoulder. Her laptop showed the main highway turnoff. I recognized it as Sparrow Creek. A car comes into view and then turns off.

"It's a Civic, right?" she said. Dark-colored, blue maybe."

"Same year, roughly."

"Now look at this," she said.

She did some magic with her fingers on the touchpad. I could never figure out the finger swipes or zooming in and out. I had enough trouble with the mouse and the clicks.

Stacie brought up a different video. "This is down that same turn-off road," she said. "See where the car goes. Turns left."

I couldn't believe it. "I know that road," I said. "It leads to Tyler Madson's parent's place."

"Who's Tyler Madson?"

I had memory flashes at the question. I was under the water, walking toward the stumps where the bodies were... I was digging tunnels with Tyler at his place and at our farmhouse... I was hiding.

> There is a different tunnel; larger, and well-engineered. There are ballerinas, feathered boas, and children with powdered faces. I smell the cigar smoke's cloying aroma. It hangs on me.

"He was a friend when I was growing up," I said.

"So, you know the place?"

"You might say that. Is there a time stamp on those videos?" I figured we were three days behind them based on what Bella told me at the Queen's Hotel.

"It's stamped 11:30 p.m. Friday," Stacie said. "We're behind at least two days."

I heard footsteps behind me; Jessica was in the doorway, in pajamas and bunny slippers. The kid had planned. All I had was my extra clothes in my duffle. "Hi kiddo," I said.

"How'd you sleep, Jessica?" Stacie said. "It rained hard last night."

"I like the rain. Didn't wake up once."

"You must be hungry," Stacie said.

That was my cue. "Let's rustle up some bacon and eggs, toast and jam."

Stacie kept tapping at the computer. I fired up some bacon and cut up a pepper, grated cheese, and made an omelette. We all sat down together for breakfast. We were too hungry to even talk.

When the sun came up after the night's rain we saw blue sky, with branches dripping silver jewels through a mist that twisted through the trees.

"I have the Madson house address here in Shaplow," Stacie said. "We can all go together, check it out, and check out the Civic."

I gave Stacie a what-are-you-thinking look. "No, you guys are staying put, right here. I'll do the legwork. Stacie, you're the researcher. And Jessica, you can assist her."

Jessica hugged me but was resigned to staying. Stacie followed me outside. "Look," I said, "here's my Glock. If you need to use it, aim for the chest, and keep firing." I didn't need to tell her that. I gave her my cell phone and the access code. "Extra insurance for you and Jessica," I said. Then I got a memory flash. "If you must hide, go down to the basement, and find the fruit cellar. At the back, there's a hole in the wall, behind the plywood. Hide there."

Stacie scrunched up her nose and squinted with her eyes, as if to say, "You've got to be kidding."

"I'm not kidding. I'll explain later." With that, I was gone. Hopefully not for long.

CHAPTER 20

I opened the glovebox, unlocked the gun box, and retrieved my Beretta. I put it in the ankle holster and strapped it on.

I drove to the Old Island Highway, then took the exit at Sparrow Creek. There was very little traffic. It was a Monday, and the ferries were not running, so I figured everyone was staying put unless they were employed on the Island. I found the road to Tyler's mom's homestead. It was less than a mile from the farmhouse, a quarter that distance straight through the bush. The road consisted of two tracks with grass struggling to survive between the tire marks. At the end of a five-hundred-foot driveway, the Madson homestead sat back from the road. The forest was creeping in. The house had a wraparound porch on three sides with a two-foot-wide overhang and a metal roof. The log home was worn down, logs greyed by sun and lack of maintenance, and failure to renew the spar varnish or whatever preservative stain they had back then.

I waited on the porch. Listened before I knocked. It was still a clear day with bright sunlight, but the porch was dark and cold. I knocked, not sure what I was going to say. Tyler's mom wasn't likely to remember me, and if she did, I wasn't sure what reaction I'd get. When they found the tunnels at Tyler's place, everyone blamed me. Thought I had something to do with the way Tyler disappeared. All this time, I'd never said a word. No one knew what I remembered and what I didn't.

I heard feet shuffling and saw the lace curtain move at the window beside the door. Mrs. Madson stood behind the door. "Mrs. Madson, I need to talk to you. It's Jack, Jack McQueen. You know, from down the road. I played with Tyler when we were kids. I used to be a police officer."

Police officer. Pulled the trigger. He had an axe. Pulled the trigger. It was all a flash without the details. I couldn't ask her about her version of what happened to her husband back then when he came at me with an axe. Not now.

"What's it about?" she said.

"Mrs. Madson, I'm looking for someone who's gone missing. Please help me out here and open the door."

"Missing. Did you find Tyler, yet?"

My heart sank. Tyler had been gone for nearly thirty years.

"Not yet, Mrs. Madson, not yet."

"I know you can find him, Jack. I know you can."

Through the door, I heard her crying. The door opened a crack, enough to see one eye and a taut chain across the opening.

"Not safe. Not safe. Jack, find Tyler for me. Find Tyler."

"I will, Mrs. Madson. Can you tell me if you've seen a car go past here? A blue car? A Honda Civic?"

She paused. Time had not been kind. She was wrapped in three sweaters. Her cheeks were sunken. Loose skin hung around her neck. I figured she'd be at least seventy.

"I don't know cars, but while I was getting the flyers from the mailbox, one did go by the front a few days ago. And there was another car, but don't ask me any more than that."

"Was it blue, Mrs. Madson?"

"It was dark-colored."

"Do you remember the color of the second car?"

"Not really. Please, find Tyler. Will you Jack?"

She closed the door.

"I will Mrs. Madson." I wondered how bad it was inside as I turned back to the Westie. But I didn't want to go there.

I followed the gravel road until it turned into a logging trail. I kept going. Stopped at each spur road that branched off into the forest and looked for recent tire tracks. After three spurs, I found recent tire tracks in the mud and turned onto the last spur. It was past noon, and I realized I still needed to find the twins' mother on my way back. The spur wound for another mile. I rounded a curve and the road stopped at a clear-cut slash. And at the end was the blue Honda Civic. I stopped the Westie about a hundred yards away.

There was an odd feeling here. Unfinished business. Too quiet. I looked out into the brush. Nothing moved. I rolled down the window. Listened. Nothing. No birds were singing. I got out and felt for the Glock before remembering I gave it to Stacie. Felt my ankle holster for the Beretta. I drew it from the holster and walked toward the Civic.

The driver's door was open. I leaned into the car. There was a folded Nanaimo and Vancouver Island map, worn creases ripped where the folds had been. Empty paper coffee cups, plastic lids, and stir sticks were on the passenger floor. I reached down beside the driver's seat and pulled the trunk release.

I went to the back. Paused as my stomach gave a dry heave, like the last push to vomit after a binge. I didn't want it to end this way. The lid was slightly open. I slowly raised it and there they were. Hans One and Hans Two, tucked together like spoons. Bullet holes in their hands and feet. They were dead. Smashed skulls and broken bones. Two shovels were visible beneath them. The trunk was an abattoir.

I turned away and lowered the lid, staggered a few steps, and hurled until there was nothing left to heave. Cold sweats followed. I still held the Beretta.

CHAPTER 21

I left the logging spur with the Civic with the trunk closed. I drove fast past the Madson place and headed straight to Shaplow Lake. I found Nemo's, a waterfront bar near the reserve on the Georgia Strait. It was still operating after all these years. A different face was behind the bar, different serving girls. I figured different owners. I washed up in the restroom before I settled in.

Barman didn't look like he'd been raised on the Island. He didn't have that slow-paced Island way of moving. He was tall which made him thin, but muscular like he'd worked hard, maybe planted trees or bucked up with a chainsaw. I always thought about the story. What was his? I saw him eyeing me. I didn't look local and came in rough.

I was upset that I'd lost it back there and barfed out my breakfast. Realized I should give Stacie a call. Patted my pockets. No cell phone. I remembered I'd given it to her.

I went to the washroom again. On the way back I checked the pay phone. Not too many of them left, with all the cell phones now. I called 911. Asked for the police. Got transferred. Made it quickly in a low voice. Told where the bodies and the Civic were. Got asked the usual. Who? Where? Where are you now? I didn't answer, then I hung up.

I ordered Scotch and a beer. Pulled out the twins' photo. "Have you seen these girls? Maybe in the past on the Island?"

He looked at me, suspicious, then took the photo and squinted his eyes at it. I could see he was concentrating, not giving it the once over.

"Maybe. But not recently. It seems I saw them around when they were younger, maybe a year ago, over on the reserve. They're band kids, right? Are they in any trouble?"

"I need to find them. I'm doing a friend a favor."

"You're not a cop, are you?"

I rolled my eyes. Opened out my arms.

"Look at me. Do I look the part? They've gone missing. I need to find them." I said it as I meant it, and I did. I could see from his face that he knew it too.

"I remember they had a mother," he said, "and I think she moved back up Island to live on the reserve."

I thanked him, finished my drinks, and left.

Even in the overcast, the light reflected off the water. The wind had turned savage, tearing at the waves. In protest, cedar and fir bent. No sign of gulls. It was going to be a blow. Something dark in the heart of things.

I walked toward where I'd parked the Westie van with my head down, then looked up and saw the big man from Brogans standing in front of me. Fuck, not followed again. I remembered Brogans and my face on the asphalt.

"I'm Tony, he said. He grabbed me by the arm. "I'll take you to her. Their mom."

I looked at him with surprise. "Is the Chief on the Island?"

"He's around. He'll find you if he needs you."

His truck was an old Dodge Ram, and I had no choice but to slide into the passenger seat beside him. He took up more than half the cab, spreading over onto the console and jammed up against the door and his open window. My window was down, and the wind whistled through the truck, but Tony didn't mind the howling. He put the truck in gear, and we were gone.

He dropped me off outside Louie Stewart's house on Cougar Creek Road. "I'll give you an hour," he said. Then he drove away in a rush of gravel. I wondered if he'd come back.

The clapboard home was a one-story rectangle like all the others. Lean-to porch, walkway up to the door. Dirt path through a bloom of cardboard boxes, plastic bags caught on tufts of grass, rusted tricycles, and a broken fishing rod. A few bees worked the last flowers of the season, wilted stink daisies and dandelions. I could touch the neglect.

Louie was expecting me. The front door opened as I stepped onto the porch. The siding had more bare wood than paint, and half the roof was battened down with faded tarps that snapped as the wind came off the water. Louie was the twins' mom, and her face looked like she'd gone a few rounds too many in the ring the night before. Or many nights before. "Come in," she said.

"I'm Jack. I'm looking for them."

"I know." Louie picked up faded papers and magazines from a brocaded couch and invited me to sit. She sat in a chair. I knew it was hers. Thick wool and knitting needles were on the end table, which was an oak barrel with a stamped label reading NAILS. This was where she knitted sweaters late at night when all the kids had finally been put to bed.

"Do I call you Louise?" I knew the answer but wanted to be polite.

"Louie. Everyone calls me Louie. Since I was a kid."

"Louie, tell me about the twins. If I know them better, maybe I could find them. Bring them home."

There was a mother's fear in her eyes, a shadow passing with a bag of thoughts not wanting to be opened. Her eyes tilted up to the ceiling, laying out the memories, deciding where to start.

"They've been gone too long," she said.

I nodded. Didn't want to get into the details that I knew, or statistics on likely outcomes after x weeks missing.

"They're good kids. They did good in school, but they couldn't stand it anymore. Couldn't stop them. I let them go."

"Did their father have an opinion?"

Louie shrugged. That was her answer. I looked around the living room. Bent lampshade and a crack in the wood column that held up the socket for the bulb. A hole in the drywall the size of a fist. I knew what she couldn't say. "That drunk. What do you think? Hasn't really been a part of our lives ever, except to keep turning up and messing with us, bringing his screwed-up anger and a belly full of booze."

I gestured to the wall and her bruised face. "Did he do that?"

Louie looked at me like I was stupid, and I regretted the question.

"Your husband is Ian Stewart, right?"

"Common-law," she said.

"When the kids left for Vancouver, did your husband know where they went?"

"He was interested to know where they were, but I didn't tell him. He'd go over and look for them and then come back and bug me to tell him where they were. I never told him. Chief had a safe home for them while they were going to school. But then they disappeared."

"Do you think your husband found them?"

"Well, most of the summer, he wasn't here pestering me, so he might have been on the mainland looking for them. Now he's on the Island and he's come by once or twice."

"I get the sense that you weren't pleased your husband was looking for them."

"He's never been a father who cared about them," she said.

"I see. Can I see their room?"

Louie laughed. "You mean where all the kids sleep?"

She showed me the room, a square with five single steel-framed beds, like a dormitory. Two beds were empty and stripped bare, tidy in amid the chaos. There was a window with a beach towel tacked across the frame.

"So, the twins took all their stuff?" I said.

"Pretty much." She started to cry. "They've been gone too long."

It could be a cruel thing to give hope to a mother who has lost her children if it turned out you couldn't deliver. I hesitated, then said, "They're on the Island.

They were coming back home. But someone's got them now. I promise, Louie, I'll get them back."

As soon as the words were out, I regretted it. Who did I think I was? Louie looked straight into my eyes as if searching for a lie. I could tell she believed me and my intentions.

As I walked toward the door, I saw a framed photo of the girls, more recent than the ones I had. "Can I take this with me?"

"Sure. But bring it back."

With the kids missing everything connected to them was precious to her.

She stood by the door as I left. Tony waited on the road. Louie shouted after me. "If you want to have a talk with him," she said, "he's in Nemo's when the strippers start." Louie's lips were a thin straight line that could be taken for a smile.

It was no surprise that Ian Stewart had a fondness for strippers.

CHAPTER 22

Tony drove me back to the parking lot at Nemo's.

"I see Louie's old man is in there." Tony said. "That's his truck, an '86 Toyota pickup."

The pickup was red and rusted, the kind of truck you might find abandoned for years in the bush. I didn't get in the Westie van since I heard the music and knew the strippers would be working. I'd find Ian inside. I wasn't wrong. I ordered a Scotch and a beer chaser and sat at the bar watching a guy I figured was Ian with a stripper. He trailed his hand along her back, his lips close to her ear, while she tried to lean away from him. Her actions shouted: Creep. Even strippers had standards, and he fell well below the bottom-feeder category. I'd seen this guy before in many shapes, many places. In dumps like this and at fancy dances.

I tried hard to listen to advice from my therapist. Be calm. Breathe, count. For a moment I thought I was getting better. Maybe the therapy sessions at Birken had worked. I stayed calm for the moment.

The wind whistled through the high cedars and the firs. The storm had finally come. It was absolutely lashing, and the late afternoon had slid into the dark hole of a not-yet winter night. The same kid who was at the bar was still on shift. "Back so soon," he said.

Smart-ass. As if I lived in these places. I nudged my head toward the muscular guy harassing the stripper on her break. "Is that guy in here all the time?"

"When he's in town."

"Got a name?"

"I think it's Ian Stewart. I think he's connected to the mother of those kids you're looking for."

"Like their father?"

"Yeah."

I nodded and asked the kid for another Scotch. I alternated, drinking it fast and washing it down with the chaser.

Someone from the back called Ian's name. Three guys were playing on a full-size pool table. "Ian, let's rack them up."

Ian waved them off with a paw like a grizzly bear. He was still petting the stripper, trying to get her into his lap. But she brushed him off and I heard a fuck-you from him.

I was counting in my head and knew it wasn't working. I went to the pay phone and called Stacie's cell. Got no connection. I told myself she and Jessica would be fine hanging out at the farmhouse. The police would have found the blue Civic by now and gathered evidence. I was trying to piece it together myself. Blue Civic and Hans One and Hans Two pick me up. Hired by Voice. The Civic is seen taking the twins from Nanaimo, and now the car has its trunk stuffed with Hans One and Two, and the twin girls are gone. Drug evidence at the 3360 West 32nd house. Two bodies at West 32nd. Russians. Mark's Russian down deep with the salmon in the river. A white panel van. Two black Escalades. Ian Stewart coming back to the reserve. Otto Strang. Anton Tarasov, Sammy Lumbar. Mike Burns and Laura Wells. All very interesting, but very little added up.

Ian had given up on the strippers who were now back, all three dancing on a small stage in the corner opposite the pool table. Ian's three buddies played a three-way version of snooker while Ian lumbered to a booth, where two women were getting wasted. Ian sat down with them, making a cluster of booze slurp, and laugher. I could see the women's glazed eyes. They were still young but practiced at making their way down the dead-meat highway.

I finished my pale ale and tilted the last drops of Scotch from the glass. Ian was on his feet. The women hung on his shoulders like bookends. They wobbled together in confusion as they made their way toward the front door. Ian partly carried them with each huge arm around their slim waists. They stumbled out into the wind and rain.

I moved toward the pool table, past the players. Took a cue from the rack and pushed the side door open. I knew this guy. He wasn't making nice. He wasn't driving them home. He wasn't brewing up coffee, giving them a warm dry blanket, and tucking them in for the night. They were meat to him, like any girl who stumbled out of a bar on drugs and alcohol.

I was in the wrong place here. Needed to make a better choice and get back to Jessica and Stacie. Not be fucking with this guy after what had gone down today.

Ian was in the alley beside the dumpster. One woman was out cold on the ground. He'd iced her so he could take the other, who was balanced over a stack of plastic garbage bags. She was hurling into the dark, and Ian had her half-naked, working his way into mounting her from behind. All my calm counting and breathing left me.

I broke the thick end of the pool cue across Ian's shoulders. He lurched forward with the blow and turned. My second swing caught him across the nose, and he dropped back. He stumbled but didn't fall. His hands reached out, and he grabbed the dumpster to keep himself upright. I moved in close. "Where are they, you fucking shit?"

He seemed dazed. Not from the blow but confused. I was out of context for him. Not on his radar. His mind was still stroking the girl's butt that he was about to mount, remembering his victim's bare body, slack with booze and slick with rain. He was wondering why some guy had clocked him. He was running it through.

I held the severed pool cue end like a dagger. His eyes widened.

"Iona. Skye. Where are they, Ian?"

Something crossed his face, a riff from a discordant saxophone. I saw he knew how everything had happened, how the pieces were fitting in. "Fuck off," he said.

"Poor word choice, pal."

I held the pool cue close to his eye, then cracked him one across his nose with my forehead. My knee came up and caught him in the groin, and then he was barfing on the trash bags.

"Where are they?" I waited for him. I hauled his head back so he could breathe and asked him again.

"I don't know where they went," he said.

"Come on, Ian. I don't have all night."

"I don't know."

I took an intuitive leap. "Where are their backpacks? Where are the drugs?"

I saw his eyes clear a little. I'd jolted him. I pressed the sharp end of the pool cue to his throat. "Don't test me in the rain or this is going straight through your windpipe, and you aren't going to be beating or raping anyone anymore."

"I don't know where the girls are. It was stupid."

I let him go limp on the ground.

"What was so stupid?"

He was still conscious, but barely moving. He fumbled one arm behind his back and pulled out a .22 pistol. I turned sideways, my shoulder against the wall. Ian didn't draw the gun up for a chest shot. His best chance. But aimed at my feet. The gun misfired. I kicked it from his hand into the alley.

I heard a scrape behind me, turned to face my assailant, and braced myself, fists out, crouched into a smaller target. A freight train from the rain-soaked darkness came at me fast. I jabbed out but felt something hard and blunt crash like a sap against my head. There was a moment of limbo, then I went down. The alley's raw surface met my face, and the night became darker and wetter than before.

CHAPTER 23

I woke, delirious, not in a grounded world but in the stomach of a vast beast. Not so much floating as being dragged back and forth by the wave's ebb and flow on the shore. Something slippery swayed like a ribbon past my face. Creeping things scurried across my chest. Saltwater swirled around me. Wave on wave rattled against the shingle. I heard heavy breathing. Not mine. Larger, deeper lungs. Ham-fisted hands hauled me higher up the beach, my boot heels trailing in the sand.

I floundered with these images. My mouth was dry as a clamshell open to the sun. A throbbing in my head. All the universal stars racing toward me through a rain so intense it could bruise and crack the skin.

At first, when I awoke in a bedroom in the homestead, my eyes were two slits that saw translucent, muted light from a draped window, my ears that heard a rustle of fabric, like two thighs that brushed against each other.

"Jessica. I think he moved."

I must be one lucky guy. I opened my eyes fully. "I need a drink."

Stacie sat on a pressed-back kitchen chair beside me. She touched my hand. She wore winter running gear. She looked half ninja; all in black, sleek, and mysterious. "Jack, you've been through a lot," she said.

"No. I need water. I'm parched."

Stacie left for a moment and came back with water. And with Jessica, who was also in running gear. I tried to gulp the water down, but it sloshed past my chin and onto my chest. I realized I was naked beneath the blankets. "I'm gone a day and you started a track and field club?"

Neither of them responded.

"What?" I asked.

"You've been gone almost two days," Stacie said. "We were frantic. You went out for the morning. What do you expect?"

"We called the police," Jessica said. She jumped on the bed and buried her face in the blanket on my chest. I felt her shaking.

"Fat lotta good it did to phone the cops," Stacie said. "I was told to phone them back after twenty-four hours. When I did, they said they'd send someone 'round. No one came."

I went to lift myself up with my arms, but my armpits felt like grappling hooks had mauled me. "Almost two days?"

"Jack, we've been running, and I mean running all over the place."

"How'd I get here?"

"That big First Nations guy, Tony is sitting on the porch right now," Stacie said.

Jessica had stopped sobbing. Her breathing was in tune with my chest's rising and falling. I realized I couldn't keep making the same mistakes.

I got it. All the events were in sequence, right up to the shooting stars and a comet pounding in my skull.

"I must talk to him. Did he say anything when he brought me here?" I tried to get up and swing my legs over the bedside and away from Jessica, who'd fallen asleep.

"We haven't had much sleep," Stacie said.

I let Jessica down gently and slipped out from under the blanket. I'd forgotten. I stood naked. From a dresser, Stacie grabbed my jeans and the checked lumber shirt I'd been wearing. She handed them to me with my black boxers and smiled. Her eyes traced me from head to toe, like a barcode scanner. "You like? You scan it, you buy it."

"You wish. Don't fancy yourself, Jack McQueen."

I got Jack. Not Mr. At least she'd slept with me, though not in the Biblical sense, a mercy cuddle after what went down with her on the mainland. But for me, it was more than that.

"Tony didn't say much. It's his nature, right? He's gone through all the liquor. Not that he drinks much. Drank steady but in moderation. You've been out a long time. I found Chief, that's how we found you. You should talk to him."

I went out onto the porch. Tony's truck sat in the homestead driveway. The weather was overcast. No rain. I sat in a handmade, chain-sawed chair, sanded cedar, thick with faded Urethane. Tony sat on another chair and stared out toward the VW Westie. He didn't look up when I came out, or when I sat down. "I'd offer you a drink," I said, "but I hear it's long gone."

Tony looked up. Every exposed feature was tanned leather. He was all over triple x, but he was not a fat boy. He was pure muscle. Neck like a ten-pack torso. Long black ponytail hair. Blue jeans, comfy fit. Wide belt with an Orca buckle. Cowboy boots. A thin smile appeared. "You took your time waking up," he said. "What do you expect? You could have had more beers in the fridge."

"Where'd you find me, Tony?"

"We searched the water. Chief got everyone out who owned a boat. He paid for the gas. We went in and out of every cove and inlet. Chief studied the tides and the currents to find you. I figured you for dead. Mr. McQueen, you don't drown in these waters; you go numb and drop off. When we found you, it was lucky you were on the shore."

"How long ago?"

We found you late yesterday afternoon."

I looked at him and wondered how long I was in the water. It couldn't have been long. Less than half an hour or I'd be dead. I stared at my hands and flexed my fingers. They were still stiff. I got the sense that whoever sapped me didn't want to kill me. I had to think about that. I could have died from exposure. That bothered me. Maybe I was never floating in the water but placed on shore at the high tideline. That would explain why I didn't die of hypothermia.

"You're one man the spirits got to, then rejected," he said. "The spirits pushed you back to shore. You were only a quarter mile up the coast. Washed up on shore. The crabs had started to work on you, and you were twisted up with kelp."

"It was you who found me?"

"Nope. I was with Chief. He found you. He figured out the currents and tides. I brought you back to the homestead and hung around out here on the porch until this morning."

"Really?"

"I wanted to make sure Stacie and your daughter were safe," Tony said.

"Thanks. But I'm wondering how Chief knew how to find me by tracking the tides?"

Tony didn't answer but stood up and headed for his truck. "Let us know when you find the girls. Buy some Scotch and cold beer for the next time I need to save your sorry ass." He got in his truck and rolled down the window.

"Thanks," I said, "I'll do that."

CHAPTER 24

We were on the porch minutes after Tony left in his truck. Jessica was inside.

"So, where in hell have you been?" Stacie asked.

"Nice to see you too."

"Don't be smart. Your kid was frantic. You left us."

"Stacie, please."

She looked at me and took a deep breath. "I thought you were dead. You left your phone with me. If you'd kept it, you could have used it to let me know what you were doing."

I waited and looked at her with real sorrow in my heart. I didn't let her see that, though.

"Mark called me," she said. "Then someone named Becky called. A Staff Sergeant Murphy also called. You thought it was smart, leaving the phone with me but then I couldn't get in touch with you."

"I guess I should tell you everything," I said.

"It would help."

"Remember the blue Civic?"

She nodded.

"I found it up the road, past Tyler Madson's mom's place. Two bodies. Hans One and Hans Two. Both dead. Bludgeoned and shot in the feet and hands. Can you believe that?"

Stacie shook her head back and forth. I wasn't sure if she was disgusted by the murders or because she knew I hadn't told her everything.

Stacie gave me that so-what-happened-then look. I told her about getting the hell out of there and going to Nemo's. Then visiting Louie's place on the reserve, and my later encounter with the twins' father outside Nemo's. After that, I said, it was lights out.

"I think you're over your head here. Someone has the kids, the drugs, and the money. The police are looking for you and Jessica. They can track you through your phone. You've probably left your prints on the trunk lid or the release, not to mention your DNA from when you were stuffed in that trunk yourself back in Vancouver."

"So, you want me to go to the police? I'm caught between a rock and a hard place as it is. Chief needs me to find these kids. You think I need another complication here, especially the force?"

"Rock and a hard place?" Stacie said.

I remembered I hadn't told her about Voice, so I told her that story too.

"Jessica's a great kid, but you've got me babysitting. Not that I mind, but we need to get her back to her mother."

"Don't you think I know that?"

"Mark is concerned," Stacie said. "I took down notes. He went on and on." Stacie picked up a notepad and glanced down at it as she spoke. "Mark said something about Russians who came back and tossed the trailer, then set fire to it. He hid in the bilge on a boat, and they never found him. He connected with a guy Chief set up to watch the kids. The kids went to 349 Anderson after they disappeared from the widow's house. He said that the woman who lived at Anderson came out the front door regularly once a week with the two kids, one wearing a large backpack. She put the kids in the car and drove them to West 32nd Street and dropped them off. Each time the woman waited at the curb for about an hour until the kids returned to the car and they went back to Anderson. He said he suspected that the couple at the Anderson address had a hold on those kids and were forcing them to make deliveries, maybe drugs and or money or both. Chief's guy once tried to follow the kids, but they disappeared on him by the time he followed the route they took along 32nd. Street. Mark figured those kids were doing things they might not have wanted to do, and that's why they're on the run."

My phone went off. I answered. It was Mark. "Where are you now?" I said.

He told me he was on the river on his Ranger Tug. I put the line on speaker so Stacie could hear him.

"I'm not going back there. I'm having nightmares."

"I've got you on speaker. Stacie's here."

"They trashed the place. The trailer is gone. The cargo container is gone. Many boats went up in flames. Cops came out. Same assholes and a few others. Wanted to know where you were. It won't be long until they do, and Del too."

"That might be a blessing," I said.

"Those cops think I'm mixed up with you. Smuggling drugs for God's sake. They took samples from the gate. Paint chips. They probably know about the Russians. Jack, I'm getting out and staying on the move. I'm keeping off the land. I'll let you know."

"Mark, stay in touch. Don't panic."

The line went dead.

I looked to Stacie, "I'm not sure he got that last bit."

"Russians? You're kidding?"

So once again I came clean. I told her about everything except Yuri Dostonovich's body in the river. She didn't need to know. It felt good to share, for her sake and mine. Neither of us could afford to be blindsided since we were responsible for Jessica.

"Let me show you what I found," Stacie said. "Maybe it will make some sense to you." She opened the laptop. "I tracked the plates on the two Escalades and the Civic. Mark probably did the same, but here's what I got. The Escalade that took you from that underground parking to the beach, where you got the money to bugger off, belongs to a Nicholas Calvino. The Escalade with the plate on the ferry belongs to Anton Tarasov. The Civic belongs to Sammy Lumbar. I looked up Lumbar. He has a twin. It is no surprise they are your Hans One and Two."

"Nicholas Calvino," I said. "You've heard of him?"

"Haven't heard about any of them," she said.

"Calvino works for Otto Strang and Strang Corp." When I said this, I got a memory flash about the Shaplow Lake Fall Fair.

> A carnival. A shooting gallery, stuffed toys as prizes. The tuxedo man stands on a platform with other men in suits. Smiles and waving hands. Important people. Children laugh and play on swings and monkey bars. A tuxedo man with scissors cuts a pink ribbon. A crowd claps.

"Can you find anything more on Calvino, Lumbar, and Tarasov?" I asked. "I think they're connected to here, not the mainland necessarily. Something might be in the papers. Could be a good place for you to start. Let's work together. We can all check out Shaplow Lake. There must be someone I know still living there, and maybe there's still a newspaper office and a library. Jessica can help you, and we can both keep an eye on her. You still have the Glock?"

Stacie nodded.

"...lesions have no starting point/cuts beneath skin/mouths that cannot speak."

I watched her lips form the words.

"A healing hum, twitchy chatter in my ear."

"I didn't think you'd memorize stuff."

"I panicked," she said. "You were gone too long. I went through the contents in the duffle. Thought I might find something useful. I listened to your recorder. Bits and pieces."

My breathing got heavy. I pushed hot air out my nostrils and tried to count. "I can't remember half of what I recorded. It couldn't have made much sense."

"Much of it didn't. But as I said before, your words are put together well."

"And how would you know?"

She moved closer and stared into my eyes like a she-wolf.

"I'm not just a pretty face, buster. I read a lot. I've always liked poetry, even at school when the word poem sent kids screaming from the room."

I couldn't blame her for going through my things. I'd left them, then disappeared for nearly two days.

"Do you ever write this stuff down?" she asked.

I laughed. "I keep it to myself."

"What's the point?"

"There is no point." I felt she'd crawled inside my head. "We're going to town. Wear a jacket. Keep the gun zipped up in your pocket."

"Sure, boss."

"Okay, you can handle yourself, but I'm worried. It's not often someone clocks me and leaves me to drown at sea." I had a weird sense there was a piece missing in the way they found me. It was awfully convenient that I was washed up and still alive. More than convenient.

Jessica came out onto the porch.

"Get something warm to put on," I said. "We're going to do some investigating."

Jessica went back inside, and I saw her grow up before my eyes. She appeared to be responsible. These moments would be short-lived. Del had to be on her way, and I needed to keep Jessica safe. I went over to the VW Westie and started the engine. Soon after, the ladies tumbled from the house dressed for combat and got in.

I dropped them off on the main street, a hundred yards from the library.

They waved, then turned and headed up the sidewalk like a mother and daughter out shopping. Stacie looked good. I patted my ankle to make sure the Beretta was still there. Then I locked the van and walked the few blocks to The Duke, the only other bar in the downtown core.

It was the usual scene. Sketchy. Loose plaster at the door. Darkness in the corners. Two regulars sat at the bar at each end with a half-full pint and were nursing it along. I took a seat; back to the wall, facing the door. I ordered Jameson and a Guinness. The J went down, and the black half followed it. I signaled. Ordered the pair again. I realized how mashed-up I was, and how needy I was for internal calm. I slowed down and could feel positive magic hitting the bloodstream. I didn't know what I was waiting for but felt certain it was coming through the door. The guys at the bar watched me without moving a muscle. They were well-practiced. The barman was familiar, but I couldn't place him. Craggy face. Deep grooves in the skin from too much smoke and booze. He looked scrubbed-up, but he'd seen more weather than the west-coast wreck of the S.S. Valencia.

I chewed on the facts. The missing girls. The Island. My memory loss since they'd dropped me from the force. The gaps in my childhood memory.

> I smell the damp earth and feel the darkness. See a buried boy. A tunnel. Is that buried boy me? No, because now I feel the boy's weight, heavy in my arms.

I gnawed on any connective tissue in my brain that could bring back these lost memories.

The main door swung open. A short guy in a rumpled shirt came in, pants cinched tight around his thin waist. The guy weaved about like a dog looking for a place to pee. He stopped, looked at me then took a seat at my table. There were stitches on his forehead. A recent fall? Missing teeth. He stank of tobacco and stale booze. The table started to vibrate from his leg pumping up and down. He was classic. "Hey," he said, "today's my birthday."

It was a great opener. Heard it before. Every day's his birthday. What the hell? I motioned to the bar and held up my thumb and index finger two inches apart. When two whiskeys arrived, the guy's eyes lit up like a small boy with presents under a Christmas tree. He didn't speak. He threw it back. I knew the feeling well. The burn, and how it spread a calm to settle into. He looked up and met my eyes.

"Happy birthday, pal," I said. Then I noticed him more closely. "Jimmy? Jimmy Walker?"

He looked surprised. Then suspicious. "Who's asking?"

"The guy who bought you that drink you came in here sniffing for."

"Do you know me?"

"If you're Jimmy Walker I do. We played baseball, soccer, and ball hockey. You had a half dozen brothers and a sister. You went to the Catholic school." I didn't say he lived in the small house on George Street in town. That the back porch always smelled of piss and his pants did too.

"Yeah," he said.

I motioned to the bartender for two beers. Figured I'd better not aid and abet this guy's habit but be at least sociable; two beers and not the hard stuff. "Do you remember outside the church the day Cross Lady beat you over the head with her wooden crucifix with the metal Jesus nailed on it?" I said.

"You remember that? The bitch wouldn't let me go. She smashed me over and over. Talk about Christ's blood." He raised his hand and pushed his hair back, and I could see the scar on his forehead. He looked at me closely, and said, "Jack?"

"Jack McQueen." The two beers came, and I pulled out the twins' photo. "Have you seen these two?"

"Yeah. They're from the rez."

"Seen them lately? In the last week or so?"

He started thinking, tracing his steps backward through his blackouts and the booze.

"Nope. What's up with them?"

"They're missing, Jimmy. They went missing this summer on the mainland. Tracked them here. Figure they came back home but are on the run. Figure someone's after them."

"Lots go missing here."

"What do you mean?"

He'd stopped shaking the table. His hands were steady, and his eyes seemed a little clearer now. "You know it's not really my birthday."

"Jimmy. Listen to me. What do you mean?"

He started to raise his glass again. I grabbed his wrist and held firm. The glass hovered, and I lowered it to the table. "Focus," I said. "What do you mean?"

"Nothin'. Booze talkin'."

He glanced around and looked at the two guys nursing beers at the bar.

I kept my hand on his wrist and pulled it toward me. He leaned in toward my face. Nicotine and whiskey stung my eyes. "Talk to me," I whispered. "These twins are children."

His eyes widened, and I squeezed his wrist to keep him focused.

"Can I get a smoke and go outside?" he said.

"Once you talk to me. Then we can go outside."

"Girls and boys, young women, babies even. They go missing. No one does anything. Never have."

I waited to keep him talking.

"Jack, you must remember the kids that disappeared when we were young," he said. "Then later when you were with the police. How could you forget?"

I wanted to tell him I'd blacked out on many memories. That I couldn't remember. That only little bits kept coming back. "Who's taking them?" I said.

"Do you think I know?"

"These girls I'm looking for didn't go missing from here. They went missing from the mainland. Are you telling me someone's taking people from here?"

"Yeah, from the rez and other places where folks are hard up or don't care."

I tried some names out on him. I whispered, "Do you know Nicholas Calvino, Anton Tarasov, or Sammy Lumbar?" I let go of his wrist.

Jimmy shushed me like I'd yelled the names across the bar. But no one seemed the least bit interested in our conversation. Jimmy was frightened now. He grabbed his beer and wolfed it down.

"I gotta go," he said.

I got up, followed close behind, and pushed the door open for him. "Cigarette," he said when we got outside. "You promised."

I didn't have any, so I went back inside and bought a pack of Rothmans and matches at the bar. I couldn't believe they cost almost ten dollars. They used to be under a buck, years ago. I went outside and Jimmy was long gone. Christ. What was I thinking? I went back inside The Duke and put the cigarettes on the bar. "I just bought these for a friend and now he's gone."

"Jimmy? He's got a habit of doing that." The bartender handed back my money. "Keep the matches."

I crossed the street and walk toward the library. I walked into a variety store, went to the counter, and bought a pack of gum. I didn't chew gum, gave me a headache, but I had to buy something. Once I paid, I said, "You know the street people, the homeless here? Where do they hang out?"

The woman behind the counter looked like a tired gravel road, with washboards on her brow, cracks, and runnels on her skin. I could see the brown burn stains on the counter behind her, where too many cigarettes had burnt down along the edge. She had a dead, gray pallor.

"Who wants to know?" she said.

Suspicion ran a tad wild in this town. I decided to be honest. "I was talking to Jimmy Walker. We went to school together. We were getting caught up over drinks at The Duke and he left, and I wanted to tell him something and give him some cigarettes."

"Is Jimmy really your friend? He ain't got many. Most around here take advantage of him and beat him up."

"Hey, I'm not going to do that. Ten minutes ago, we shared beers."

"You know his brothers and his sister?" she asked, reaching back for the cigarette burning on the counter's edge.

My mind started to race, and from a buried memory layer the names came: Eddie, Johnny, Mikey. Forgot the sister's name. Didn't have much to do with her since she was the last one born, an infant when I hung out with Jimmy. I rhymed the names off, and she smiled.

"Most hang in the park down near the lake, and some you'll find burrowed beneath the overpass across the river that leads into the lake. They're a cautious bunch. Don't go barging in there, especially at night."

"Thanks for the advice."

I walked up the main street to the local newspaper office, the Shaplow Daily News. I remembered that Bob and Betty Roland owned the paper and had run it since at least the time I started on the force. Bob was in the back with the guts of the business, while Betty greeted me at the counter. "If you've come to place an ad, you're in the right—Jack McQueen. Now there's a face I haven't seen for quite a while. Are you on the Island?"

"It's good to see you, Betty. No, I'm visiting. I'm wondering if you can help me. Do you keep all your copy?"

"Everything's computerized now, so all editions are in pdf digital files, and the old stuff we arranged to have scanned in jpg or pdf. Don't have much call to go back to the old stuff, but we have it for historical purposes."

"I need to see articles referring to Otto Strang and your annual fall fairs. Thirty to thirty-five years ago."

"Are you working for the RCMP again?" Betty said.

"No. I'm done with that. Private Investigation. I want to pay you for your time if you're willing to do it."

"It would take me an hour or so. You can pick it up later today. How about fifty?"

"That's great, Betty. I'll swing by later." Then as the last thought, I said, "What's your impression of Mr. Otto Strang?"

Betty's lower lip quivered. Her eyes looked at the window, and the street, then she turned to the counter at the back where Bob worked.

Bob answered for her. "Think about an ugly portrait crossed with a goat-footed balloon man. If you want, you can also look in Mr. Otto Strang's gun-barrel eyes."

I shivered. Walked to the door. Turned to Betty and said, "Sorry I asked, Betty."

I stepped out and turned toward the library. As I got to the library's glass door, I turned back to the street and saw a uniformed RCMP officer coming up the sidewalk. I swung the other way and saw another moving toward me. And across the street, two obvious undercover cops leaned against an unmarked police vehicle. I stepped into the library foyer.

Stacie and Jessica came toward me. A thick brown envelope protruded from Stacie's coat pocket. Jessica spoke first. "Jack, we found out a shitload of stuff about this town and you."

I let the "shitload" slide. I looked back through the glass door. The two undercover cops were running across the street toward the library entrance.

The two envelopes with money were inside my plaid lumber jacket. "Here, take these," I said to Stacie. I passed her the envelopes and the keys to the VW.

"Go back into the library. Find an emergency exit. The police are outside. Take the van back to the homestead. Don't let anyone in, no matter who. You've got the Glock. Remember the fruit cellar. Look behind the shelves at the back."

Stacie was quick. She didn't question, but grabbed Jessica's hand, spun on her heel, and headed back into the library and toward an emergency exit door. Jessica clued in quickly too. She was so smart, but Del was already going to slit my throat. I'd let this go on too long.

I went out the library's front door. One uniformed cop was close now. He braced himself. At that point, I turned in the opposite direction, but it was too late. Then I felt it. A low-side tackle and I was down. The undercover guys had dropped me, then the two uniformed officers piled on. All I felt was their weight on my back. I smelled their sweat and after-shave, then heard the VW's engine tick as the van moved into traffic.

CHAPTER 25

The interview room was square. Opaque window on one side. The door at the end. Metal table bolted to the floor. Three chairs, two on one side, one on the other. All bolted to the floor. The walls were pea green like an old kitchen. I was in the single chair at the table, back to the door.

The door opened. A guy walked past me and turned to face me. I knew him. Reilly. Hard head. Irish. He knew me. He wore a tight suit, off the rack, and tired from overuse. A cream shirt. Slept in. Open collar, one button, and a tie knotted in a hurry without a mirror or tied yesterday and slipped over. "Did you just wake up, Reilly?" I asked.

"Shut your face. I'll be asking the questions." He sat across from me. "Why are you here, Jack McQueen?" He drew out the McQueen.

"Go ask the rugby thugs who tackled me and hauled me in?"

"You always were a smart-ass. I mean, on the Island."

"I was homesick. Thought I'd catch a glimpse of your ugly mug."

He didn't blink. He'd gotten better at controlling his temper.

"Do you know why you're here in this room?"

"No, but I think I'm going to find out."

"Let's start with kidnapping."

"So that's what all this crap is about," I said. "The kid is my daughter for Christ's sake. How can that be kidnapping?"

"We'll see about that once the next storm's over. The mother's going to be here soon enough."

"Good to know. She'll go back with her."

"Where were you yesterday? Start from the beginning."

"Tell me why I should tell you anything."

"Jack. I know your background. I know what happened. Why you're off the force. So don't fuck with me."

I remained silent and thought back.

Parts of my body are broken..

Something inside has collapsed.

But it is all shadows, dark movement in a fog.

I snapped back.

"Shouldn't you be out catching taggers, graffiti vandals, and dopers instead of harassing me?"

Reilly's tone changed. I saw it in his eyes before he spoke. "It's murder. It's serious. Tell me where you were yesterday. All the steps. All the places. Who you saw?"

"You think I'm involved? You think I murdered someone?" How many bodies did they know about.

The door opened and Reilly tried to make himself look neater, straighter, more composed. I turned my head and there was Murphy. I'd forgotten many details, but I hadn't forgotten Brigit Murphy. She was my partner when we worked undercover homicide when I'd crashed and burned. Now she was Officer in Charge.

I watched her walk across the room in sensible shoes that still made her legs look inviting, a grey skirt to go with her suit jacket, white silk blouse. She looked too refined for the Murphy I used to know. She passed behind Reilly and sat down. It was obvious she was taking over. I watched her lips move, imagined they were close to my ear, whispering something sweet, like a flow of honey. "How are you?"

I believed she was genuine. Good people don't change.

"I've been better, thank you."

"Now, let's get down to it so we don't waste time." She pulled out a small recorder. Said the date, time, and interrogation session name. "This is where we are, Jack. There are two bodies in the morgue here. Found them stuffed in a Honda Civic not far from your family homestead. There are two bodies in a morgue on the mainland with bullets in their heads. Your ex is on her way here to claim the daughter she says you kidnapped. Rumor has it you're tracking down two missing girls. I want you to tell me what you know about all this. We have forensic evidence that ties you to these murders. Fingerprints on the trunk lid and the interior release. DNA. A surveillance photograph of you entering a crime scene, courtesy of VPD."

She was all business, more intimidating than Reilly could ever be. Surveillance photograph? I was surprised that VPD would communicate with the RCMP. City police and the force weren't known for sleeping together, even in big cases. Fingerprints? Sure, mine are on record with both Canuck and U.S. armed forces since I'd worked in special operations for both, and with RCMP. But DNA?

Bullshit. That takes time. But then I remembered Reynolds mentioning the Combined Forces Special Enforcement Unit.

"Start yesterday morning. All the steps," Reilly said.

"I visited Mrs. Madson, my childhood friend's mom. She's still in her homestead up the road. I asked her about the two girls, the twins I'm looking for. Iona and Skye Stewart. Louie's kids from the reserve. She hadn't seen them. Then I followed the road further since I thought this Honda Civic would be somewhere along."

"How did you know that?" Murphy asked.

"I have someone helping me with the computer stuff. Research, and she found some videos that pointed in that direction."

"Yeah, but why the blue Civic?" Reilly asked.

"It's a long story."

"Try us," Murphy said.

"A while back when I got hired to find these girls, someone roughed me up a bit and threw me into a beat-up, blue Honda Civic. Tried to scare me off looking for the girls. Then back in Nanaimo, someone saw the two girls get into a Honda Civic, so I figured it was the same guys and the same car."

"Go on," Reilly said.

I could see the prick was enjoying this, getting the upper hand on me with Murphy taking over. Weasel. "I follow the road to the end and find the Civic in the woods. I wait. Nothing happens, so I creep over toward the car. No one was inside. There are cups and wrappers on the floor. I think the worst for the girls. I pop the trunk release. Turns out the two guys who roughed me up are in the trunk with bullet holes in hands and feet. They'd been beaten to death."

Reilly and Murphy gave each other a look.

"What?" I asked.

"We found your breakfast in the grass," Murphy said. Your DNA."

"I threw up. I didn't kill them. If I'd killed them, do you think I would have left fingerprints? Thrown up? Come on."

"Then where did you go?" Murphy asked.

"I got a sense you already know."

"Humor us a little," Reilly said.

I counted in my head, and took deep breaths, but I wanted to jump across the table and smash my forehead into his nose. But I was getting better at working on this. "I went to Nemo's to settle my nerves. I used the pay phone and called the detachment. Then I went to the reserve to see Louie. Asked about the kids. Then I went back to Nemo's to settle my nerves some more."

"That was you?" Reilly said. Why didn't you leave your name? Appears very suspicious."

"I called, didn't I?"

"That night," Murphy said, "when you were in Nemo's for the second time, did anything happen? Did you confront anyone?"

"I met up with the old man. Ian Stewart. Had a word with him about his girls."

"We heard it was more than a word," Reilly said. "You took a pool cue to him."

"I roughed him up. Gave him what he deserved for that night."

"We know," Murphy said. "We found Ian Stewart dead with that pool cue stuck in his throat. Your fingerprints were on the cue."

They'd waited patiently. Let me reel it all out, then gave me the hammer. I let it sink in.

"I don't expect you'll believe someone clocked me and I was out when Ian Stewart got whacked."

They looked at each other. Hell, I wouldn't believe it either.

Murphy got up. Switched off the recorder. She walked over to the door. Didn't look back. Reilly got up and trailed after her. He swung his head back toward me and said, "Do yourself a favor. Get a lawyer, asshole."

I sat in the chair, staring at the puke-green walls, and the one-way glass. Who'd been watching me if anyone? Maybe they went for coffee. Yeah, let the killer stew in his juices.

A short time later Reilly opened the door and walked in. He sat down with two coffees and slid one toward me.

"It has been two years," he said.

I looked at him. Wondered if he'd come to gloat and call me an asshole one more time.

"You've got the wrong guy."

"You can't blame them for dropping you off the force. That day you went from paralytic to homicidal."

"That's what you believe?"

"It's all in the file. Well-documented. The situational. The medical. The psychological."

"He was a killer. He molested little boys."

"So, you say," he said. "There was no proof of that."

There was proof, but I wasn't about to tell Reilly how I knew that. I know Murphy knows because I told her. And I know she's not telling. Ever. That was the deal we made, back then.

"Jack, if you remember, you emptied the clip into his chest. A bit excessive, don't you think?"

He let me chew on that. I could almost taste the memory, but not quite. Images had been mauled into a blur. The whole clip?

"You're lucky," he said, "that you're not behind bars playing happy bitch to some burly Aryan gang leader putting your ass up as another notch on his tattoos. Murphy saved that ass of yours. You know it. She knows it. The old guys who were around at the time are aware of it."

I sipped my coffee. Wondered where this was going.

"Jack, did you go berserk and beyond two nights ago and beat up Ian Stewart because you thought he'd been molesting his missing kids? Did you go too far and drive a broken pool cue's sharp end into his throat?"

"Reilly, c'mon. Really?"

"You've got anger issues. We've got witnesses who say you followed him out back at Nemo's. They heard the fight."

"That's it. They stayed inside. They saw nothing. They heard the fight. They didn't see someone clock me. They didn't see that same someone kill Ian Stewart."

I finished my coffee and Reilly picked up the cup and took his own with him behind me. I heard the door close. Two hours passed. I chewed on mangled memories. It felt like Birken all over again. Questions. No answers. Hypnotic guided journeys. I kept it all inside. Got the hidden details in sporadic spurts. Part strategy. Part survival. A part that couldn't help me.

> "Give me a raging forest stream,
> a flooded alpine meadow,
> last marsh marigolds in bloom."

The next time the door opened, Murphy entered. I turned my head to watch her come over to the table. She was still in her business suit. One more button on her blouse was open. My benefit? An absence of protocol? Some message? I wondered why they hadn't yet arrested me for Ian Stewart's murder, the two guys in the trunk, and the Russians on the mainland. Or at least booked me for skipping to the Island when I'd been instructed not to leave Vancouver.

Murphy had a pale manila folder. She placed it squared up, parallel to the table's edge, and sat down. "I didn't think I'd see you here again."

She was hot in her power suit. Better than when we'd worked old clothes together when we shared most everything.

"Wasn't planning to be here," I said.

"Over two years and the homestead stayed vacant. You should have at least rented it."

"I didn't want anything to remind me."

"I kept tabs on you."

"You did?"

"You have been a PI during that time. You're not exactly clean of your addictions. I know you've recently come back from Birken Psychiatric Hospital. I understand you and Adele are not working things out so well. And here you are out on a limb, feeding your obsession with missing kids."

"It's not an obsession. No one seems to care unless some rich kid goes missing, or there's ransom money. Who cares about the missing when they're invisible in the first place?"

"That's not fair," she said. "The force has got only so many resources at their disposal. Everything's prioritized from the top."

I knew she was right. Even as a staff sergeant, she didn't have a choice. Further up the chain of command, power and influence were in control.

"That's why people come to me for help," I said. "That's why despite the past I'm back on the Island."

"Sad for you, but you had to leave the RCMP."

"I know, Murphy. And thanks." I'd always called her by her last name. Brigit seemed such a mouthful of harsh consonants. She liked it, but I couldn't bring myself to use her first name. For a while, we'd had a thing. Maybe six months, but we both knew it wouldn't work in the long run. She was on the way up, and after Del and I split, I was cruising. I knew I'd get in her way. She was tidy. Everything by the book. I'd never been tidy. We stayed friends when it ended, two years back. After I left the Island, we lost touch. Staying friends was hard to do.

Murphy flipped the folder open. She kept the edges parallel to the table edge. I watched her hands. She had long fingers. Pale nail polish, hardly noticeable. Her hands and wrists were white, not tanned as they were when we worked the streets. I glanced at the open button on her blouse. She hadn't changed much. Smooth tight skin, but pale, like she was always inside. The whole package was packed muscle, balanced with an overall impression that said don't-mess-with-me. Her hair was clipped short, businesslike.

"So, are you going to arrest me?" I said.

"Don't jump too far ahead."

I sat quietly and let her turn each page in the file. I couldn't see them well, especially upside down. Reports. Statements. Blurry photographs. Press releases. Newspaper clippings.

"I want to go back in time," she said.

For a brief second, I thought she was talking about us. Then I realized she was referring to the incident. My discharge. "Jack, first I want you to tell me you didn't kill anyone. You didn't kill those two guys in the Honda Civic or drag Ian Stewart into the undergrowth along the shore from Nemo's and in a blind rage stab him in the throat."

I looked Murphy in the eye. "I swear it. I didn't kill them."

I could feel her tension dissipate a little.

"Going back, what can you remember when you shot Frederick Madson?"

"Are you recording this? Can anyone else hear this?"

"Only you and me."

"Why are we going back there?"

"This is my file. No one else knows about it. I've kept it open for two years. For you. I think there's a connection. I know you had trouble coming forward after the incident. I'm still not sure you were evasive, more like something closed you down. I want to unlock all that."

"What makes you so sure you can do that when all the shrinks who harassed me after the shooting couldn't, and the therapists at Birken didn't help? Oh yeah, it was partly anger management, but they tried to crack me open."

"Talk to me. Tell me what you remember."

"Are you sure no one's taping this?"

"Positive."

"And you're not going to arrest me?"

"Currently, I'm not going to arrest you. You can't leave Shaplow until we clear this up. I'm putting a detail on you."

"So, I'm free to go?"

"I'm investigating an inquiry that's two years old. What we were working on back then has been deliberately put in storage. We can't touch it. Do you even remember what we were working on?"

"So, I'm free to go?"

"You're trying my patience. I can put you in a cell right now. Hold you without a charge or if you want, I can slam you for not cooperating with the police. You left the mainland after receiving instructions from Reynolds not to leave Vancouver. See I know about that, and I know about a photograph of you leaving a murder scene over there. The force does talk to VPD. And we got DNA on you here, and fingerprints, and witnesses. Enough to hold you if I want. Are you going to cooperate with me?"

"DNA?"

"Well, not yet, but that vomit in the grass and the saliva on your coffee cup will match, along with what you've said about throwing up."

"Cooperate? Are you asking me to work with you? Tell you about the past. Tell you about the present. And are you going to tell me about the past and the present? And are we going to be partners again? Can you help me find these two girls? Are you going to put closure on this two-year-old file?"

Murphy closed the file. She adjusted the spine to line up with the table's edge. "That's about what I want," she said. "Nothing is what it seems here on the Island anymore."

"So where do we go," I said, "because I'm sure as hell not talking here, and I don't think you want to be talking here either. For all you know someone's listening to everything we say."

"I don't think so, but you might be right."

"Well, am I free to go?"

I reached across the table, picked up her pen, and scribbled a word on the folder.

"I'll escort you out," she said.

CHAPTER 26

I sat in a corner booth at The Duke. I'd left the police station with the contents of my pockets after the desk sergeant poured them from a brown envelope. They were kind enough to give me back my Beretta since I had a permit. I'd written the word "Duke" on Murphy's folder, and figured she'd arrive when she could. So, I waited. I dialed Stacie's number on my cell. It rang twice.

"Jack."

"I'm out. Are you guys, okay?"

"Yeah, we're sitting here with the Wi-Fi and the newspaper clippings. I have an old photograph of your parents that was printed in the newspaper. You don't look anything like your parents. We've got the munchies but there's nothing to munch on."

I wasn't sure if she was pissed at me. "I don't much want to look like my parents. Seriously, are you okay? I'm hanging out at The Duke, waiting for Murphy."

"Who's Murphy?"

I forgot I hadn't told her about Murphy, so I said, "Long story. She's the staff sergeant at the detachment in Shaplow. We used to work together. She got me off the possible arrest. She's with us."

"Don't be long. The Glock is fully loaded, but I don't want to use it. Jessica's on the computer, playing games. I have her close. The doors are locked and only one light is on. I've got a plan, but don't be long."

She was making me nervous. "I'm going to wait here half an hour. If Murphy doesn't show, I'll walk home."

"That's still going to be more than an hour."

"Don't worry, Murphy will show, and I'll get her to drive me. If I must, I'll jack a car."

"Right. As if you're not in enough trouble." Then Stacie was gone.

Before I arrived at The Duke, I'd dropped into the Shaplow Daily News and picked up an eleven by-seventeen-inch envelope from Betty. When I gave her a hundred, she tried to protest. "For the cause," I said. "Keep printing all the news that's fit to print."

The envelope was beside me, on a chair's wooden rungs. I hadn't opened it. I looked up and Murphy came through the front door. The Duke wasn't full. A few guys were at the bar. The regular bookends were nursing beers. Murphy saw me in the booth and came over. She had ditched her business suit and wore blue jeans and a blue cotton blouse tucked in with a thick all-weather quilt-lined shirt, loose and oversized. I knew she had her gun beneath the shirt. She sat down beside me, so we both looked out into the room and had a good angle on the door. Basic stuff.

I watched the others in the room. The bartender looked Murphy over when she came in, but everyone else stayed with what they were doing. "What'll you have?" I said.

"Beer's fine."

I went to the bar and brought back two pints of pale ale.

"Cheers," she said.

After the first sip, which for me was a long one, I said, "So tell me about that file."

"It's on you. The incident. Everything that happened then. Everything that's happened since. It's my file. I keep it with me all the time. Can't trust anyone in the force on the Island."

I looked at her carefully. "You can't trust anyone?" Then I smiled.

"You were always a cynical bastard," she said. "And I found out over the last two years that you have a right to be."

"Tell me what's so special about this file."

"I want to question you," she said, "then I'll tell you why."

I looked around the room and figured we were safe enough. A CD was blasting out Boom Boom by John Lee Hooker, and I figured the trend would continue for a while. "Go ahead," I said.

"You were always a loose cannon on the force. You know that. And I always wondered how you ever got past the psych tests for the army, Special Operations, and then the force. When we worked together, you know. Got together. I saw something that wasn't in your psych bio. The foster home life after your parents died, how you were trained in the army, and what you brought to the job on the force. There was something all those people who dealt with you never knew. And I sensed it in the dark when we were alone. I know it sounds crazy. But it's in my gut and when you killed Frederick Madson that day, I saw it. I saw the look. I saw the panic."

I looked into her eyes. She looked inside me. I knew what she was talking about, but I wasn't sure I had the words. I could see the images I saw at Birken. He had an axe. I knew that axe. I'd seen it before, and I'd seen him use it. Mrs. Madson knew about the axe, but she was terrified. Couldn't speak. Tyler couldn't speak. I squeezed the trigger, squeezed the trigger, over and over and over. Silence. Metal axe blade falling on the rocks.

"Mrs. Madson must have known all along when I was a boy," I said. "When Tyler was a boy, did she know what was going on? Back on that day she was frozen. The axe was what gave him away. Ran at me with it. I had no choice. I recognized the axe."

Murphy was silent for a minute, marinating in my words. "I traced a few things back before you shot him," she said. "I know that young kids were going missing when you were a boy when your best friend Tyler disappeared. No one ever did anything then. Leads always went cold. Bodies were never found. People figured those kids ran away from home. Same with the missing kids when we worked undercover and now."

"Are you telling me it's all connected?"

"I'm saying something has been going on since you were a child. You were part of it then, and when you were on the force. After the shooting someone wanted you to be gone from the force. Someone with influence. You're a part of it now. I'm not sure how it all connects, but I think you have the answers locked up inside you. In that childhood trauma, and the trauma after you killed Madson."

Madson had the axe. Mrs. Madson wanted me to find Tyler for her. I knew where Tyler was, but I didn't know where Kat and Peter were. I couldn't speak this. I couldn't go where she wanted me to go. I didn't even know how to find Tyler. I'd blocked that out.

"People around here are afraid," Murphy said. "They've been afraid for a long time. No one really speaks."

I deflected her. "Anton Tarasov?"

"You know him?"

"Heard the name," I said. "I had a guy from the mainland checking out a few things and his name came up. You know about the two dead Russians on the mainland. Reynolds or someone must have sent a report when I left."

"I've seen some information on it. Those two guys were known associates of Anton Tarasov."

"And you know this Tarasov?"

"Tarasov calls the shots," she said, "and no one does anything but jump high. We know he deals in drugs and maybe more, but apart from nailing a few small mules and two-bit punks who are bottom feeders, we can't get near him. We have orders from higher up to stay away. He owns an estate about twenty miles up Island, near Campbell River. We can't get near it."

"Higher up? Like in the force?"

"Hard to tell if it stops there," Murphy said. "Money. Politics. Influence. You know the story. It's an old one."

I shook my head. I wasn't surprised. "What's Tarasov like?"

"He is old school and comes from a prominent Russian family in the day. Honor code. Mean and ruthless. He is into illegal gambling, arms distribution, and drug trafficking. I heard he's got an army of bodyguards up at the estate. The involvement in his pachka or pack is not ethnically exclusive. If you have the skills he needs, you can be Latino, Asian, Sikh, American, or European. He owns a small island in Desolation Sound and has connections with the port on the mainland."

"What about Nicholas Calvino?"

"You've heard of him, too?" she asked.

"I get around. Remember, loose cannon."

"He's the business manager, if you like, for the Strang family. You know the Strang family, right?"

"Same family as when I was a kid. Do they still own most of Shaplow Lake, the town, the actual lake, all the shoreline pretty much?"

"They do. And that family is hands-off. Always has been."

"Untouchable? Fuck. Strang," I said. "I've suppressed all that. It is going to take a lot to get it back. He must be old by now if he's from my childhood?"

> A man stands in a well-lit concrete tunnel. A young, handsome, athletic man with white skin and a hairy chest, flat ribbed abdomen. I smell the aftershave and the cigar smoke.

Murphy looked genuinely worried for me when I admitted I couldn't remember. "Otto Strang is a lot older now," she said, "but he's still in charge up there on the hill, looking down on Shaplow Lake. Can't get near that place either. Calvino sees to that, along with Strang's two sons, James, and John. But the sons deal with business on the mainland."

"I don't remember them."

"They're your age. They'd have been kids when you were young. Likely they wouldn't have gone to any school on the Island. Probably went to a private school on the mainland."

I slip back to the immediate present. "Sammy Lumbar?" I asked.

Murphy came back with, "And his brother, Frankie. The lookalikes. They were pretty boys once, weren't they?"

"Did you figure out how they came to be shot in each foot and each hand," I said, "and battered to death and left in the trunk of the Civic?"

"I Got My Mojo Working" by Muddy Waters took over from John Lee Hooker. Murphy said, "Do you think the same people shot them in the feet and hands also beat them to a pulp and killed them?"

"That would be logical," I said. "Did Reynolds say anything about the same MO in his report on the two Russians killed in Vancouver? And do you think we've only got two choices here? Tarasov or Strang?"

"Reynolds didn't put in the detail on the hands and feet. But that looks like a pattern. Strange though to go to the trouble of doing that. Any thoughts?"

"Must be a way to torture them. Get information," I said.

"Jack, I think that one of them is mixed up in this. But we can't touch them."

Whoever shot the hands and feet had a motivation. Pain. Incapacitation. Little blood loss. The result, well, pure brutality. My bet was on the Russians for Hans One and Two. And maybe they popped two of their own to find out where the cocaine went, and maybe the money. I kept this to myself.

"I'm wondering why they're dead," I said. "They're the two guys I called Hans One and Hans Two. The last time I looked at a program, they weren't working for Tarasov. So maybe they worked for Strang or at least Calvino. He was on the mainland and got them doing something, maybe it was moving drugs, short hauls around the city. Something went wrong. I have my suspicions that the girls skipped with the drugs and the Russians were involved but it's pure speculation."

"So, who has the drugs?" Murphy said. "Where are the girls? Is there money involved?"

I looked down at the folder. She saw me look. "What's in there?" I said.

"You remember what we were working on when you shot Madson?"

I wanted to tell her I knew everything. Clear as a bell. I wanted to prove that I wasn't still messed up by everything that had gone down in my past life. But I couldn't. I remembered that when I was a boy, there were missing kids. But I no longer remembered the details.

"Some memories are there," I said, "but not everything."

"I have all the reports. The ones on you. The missing person reports. The newspaper articles. All the dead-end leads we had. The letters back and forth trying to get the case re-opened. The interview transcripts we did. The ones with the First Nations community. The ones with the homeless. It's all in here and I want you to look at it. I'm blocked here at every turn because the case we worked on is sealed, but you're not prevented from investigating. You can slip under the radar. Maybe visit these people again. You might remember lost details."

"We can do this," I said. "I'm getting flashes. I went to The Shaplow News. Got articles about Strang in connection to stuff that went on in the past."

I pulled out the envelope and opened it. There were at least five stories. Strang cuts ribbon on children's playground. Strang Corp funds Oceanside Ball Park. Free Fall Fair attractions. I scanned the last article: face painting, blow-up trampolines, carousel, bumper cars, clowns, kids' ballet, and fairy costumes. "These articles are from when I was a kid," I said.

I read her the headlines and passed the articles across the table so she could take in the details.

"Remember, Jack. Many people in town loved the guy. He was always there for the kids. If they needed swings and monkey bars? He paid for them. That ball diamond wouldn't have happened without Strang's money. Every year the kids loved the Shaplow Fall Fair. Otto Strang would come down off the hill dressed up in some costume. Sometimes it would be a tuxedo. Sometimes he'd be a clown. Sometimes a cowboy or a lumberjack. He'd make a speech. Donate more money. Then mingle with the crowd. The moms and dads and the little kids. There were some parents who felt uncomfortable having this guy dressed up and mingling with their kids, but for the most part, people thought he was a generous, stand-up guy."

Kat pushes her face forward toward the paintbrush. She sits on the tuxedo man's lap. His hands rub the soft fuzz on her arms. White feathers stick to her tiara.

A clown in a yellow suit, with oversized red shoes and tufts of red hair, a white face, red lips, and a red nose is in a crowd of little kids in fairy costumes. He hands out candy and helium balloons.

"Are you okay?" Murphy asked.

I finished my beer and heard Murphy's cell phone vibrating.

"I have to take this," she said. "Murphy." She listened for a minute. "I'm on it," she said and clicked off. "Jack, I have to go and you're coming with me."

"But I need to get to the homestead. Stacie's waiting up with Jessica "

"Jack. That's where we're going. There's a fire."

CHAPTER 27

We left The Duke with the rain lashing and the wind whipping the fir and Arbutus trees into a demented fury. I barely had time to close the passenger door before Murphy pulled into the deserted main street and roared the engine through its gears.

"A fire? Where? The barn or the homestead?" I asked

"Everything."

"Jessica? Stacie?"

Murphy had no time for complete answers. She was on a mission. I fell silent.

The road was slick with leaves and small blown-down branches from fir trees. We curled around Shaplow Lake, rain pocking its surface. Murphy made the left onto the gravel road leading up from the lake. We crested the ridge that ran parallel to the lake's south end. I saw the glow in the distance. The homestead was on fire.

Murphy wasted no time entering the upward-sloping gravel road that led to the driveway. The car kicked over the humps like a bronco. We both lurched forward with each washboard bump in the road. A fire truck, a cruiser, and an ambulance were parked by the house. Murphy slammed the brakes. The barn was gone. All I saw was its thick-timbered skeleton in flames through the pouring rain. The air was thick with smoke, burned rubber, and old paint. The VW Westie was lit up like a torch, and the main home was ablaze.

Murphy was out first and rushed toward the uniformed officers standing beside the cruiser. Firefighters hosed the house through the rain. Tony's truck was parked off to the side away from the fire truck and other vehicles. He was dressed in personal protective gear, coat, pants, helmet, boots, and gloves. He was helping the firefighters control the blaze. Add rockets and explosions and it would have been Apocalypse Now. I jumped from Murphy's car and ran toward the house door. The firefighters were busy and couldn't stop me without dropping their hoses, so I busted into the living room, right into Dante's Inferno.

Inside. The fire. I searched. Smoke drifted and curled in waves around the open interior doors. The satin ribbon edge from Jessica's blanket lay beside the flaming couch. I rushed toward it. The end was tattered, scorched black like everything around me. The stone fireplace stood like a huge tower, and flames leaped around it and up through the roof.

I broke toward the bedroom on the main floor, the air filled with smoke and ash. Flames licked up the walls, twisted around the door, and up the staircase leading to the second floor, now engulfed and raging. The heat pressed at my mouth. I stopped breathing. Heard my heart pumping. My lungs screamed for air. The heat. I couldn't take the heat. The upstairs was impossible to attempt. I left the bedroom and tripped into the kitchen. A charred shape lay on the floor beside the table. Arms bent as if in prayer. I wanted it not to be the worst. Looked closely at the shape and size. It was a male body. Flames darted back and forth. Vertigo set in.

> I keep Kat and Peter safe from wolves. I bring them back to this house. To a place where we're not wanted. To a place, we don't belong.

> Light flashes from a moving window on a sunny day. I hide behind the closet door in the kitchen. I see two teeth from my mother's mouth lying on the floor.

> There is a hatchet honed sharp in my hand. So sharp its thin edge can shave my fingernail. A fragment of my mother's head lies in her blood on the kitchen floor. I hide from the anger in the room. I open the closet door with my fingers. The space is wide enough to see my father. His huge chest was built by work heaving bales of hay into the barn. His muscular hands slap us across the room.

Now in the present everything was flames, not blood and teeth and me.

> I watch my mother canning peaches and making jam. The air was all peaches, sticky with the sweet scent of boiling… I see her hanging laundry on a line, the wind snapping the white sheets against a blue sky… I see her dusting. Always tidying. Feel the clean, slick surfaces where dust knew better than to settle. I see her work on everything but things for herself.

> We are bundled together with a woolen blanket, against the wind. My mother and I sit in a sunny spot in the field with Max sleeping beside my knee. My mother reads a picture book to

me. There are fairies, toadstools, small houses in the dark forest, and a happy ending. This is once. Only once. Her arms are around me. The sun shines down on us, the blanket, and her body close to mine.

I see her beneath the kitchen table. The bone fragment from her skull. The teeth resting in her blood.

Then the hatchet is in my hand. My father is dazed and in a trance. I step out of the room. He doesn't see me, and I plunge the hatchet deep into his chest. I watch him stagger to the tabletop, lurch back against the counter, drop to his knees, and fall forward on his chest, burying the hatchet blade deeper toward his heart.

Now in the present, the house was flame and smoke, and my legs were buckling beneath me. A hulk moved toward me, through the inferno. I dropped and felt my body lifted and carried out through the curling flames into the black wet air. Where were Jessica and Stacie?

CHAPTER 28

Many minutes later I saw a fire truck, lights spinning in the rain. Ghost figures, bulked up by protective gear meandered the house's wet smoldering wreckage in the constant downpour. One ambulance. One cruiser. One grunt constable secured the scene behind the yellow crime-scene tape. His cruiser at the homestead's entrance to the driveway blocked access. No other cars, except Tony's pickup and the burnt-out VW Westie: a hulk of twisted metal. The tires were black melted rubber, the wheels chaotic skeins of wire mesh.

Tony sat beside me, his butt planted on a downed cedar log, bark long gone, and its inner wood smoothed and bleached by sun and rain. I'd been uncontrollable when I was carried from the blazing kitchen. I wanted to rush back in. I was carried back exhausted to the cedar log. Then I must have dropped unconscious after that.

I lay on the ground, my back against the log. Tony passed me a bottle of Scotch. I took a small bolt and felt the warmth hit my mouth and throat and settle in. Tony grunted. There was no pleasure in the process. To myself I said, "Don't do this, Jack." Then I spoke to Tony. "You carried me out?"

Tony grunted again.

"We have one body. Too big for your daughter or Stacie," he said. "Neither one of them was in the house."

He handed me the bottle again. I put it to my lips but stopped, didn't take another sip, and passed the bottle back. He seemed to need it more than I did. He finished the rest and threw it down, glass rattling on gravel. Fruit cellar. Jessica and Stacie. Stupid. I needed to do something.

"How long was I unconscious?" I asked.

"Five minutes."

The lights from the fire truck revealed the only structure still standing: the charred stone chimney. Surrounded by burnt lumber, soot, and ash. The rain still dropped heavy on our shoulders, down our necks, and dripped from Tony's baseball cap.

And then it dawned on me.

How stupid. "Beneath," I shouted. "Beneath."

I stepped up to the crime scene tape, ducked under, and walked toward what remained of the front veranda, got my bearings, and visualized the house before the fire. The two firefighters looked up from prowling through the drenched wreckage. I saw the officer on duty get out of the cruiser. Everything was converging. I entered where the front door used to be, moved over the uneven, water-soaked terrain of the living room and into the kitchen. The world was twisted. There was a staircase beside the kitchen, that once led down to the fruit cellar. But the space was now a gaping hole. I heard shouts telling me to stop, then the firefighters grabbed me.

"She's down there," I said. "I know exactly where she is. I've got to go down. I know this house. I've got to go down." The firefighters swapped glances.

"We'll help you," one said.

The other one tested the flooring, roped himself to the refrigerator's charred mass, and lowered himself into the basement. The other firefighter lowered me by the armpits. The first guy caught me by the feet and waist as I descended.

Once I was down, I oriented myself to where the cold cellar was. The firefighter handed me an industrial flashlight. I found the door and entered a gritty swamp of broken glass and an entire archeological dig of smashed preserves from years ago. I found the moveable shelf at the back and swung it open. I pointed the flashlight toward the tunnel that Tyler, and I dug so many years ago. The light showed encroaching roots, but nothing I couldn't get through. "It's a tunnel I built years ago," I said, "when I was a kid,"

"I'll follow you," the firefighter said.

Many roots followed the tunnel's sides and ceiling; only a few crossed it and created impediments. I moved slowly, searching the ground with every step. Not wanting to find Jessica and Stacie just yet. Not wanting to find that they hadn't made it. I knew where the tunnel led: toward the boundary with the Madson property, where Tyler and I dug a large underground room, covered the ceiling with cedar plank ends, and braced it so the earth would not cave in.

Halfway along, I remembered how I'd dug into the tunnel's wall. I remembered what I'd buried there.

There was a closed door at the tunnel's end.

"Stacie. Jessica. Are you in there? Jessica, honey. Shout to me."

I waited and listened.

I pushed on the door, but something heavy blocked its movement. I pushed harder. It still wouldn't budge. The firefighter came up behind me.

"Stacie and Jessica," I said. "If you're in there, yell. It's Jack."

We waited again. Then we both pushed. Nothing. "Step back," he said and took the fire axe from his belt. The blade shone in the light and triggered a memory flash; I visited the digging, and what was buried farther back in the tunnel.

He swung the axe taking three hits to break through. We stepped into a large room. "Jessica? Stacie? It's Jack."

I swung the flashlight in a circle, then heard a small voice. The Glock stared back at us.

"Don't move. I'll shoot."

It was Jessica. Blinded by the flashlight, she couldn't see me.

"Jessica. It's Jack."

She hesitated. "Daddy?"

"Jessica. It's all good now. It's Jack and here's a firefighter. Thank God, we've found you."

I took the gun from her hand and slid it into my pocket.

"This is my gun.' I said to the firefighter. "It's licensed. Please, don't mention it in your report."

I found the old side door, about three feet tall. I crawled out, followed by Jessica and the firefighter. We were in a fallow field, close to where the trees started. I could see the Madson house in the near distance. The firefighter radioed his partner and let him know we'd got through and were safely out of the tunnel and away from the house.

"Where's Stacie?" I asked Jessica.

"She had to leave. She said that I'd be safer hiding here and gave me the gun. She has another gun that she took from a man who came into the house."

"Who came? How many?"

"Daddy, I don't know. We were so scared."

"Okay. Okay." I lifted her into my arms, one arm behind her knees and the other at her shoulders. We walked slowly through the wet grass in the pouring rain, back toward the spinning fire truck lights.

A firefighter wrapped Jessica in a blanket and put her in the back seat of the police cruiser. She was asleep a moment later.

Tires rolled over gravel and headlights searched the sky as a car lumbered up the gravel road to the driveway.

This early morning marked the second day of a wave of storms that were piling onto the Island. Now even the once-a-week ferry was canceled. All water travel had been prohibited. All air traffic was grounded. I wasn't expecting Del, but there she was walking toward me.

Del was prepared. Sturdy hiking boots. Rain gear. Wool hat. Hooded jacket. Rough. Full of mind-your-own-business, like she was when we met and got married and made a family.

I returned to Tony who stayed to give whatever help he could. He grunted and shifted his butt along the log away from me. He needn't have moved. He wasn't the target. I was. Del stomped toward me through the rain and punched me in the face. The blow rocked me back. She followed it with another and another until I toppled back into the salal. Then she jumped up onto the log and came down with both feet on my chest. I rolled so each heel merely glanced off me, and she stumbled and lost her footing as she landed. We grappled. Her close-fisted hands beat me.

I blocked each punch as best I could and rolled away. She pounded my back until we were both exhausted and slid over each other along the slippery, salal leaves. We cried together. She clung to me. I clung to her and shook. "But Jessica's—"

"Where's my baby? What have you done to my baby?"

She was full of sobs. I'd never seen this side of her, berserk and fearful that her child was dead.

"She's sleeping in the cruiser," I said. "She's safe."

CHAPTER 29

Del ran over to the police cruiser where Jessica was sleeping. I followed her.

"How did you get here?" I asked her.

"I have connections. I managed to bypass the restrictions and flew on a Cessna floatplane. I arranged for a cab to pick me up at the Shaplow marina at Beachcomber. I'm taking Jessica to the clinic to get checked over, then we are going back to the mainland immediately."

I left it at that and watched Del carry Jessica in her arms toward where the cab that she arrived in, was still waiting.

Murphy drove me to the emergency clinic in town. Behind me I watched Tony's truck follow the cruiser. He was going to look after me.

The doctors fixed up my superficial burns. They cleaned the wound on my arm, which I'd been nursing since the fight outside Del's house, and they prescribed meds for the pain and released me.

Tony had taken off his firefighting gear and was waiting for me. He asked me where I wanted to go.

"I need to get to Beachcomber Marina. You know where it is?"

He did and we arrived before the Cessna took off. I walked over the grass toward the dock and the Cessna. Del, Jessica, and Murphy stood beside the aircraft and turned toward me. I approached them hesitantly, but Jessica took two steps forward and hugged me. She still clutched a different piece of her blanket's satin trim. A charred piece was in my pocket. Del hugged me too, but there was a small force field between us, like magnets repelling each other. It was subtle, built on fear and memory. When we separated, she wasn't Del but Adele, and Jessica was hers, clinging to her thigh. I heard my daughter say, "Mommy are we going home?"

"Yes, dear. We are," Adele said.

Murphy moved over beside me. In her eyes, she had a mix of we've-got-to-talk, what-an-idiot-you-are, and maybe-we're-too-deep-in-this-shit-to-escape. "It's still dicey, but the wind has dropped," she said. "Pilot says they have lifted the restrictions."

I worried for them. A single-engine plane ride was dangerous. "Del, you don't have to go," I said. "Murphy can arrange for you to be safe here on the Island."

Adele looked at me. Adele wasn't having any part of it. She wanted Jessica back on the mainland, far from the grime that I always seemed to channel toward them. They could both be targets. And what was safer, staying here or risking the weather?

Del and Jessica climbed into the Cessna. Del didn't turn her head. Jessica pressed her face to the window and waved at me as the plane motored from the dock.

The Glock was stuffed in my coat pocket. The Beretta was strapped to my lower right leg, above my ankle. Tony looked at me.

"Take me to The Duke," I said. And he did.

He physically took me into the hotel and stayed with me as I checked into a room that was rented by the day.

He gave me a small bag with a bottle of single malt and six beers.

"I didn't know you were a volunteer firefighter?"

"I'm full of surprises. I'm going to be watching you, rest and get some sleep."

I came up to the room with the bag, the smoky clothes on my back, and no cash since I'd given all the money from Chief and Calvino to Stacie. That was it. Like starting at square one.

I eased into the only seat in the room, a heavy living room chair that had seen more ass than a whorehouse. Thick upholstery was worn thin at the arms, but with a deep seat that invited you in for the night. It was late afternoon. I broke into the Scotch and drank the beer from the can. It was light summer swill you drink when you're thirsty, not Guinness or Pale Ale. I was thankful Tony thought of me. He left me his cell number.

The beer and Scotch made good partners. Before long they blended with the drugs. "Oh, sweet Jesus I shouldn't feel so good," I said aloud to the light glinting through the amber liquid in the glass.

In the hotel room, I walked myself through three more glasses of Scotch, neat, and took down two more beers. This was my home. A double bed. One chair. One sink. One toilet. Shower down the hall. Cigarette burns on the bed cover, ashtrays on each end table—both tables streaked with brown grooves where cigarettes had been left to burn across the veneer. It was a perfect place to drink Scotch and beer and wash away my sins.

Someone knocked on the door. "Come in," I said from the chair. Careless, but I was starting to not care. I gave my head a shake. She was gorgeous. Tight black leather pants, cream blouse, a little on the small side for what she was covering. Tony, you're too good to me, I thought. Then I realized she was carrying a tray of sandwiches from the bar.

"Hey that big guy who brought you here, wanted you to have these. Said you need to eat. He's coming by later and he wants all these sandwiches eaten. He said it was an order. Told me to tell you I wasn't to let you mess around. He knows my sister and my brothers."

"Oh, he's a smart-ass, isn't he? Wouldn't think of it."

She put the tray down on a small dresser. "Just kidding about that messing around stuff, but I thought you'd try."

"Maybe next time," I said. "Thanks." And she was gone.

The sandwiches balanced the booze and kept me lucid. Right.

Scotch. Beer. Sandwiches. Minor burns. Jessica and Del on their way to the mainland. The weather still bothered me. I worried that they could be grabbed to get at me. Stacie MIA. Murphy needed me. I needed Murphy. The Scotch continued to work its magic, blending with the painkillers. I drifted in a swill of thoughts and narrative.

Something made the Stewart girls leave for the mainland. Their father. Probably abuse, but no one's talking. How did they get from being safe and attending school, living with the widow Milroy, to something more adult? They were victim material that fell prey to someone darkly evil. My thoughts drifted to Tyler Madson.

Tyler lives by the river that flows into Shaplow Lake. We make up games to play together. His mother adopts me as a second child. "Oh, meet my second son, Jack," she says.

Tyler likes to dig. He gets me involved in projects, the biggest one being the tunnels with compartments, complete with PVC tubing for air. We dig a hundred yards behind his house and cover the hole eight feet by four feet and six feet deep. We use old planks and small logs salvaged from the ocean, or deadfall branches from the woods. We conceal the hole with planks and put grass and forest debris on top so, from above, the ground looks natural. Tyler doesn't let his parents know, so it's a secret place, the sanctuary where he can hide from his father. A place where Tyler runs when his world turns small and ugly. When his father comes home wanting him. We build the tunnel to my house so I too can run when I must. And it's there I lay the body. Below the floor, so he can rest.

This is the place where I found Jessica by following the tunnel from our homestead to Tyler's secret place.

I sweated through the booze and painkillers. The Scotch and beer were gone. The darkness and the room became a spiral tunnel, and I was deliriously tied to a bullet, screaming through the shiny metallic night. It was all garbled and repetitive. Skin was itchy and nerves twitchy.

Today I enter my mother's room.

A thick handwoven curtain blocks the light from the bedroom window. I follow the light toward her dresser. The light strikes a music box. One corner glitters and draws me to it. I know the music. I know the memory, sound upon sound.

My hand opens the lid. A ballerina in her faded pink tutu flips up. The music begins and she dances to each pure, plucked metallic tine. Every note grips my heart. I want to ask her who she is in her lost silent dreams. Who are you as you watch him beat us beside the barn? Where is your heart when we are in the long tunnel, with that man waiting for us at the end? The ballerina is you dancing round and round to all your life's sad music.

> "You open your mother's chest of drawers
> You lift the lid of her music box,
> And listen to the metallic notes."

CHAPTER 30

I woke to more rain hammering the roof. Would it ever end? My mouth was fouler than a dirty sock. I was eggshells and felt as if my fingernails were peeling paint. There was a floating twitchiness. I was in the bed, naked with a faint smell of smoke and Scotch about me. The last I remember; I was sitting in the chair with sandwiches and beer. Now, I was not alone.

"Aren't you a ray of sunshine?"

I looked across to the chair where Murphy sat cross-legged, in jeans.

"Fuck, what hit me?" I said.

"When you decide to dive down a rabbit hole, you do it in spades."

"Never did a half-assed job at anything."

I saw new clothes on the dresser, almost identical to the rags I'd worn the night before. Murphy saw my glance.

"Thought you'd need new clothes to put on," she said. "I've kept the bills. A couple hundred should cover it. I know you're good for it."

"Yeah, sure."

I saw the Glock and the holstered Beretta beside the clothes. The sandwiches, the beer cans, and the Scotch were gone. "Who got me into bed?" I asked.

"I'd like to say I did it all myself with guile and promises, but you're not that lucky. Besides, who'd have wanted you the way you were? Tony came by. Got you showered and tucked in. Can't say he was gentle, but then again look what he had to work with."

"Why would you even care? I nearly got my daughter killed. The homestead is gone. Stacie is missing, and I'm no closer to knowing what the hell's been going on. I feel I can't continue."

"That's not true. Now pull yourself together. Dammit, you've dropped back into my life and I'm going to damn well use you to help me find out what has happened to everyone who has gone missing over the years."

Settling into the pillow, I said, "I don't know anything."

"Jack McQueen, you know a lot more than you think you know, and we're going to find out what it is. The Chief's still counting on you, and I can't work for the force here without making changes. I can't do that alone. If you don't pull yourself together, we'll all be dead. We're at a point where no one's pulling punches. There's too much at stake for these guys. We're doing this together."

I looked at Murphy. I believed her. "Do you have a plan?" I asked.

"I'm counting on you," she said.

"Did you bring that special file you have on me? All the secrets. All the times I cracked someone's head open. My school record that said "incorrigible?""

"I did."

"Also, I left the envelope with the old newspaper articles in your car. Do you have that?"

Murphy nodded.

"Stacie did research at the Shaplow library and had an envelope full of stuff the day you guys brought me in. She still has it. All the other information she has on her laptop, along with the files I gave her. Any word?"

"I have Reilly and two constables out looking for her. Either whoever came to the homestead's got her, or she's lying low, or…"

I didn't want to go there, so I looked up at the peeling wallpaper above the door and thought about the Stewart twins. About them coming back to the Island after all this time, their father showing up in Shaplow Lake, how convenient it was that he was dead and how it looked like a tidy frame that Murphy hadn't fallen for. "Why didn't you arrest me since you had evidence? You must be getting heat right now."

"Let's say I'm not taking the easy route. As I said, there's no one I can trust. I'm not even sure about Reilly. I'm going to the bathroom. Get dressed."

When she came back out, I was basically dressed the same as yesterday, but cleaner. I was grateful. I wondered where Stacie might be. I thought about my spare clothes, the recorder, and the other stuff in the duffle. I wondered if the bag had been destroyed in the fire or if she had it. "I've been thinking about the twins and their father, Ian Stewart," I said. "I know there were drugs, and where there are drugs, there's money. I'm piecing it together. How could this have happened? From what I saw of the father, I'd bet he was touching them. That's why they left. Couldn't stand it anymore. Maybe their mother helped them escape because she didn't want it to escalate. Didn't want him to start beating on them too. It's a familiar story, isn't it?"

"There are always 911 calls from the reserve, but no one goes out. Most figure it's better to let them settle it themselves."

"You figure that?" I said.

"Not really, but after you go out a few times and no one's talking, and when you do intervene and want to drag the guy off for the night—and you end up in the middle and the victim's beating on you—it's hard not to be jaded. I've seen too many young officers full of piss and vinegar race right into a domestic and the next thing you know, someone kicks them in the knees, sends them down the stairs and they're on disability for months. After a while, you get cautious and look out for number one."

"Once the girls got over to the mainland," I said, "Chief set them up in a safe place. He had them watched. But I think Ian Stewart went over and tracked them down. Started to watch them too."

"How do you figure that?"

"I found out the twins ended up at 349 Anderson in a safe house. They'd been conned into transporting drugs to a house on West 32nd Avenue. I went there. Found the two Russians dead. Mouths, wrists, and ankles were duct taped, and neat small bullet holes were in their foreheads, but they had also been shot in the hands and feet. Same as the guys in the Civic."

"And the connection with Ian Stewart is?"

"Do you think Ian Stewart is the hands-and-feet shooter? I don't think he had it in him to kill anyone, just incapacitate them. You know the night I fought with him in the alley before I got whacked on the head?"

"So, you say," Murphy said.

"I hope you're pulling my chain here." I was on the brink of trusting her.

"Go on," she said.

"When I fought with him. When I thought I'd knocked him limp, he pulled a gun from behind his back and for a moment I thought, here it comes. But he tried to shoot my legs when he could have just as easily hit me in the chest."

"You didn't mention anything about him having a gun."

"Must have forgotten. Anyway, it didn't fire and the last thing I did before I was hit with a sap was kick the gun deeper into the alley. Maybe the gun is still there."

"I'll have homicide search for the gun," Murphy said." I'm not sure your theories are clear on the murders. You hit Ian Stewart hard with the pool cue. That could have disoriented him. You were fighting in a storm. What I remember about Ian Stewart that's locally on record for the RCMP would put him in the category of a desperate man who might do anything to survive. He was certainly a wife-beater, but Louie never ever filed a charge against him. This might sound like a cliché, but I recall Ian Stewart was known for torturing animals. He was a large strong man used to working with his muscles logging in the bush, and he was violent. I believe he could commit murder."

"If you think Ian Stewart has the personality to murder," I said, "he could have put bullet holes in the Russians in the West 32nd house, and he could have killed Hans One and Hans Two."

I was starting to get restless, so I stood up and began pacing. I looked for some alcohol to pour into a glass then I realized what I was doing and focused on Murphy instead. "Maybe Ian Stewart takes the money the Russians had to buy the drugs the twins were delivering to them."

"Reynolds didn't say anything about having photographs of other people on surveillance at the house," Murphy said. "Doesn't that seem strange? Why wouldn't the twins, the Russians, and Ian Stewart not be photographed?"

"I wondered why the police were only interested in me," I said. "Maybe surveillance was one copper with a camera near the front? Maybe the twins and the Russians used a back entrance? Maybe we have a corrupt copper in the Van PD who messed with the photographs? I've wondered why the Russians showed up at Mark's marina looking for me. Reynolds saw my license plate on the surveillance and traced me to the marina. If the Russians were fed that same information about me, that would make sense."

"Now you're starting to make this stuff up to make your theory fit."

I leaned against the window frame and smelled the dusty drapes then moved away in case the bugs started jumping.

"You can call him," I said, "Ask him if there were other photographs. I think you might find one for at least Ian Stewart."

"I'll do that. Go on."

I watched Murphy change her legs. Crossing one over the other. She was getting antsy too. "So," I said, "the twins arrive with the drugs but find the dead Russians, get scared, then bolt with the drugs. They decide to go into hiding, and what better place than back on the Island."

She came back with, "Who whacks the two Russians if this is true?"

"Whoever was supplying the drugs," I said. "Whoever had the twins making deliveries across town."

Murphy kept pressing, "And the two guys in the Civic?"

"See, I know the two guys in the Civic picked the twins up in Nanaimo a few days after they came off the ferry. I have a witness who saw them get into the car and head up the Island."

"You like Ian Stewart, their father, as the hand-and-foot shooter for the bodies in the Civic trunk?" she said. "If that's the case, he managed to get the drugs from the twins, and the twins are in the wind or someone else has them and is pretty pissed off they don't have the drugs or the money."

I couldn't have summed it up better. "Sounds plausible. Someone angry enough to execute their own people," I said.

We locked gazes. She was with me now.

"Are you thinking what I am thinking?" Murphy said.

"Where's the money and the cocaine? Too bad Ian Stewart is dead."

"Yep," she said. "Assuming Ian Stewart took the drugs and already had the money, where is it?"

There was a rap on the door. I opened it. It was Tony. I grabbed the Glock and the Beretta. "We must get to the reserve," I said. "Louie's house.

CHAPTER 31

I jumped into Tony's truck, and Murphy followed in her car. Tony phoned Chief. He asked him to go to Louie's place and get her and the kids out. If Ian Stewart had the money as well as the drugs, where would he hide them? Somewhere familiar where no one would stumble upon them. If I was right, they'd be around Louie's house. We needed to find them. I feared the Russians had put it all together already and were headed there themselves.

Tony pulled the pickup into a driveway three doors down. Murphy left her car on the side of the road away from Louie's front door. A rain had let up earlier but was now steady, and the late autumn light was fading, making the gray sky darker. No lights were on in Louie's house. The same boxes lay scattered on the lawn, but the rain had pounded them into the grass. Tony had his hunting rifle—a Remington 700 SPS Tactical—at his shoulder as he ran for the side of the house. I held my Glock. Murphy had her service Glock G30S out. She and I entered Louie's front door as Tony came in through the back. The house was empty. Chief had come over and taken Louie and the small kids to a safe location. I could make out the furniture in the dimness. Everything was in its place.

With the reserve located on Georgia Strait, the wind had picked up and was swaying the shoreline firs and cedars into a frenzy. A sure sign the next storm was coming. Rain hammered on the roof. It would be nearly impossible to distinguish sounds: the scrape of a boot, the twist of a door handle, the slow movement of a poorly hung door opening. Tony was in the kitchen, back to the counter, facing the rear door. Murphy had tipped the coffee table over and was crouched behind it, using it as a shield. I waited by the window, nudged into a corner beside the couch. If I couldn't hear it, I wanted to see what was coming.

"Don't wait for me to try to arrest these guys," Murphy said. "Do what you have to do."

It was still early, maybe 6:00 p.m., and it could be a long night, so I stayed alert at the window and started thinking about where Ian Stewart could have hidden the drugs and the money. I remembered there was enough crap stored in the bedroom closets that money or drugs could be hiding in a plastic bag beneath some stuffed animals. The ceiling was fiberboard squares on a metal grid. Another possibility. I put my focus outside. A wooden boat sat rotting, leaning to the left where it had rolled off its keel. It was derelict. Maybe there, beneath the flooring or behind a side panel. Many choices. Or maybe we had it all wrong. Maybe the Russians were not coming.

Headlights flashed and hit the back wall for a second. I watched the light move along the street and disappear.

Two hours went by. The rain grew more intense, a heavy sheet slapping the ground.

I heard an engine's low-throated growl, then silence. I strained to hear the car motor's metallic ping as it cooled in the rain, but the rain dominated and lashed the window where I was hunkered down. No lights. Rain. Wind. Lightning flashes. Everything was blue ice, jagged. A white panel truck and an SUV were on the road out front. Stopped. Silent. Another flash. Men moved across the lawn toward the house, wavering figures against the lightning after-print. I heard movement in the kitchen. The wet scrape of a foot. An uneasy yawn at the back door.

I expected a rifle shot from Tony, but all I heard was his rifle stock's muffled thud hitting soft tissue, and a body falling to the floor.

I started to move. Wanted to shout that we couldn't wait for more men to start coming in. Too many, and after one doesn't come back out or respond, they'll know. I could see Tony back against the wall, rifle ready to shoot from the hip or swing like a club. I motioned with my finger. Let him know I was going through to the outside. I could see him track me and swing over so he could see where I was going. Murphy was dug in.

Once outside the door, the rain engulfed me. A racket was raging inside my head. I crept across to the boat, blended into its shape, and waited. The front door of Louie's house protested. Splinters of wood, a mélange of bullets. Murphy's Glock and Tony's rifle returned fire and the house lit up with crisp flashes, followed by each explosion's crack. I waited. A figure moved toward the back door. I fired. Two quick rounds and a body dropped. I waited and listened in the din of the rain.

My neck hair bristled. The air movement changed. I started to turn, and a heavy body crashed into my arm, a pass rusher cutting off my corner. The Glock flew from my hand and slid across the boat's hull. I twisted and got my elbow up, then a heavy man crashed into me again. He was slick with rain. I grappled, feeling the pain jumping all over my skin where the burns started to protest. I bounced off the gunnel and dropped, but not before I grabbed him by the shoulders and let my fall and his momentum topple him toward me. Both my arms got pinned by his chest, but I kicked back at his ankle, and he rolled, allowing me to slither sideways and grab the Beretta from its holster. I fired. The bullet caught him in the upper thigh. I jumped toward him and smashed the gun down onto his head until he was unconscious.

I heard sporadic gunshots, car doors slamming, ignitions starting and the growl of tires retreating over gravel.

The remnants of the intruders had left in their vehicles. Murphy called the incident in, and there were cruisers everywhere and bodies were found. Two bodies were located inside by the battered front door. One body lay on the kitchen floor, and another at the back door. Spent adrenalin was hot musk in the air. We all were drained and traumatized.

Duct tape hung on a hook near the door. I used it to tape the guy I'd shot in the upper leg, a through-and-through hole. I taped first his mouth, then his legs and wrists. He lay still under a tarp in the boat's hull. I bandaged the wound with his shirt. No arteries were hit, so he wasn't bleeding out. He was unconscious, with a large headache in his future.

Reilly was on-site. I knew Chief had the place covered too, but he was nowhere to be seen. Just Murphy, Tony, and me. We needed to wait until the scene calmed down. Murphy sat at the kitchen table with Tony, and I was outside with Reilly. We watched as the bodies were zipped into body bags and hauled to the morgue van.

"How'd you know they were coming?" Reilly asked me. He swayed back and forth from one foot to the other, like a small kid who needed to pee but didn't want to waste the time. It was his tell. He was nervous. Unsure.

"Didn't really," I said. "Came over to talk to Louie, but she wasn't here."

"Sure pal. You think I was born yesterday?"

"Okay. With her husband getting whacked, I thought she needed protection."

"Yeah. Maybe protection from you. I still figure you for Ian Stewart's murder. You might have Murphy in your pocket these days, but that doesn't make me think you're going to get away with it."

"Look, Reilly. You can't tell me these Russians weren't after something."

"How do you know they're Russians?"

I looked at Reilly like he was stupid. Tried to figure out who'd had a hold on him. "You just have to look at them," I said. "And who acts this ruthlessly?"

Murphy came outside. "Once the bodies are gone," she said to Reilly, "I want you all back at the station. Leave a cruiser at the main entrance to the reserve. No one is in or out unless they're aboriginal. Got it? And try to ID these guys and let me know what you come up with."

Reilly flipped into subservience. "Right," he said. He headed for the nearest cruiser to call everyone off.

Murphy turned to me. "Tony and I have been talking," she said. "He figures we need to find a safe house here in case they come back. So once the circus has gone, we're going to the abandoned cannery in his truck. You bring my car over."

She handed me her keys. "I think I need to watch Reilly."

"No kidding," I said.

Once the force left, Tony and Murphy placed the tarp-wrapped duct-taped guy in the back of Tony's truck and drove off. I waited at the front door, wishing for something hard to throw back and sting my throat. My body was twitchy, a flaming trigger and I needed something. Since we didn't have time to search the house before the attack, I rummaged through the rooms and looked in the usual places like kitchen cupboards and under counters. I came up empty. I searched in earnest not only for booze but for money and drugs. The closets were piled to the ceiling with pillows, large and small stuffed toys, old towels, and used clothing, and seemed like the best place for a fruitful search. Snake eyes. The lack of organization was unnerving. Worse, I didn't find any bottles either.

I checked the space above the ceiling and found nothing.

I went outside to the boat. The rain had stopped. I crawled up over the gunnel and slid into the wheelhouse and under the bow, where the boat stuff was stored. Not much there, other than moldy life-saving PFDs, oily rags, and a first-aid kit that had seen better days. The boat's side panels were teak sliders. I removed one, and there it was: a taped-up plastic kilo packet. I removed more panels and found more packets lining each side of the boat. There was a dusty sack stuffed in there too. I loaded it up with the drugs and took it into the kitchen. I wondered why Louie's home was searched, but not the boat. Maybe too much exposure if it happened during daylight.

Then I thought about where the money could be. I glanced at the closets I'd rummaged through and concluded that if the money had been here, it was long gone now. Maybe the previous searcher found it and stopped looking. At least I had the drugs with which to bargain.

My pain was overwhelming, especially after crawling around in the boat. I needed something. I thought of J and G, but now wasn't the time for that. I looked at the packets. If it was cocaine, I could get a short-lasting euphoria rush to get me through.

I took a carving knife from a drawer in the kitchen and made a small slice in one of the packets. I found a spoon and scooped some powder onto the kitchen table. I used the knife to make a few lines and wet my finger to be sure it was cocaine. The powder was off-white and had a sweet floral scent. I rubbed it on my gums and felt the numbness. Hauled out my wallet, extracted the least tattered bill, and rolled it into a straw. I leaned down and was about to take the first line up my nose—and hesitated. I heard my therapist's voice from Birken. And Jessica who told me I needed help. I stopped.

I tried to block out the pain from my burns and bruises. I closed the packet with duct tape and put it with the others in the sack. Then I went out to Murphy's car and drove over to the cannery.

CHAPTER 32

I drove along Cougar Creek Road and turned right along the cove shore. I was almost out of the reserve when the cannery came into view with its long sloping roof, cedar plank sides, and stilted moorings at the water's edge. It was derelict, as were many canneries along the coast. I took the canvas bag from Murphy's trunk. I wasn't yet sure what to do with the drugs and needed flexibility. Should I turn them over to Chief because I found them on the reserve? I don't think so.

Discarded seine nets and wooden crates ran along the docks attached to the cannery. I slipped the bag beneath the nets and went inside.

I found Chief, Tony, Murphy, and the guy we caught at the house, who was tied to a metal chair. The place had gaping holes in the roof and on the siding, and the odd gull flew through one opening and out another. The smell of salmon oil, machinery grease, sweat, and hard labor still hung in the air. It seemed everyone waited on me to start the party. "Chief," I said. "You let a rough crowd on this reserve."

"Always a smart-ass. You've come into the center of the fire but have only begun to face your demons."

"Meet Ivan Barsukov," Murphy said. "If we look back far enough, he's not a nice guy."

Ivan's hands were tied behind him, his feet strapped to the chair legs. His black hair hung over his defiant eyes. His jacket lay on the floor, and his undershirt was ripped open at the front. I saw his tattoos and thought of Lobelia and her art. But these were hand-carved, with crude blades fashioned out of anything that could be made into an edge. The most prominent tattoos were two spider-in-web images centered on his shoulders and a bull on his chest.

Murphy watched me reading his skin. "So, do they mean something?"

I stepped back from the others, far enough so no one else could hear. "The webs mean he has or had a drug addiction. Not unusual for a communist prison population. Spider means high rank. The bull means he's a hitman. I don't expect to get much out of him."

We moved closer. He lifted his head theatrically and stared at us through his greasy hair. Ivan was as still as frozen water. I could usually detect a tell, whether it was the way a guy moved his hands or how he swallowed. He waited, looking like he knew he could take whatever we could throw at him. "You came for the drugs, or the money, or both?" I asked.

He smiled. His eyelids dropped and came up again. He was surprised I knew that much. "Ivan, I'm interested in people. Two twin girls. I'm interested in finding them alive. If you help me, maybe you don't have to die."

He smiled again, this time with the smugness of a man who didn't believe in threats. Didn't care what might happen to him. He cared about the present moment. That was what made him a survivor.

"We know who you work for," I said. "We know about Anton Tarasov. He's a dangerous man, so I understand if you don't want to say anything. Code of honor. I know a lot about that." I leaned in close and smacked my forehead hard against his nose. He toppled back with the chair. Tony picked him up. His bloody nostrils leaked down into his mouth. I stepped back and saw Murphy move forward.

"We're going to take Tarasov down no matter what happens here," she said. "You're not going to escape incarceration. And once you're inside, who's to say if you told us anything or not? They're going to assume you did, so as tough as you are, and as high up the food chain you are, holding out isn't going to help you."

Ivan spat a heavy gob of blood and phlegm at Murphy. Big mistake. She ripped off the shirt bandage I'd tied around his wound and took her thumb and pressed it into the bullet hole in his thigh. Ivan was tough but his eyes fluttered, and his mouth opened with the pain. She worked her fingers into the wound until he passed out. She nodded to Tony, who threw a bucket of salt water on Ivan. Ivan groaned and gasped back to consciousness.

"Ivan," Murphy said. "Listen to me. I'm very close to the femoral artery. I could nick it right here and leave you to bleed out." She pressed down on the wound, with the nose of her Glock this time. Ivan drifted off. Tony splashed him with more salt water. I could feel my gonads lifted into my throat. Never thought Murphy had that in her.

When Ivan came to again, Murphy said, "We're going up island to talk to Tarasov. A small amount of intel would be helpful. Then maybe you won't be left in the general population. You're a survivor, Ivan. Think about it." She held a knife below his groin. "Won't take much, Ivan. You'll get thirsty, feel weak and fall asleep. Is that what you call survival?"

Ivan rolled his eyes. His tell was a small twitch of his right cheek.

"How many are up there, Ivan? Where are they usually deployed?"

There was a long silence like he was gambling at a table, fumbling with poker chips, wondering whether to go all in. His head lolled to the side, and he spat on the floor. "Twenty-three. Ten outside. Six on the main floor. Six on the upper floor, and Tarasov." Then he said, "Crazy idea. Crazy idea."

"And the missing girls?"

"Don't know anything about missing girls."

I believed him about the girls. I believed an assault on Tarasov was a crazy idea. I didn't believe anything about the numbers and deployment of Tarasov's men. Too easy, even for a tortured Russian. I looked at Murphy and realized no one was going after Tarasov right now.

Murphy stepped back and walked to the far end of the cannery, away from us. I knew she couldn't leave him here. Too risky. She didn't know whether she should take him in but had no choice. She took out her cell and called Reilly to bring a cruiser over to pick up Barsukov.

I looked outside. The storm was kicking up again. The wind was raging over the water in the strait. My body twitched. I felt something dark approaching. I should have known what was planned for me. But I didn't. Murphy was getting ready to transport Ivan. Chief and Tony sat and waited. I felt like I could keep going. Maybe Chief had some Scotch and a few beers. If so, I knew I could continue.

CHAPTER 33

Chief along with Tony walked me over to his house.

"Tony and I have to secure the reserve against future attacks, Jack," Chief said. "We need to set up roadblocks and sentries. Sit tight. Have a beer."

They left me at the open front door and jumped into Tony's truck.

I went inside and sat on the couch. I helped myself to beers in the refrigerator and the half-bottle of Scotch on the coffee table. Stacie kept crawling into my head. It wasn't like her to drop off the radar. Where had she gone, leaving Jessica underground with a loaded gun? It didn't take long for the beer and Scotch combination to whack me upside the head and send me drifting in multiple directions.

I saw Iona and Skye caught up in a web, hauling drugs across the city and being groomed for a life of abuse. I didn't see them as spent, but as young women determined to escape. I saw Kat and Peter as murky figures caught in the same web.

The Scotch and the beers eased my pain. Something told me to rein myself in. But I couldn't, and I knew this wasn't going to end well.

I was the lost soul who hadn't found himself. The Scotch and beer went. No focus. Only sleep and memories came in unconnected pieces.

I watch the little ones gather berries in the lunch boxes that were filled with stones... We sit, numb beneath the gnarled Douglas-fir where we first opened our lunch boxes. Two Arbutus trees with flaking bark curl into the air. Meadow. One side is jeweled with dew. No one speaks. Kat and Peter wrap their arms around their chests for warmth. I need to take control, but my burden is a hawk trapped inside my chest. We are deep inside the forest. We have no place that wants us, no one who can save us. I hear their hearts and imagine the sparrows' brief erratic flutters inside their winter coats. I'm their only hope...

Kat and Peter are seven, and I am nine. We wear canvas running shoes, jeans, sweatshirts, and winter coats. The ground tumbles below our feet as we step down through waist-high sword ferns and over-blown down trunks covered with thick moss. I can't tell where the bottom is and reach with my toes to find it as we wind back and forth in dense undergrowth.

"Stay close," I say.

"Why are our lunch boxes filled with stones?" Kat asks.

"I can't go any farther," Peter tells us.

"They're playing games with us to make us strong," I say. "They want us to find our way home, so we've got to keep moving. We must find a path or a road. There'll be a road."

They don't want us to die because they made us bring winter coats. They're punishing us for the painted raven, and all the times we made them angry when they came home after drinking in town.

Some nights they put on the radio, push furniture to the kitchen wall, and dance. They swirl around the floor, bump into the furniture. Laugh. We sit and wait to be asked.

"Come on," my father says, offering his cracked, creased hand. And he swings me, and I stand on my father's shoes as he sways back and forth and spins me 'round and 'round...

I make a bow drill fire. Can't be in a rush. Weave plants into a string. Make containers for water. Break stones from streams and rivers by setting them in a fire and cooling them in water so they split into sharp-edged pieces. Make deadfall traps. Peter and Kat don't want me to kill the rats and squirrels, but they eat them once I skin them with the stones and cook them on the fire. I tell them we need to thank the creatures for giving up their energy. I don't sleep. When Kat and Peter aren't close, I startle easily. But I have clarity. I am the cougar. I am snake fang. I see the future. That moment before the moment. I am forged in fire. I am what does not come easily.

We're skinny. I use a sharp stone to cut extra holes in our belts, so our pants won't fall. And we walk and walk and walk from spur to spur to gravel road to paved road to home, three abandoned children who survived. We don't ask questions. We come home and our father sits us down at the table and our mother puts barley soup in bowls. We eat in silence and go to our beds in the cages in the barn, and we fall asleep with all the other children's muffled noises from their cages. We do not ask the question about the stones in the lunch boxes, nor do we talk about our journey home...

I clutch a five-pound stone to my chest and walk into the lake where the bottom is sandy. The water reaches my chest, but the stone holds my feet to the bottom. I trust and step out farther until the water closes over me. Shaplow Lake is streaked with yellow pollen as the sunlight penetrates the water from above. I keep walking, my feet feeling the uneven bottom. My ankle is tethered to the stone so when I get to the bottom, I can maneuver with my hands.

The bottom drops away with my next step, and the stone pulls me into deeper water. It's cold, and the surface light winks silver as I drop. My feet hit solid rock. My eyes adjust. I see the driftwood stumps, severed trunks, and truncated roots—a tangled jungle. The pressure builds in my lungs. My brain sends frantic messages for air. I know I have time, though I've hit the first wall. I lay the stone on the thickest stump and hold onto its woody top, resisting my body's natural buoyancy. I peer down over the severed stumps and see the bodies.

Hollow eyes. Tags of flesh. A flow of hair. Skulls. Vertebrae. Legs and arms pinned down with cables twisted around stumps. I am startled. Air explodes from my chest, and rushes upward from my mouth and nose in a bubbled silver flash. I kick and pump toward the surface, it's white light far above me. The rope pulls taut against my ankle. All my oxygen is gone. I reach into my brain for the energy to dive back down and wrestle some slack for my ankle. I panic. My eyes protrude from their sockets and my heart pounds. I turn. Fumble with the line still looped around my ankle. I widen its noose and release my foot. I rise, push against the water with my cupped hands and thrash with my legs until I break the surface. I suck in air like a great rasping maw...

On another day, I pick up the stone as I've done before. Hold it fastened securely to my waist, clutched close. I feel its grounded power. Feel the gravity pressure pushing my feet into the soft earth beneath the lake's surface among spiny weeds. One step after another until I'm waist deep, then chest deep and the stone begins to lose its heaviness and becomes a part of me. My head beneath the water. I can do this forever. I can wander here as in this sleepy world. Again, I feel the familiar pressure as my body uses up its oxygen and the tiny messages begin to filter in. But I persist and keep walking. There's something I need to find here. I have seen two men drop a wrapped bundle from the back of a rowboat. One man slips into the water and takes the bundle below the surface. I know I can find it…

In my memory what once was a shadow had come back into the light. The smoke and steam closed in around me.

The shadow figures chanted to the drums. The rain hammered on the roof.

CHAPTER 34

It was morning. I sat cross-legged on a blanket. The rain had stopped. The shadows had retreated. Smoke and steam were gone, and a crisp fire crackled into life in the sweat lodge pit. I felt the world seeping into all my pores. No wind. Silence.

Chief sat across from me. Tony stood at the entrance.

I wasn't sure where I'd been, or where I was. But I felt safe for maybe the first time in my life. I wasn't alone, and not lonely, as if on my last bed, and nothing could be done. Ice chips for my lips, a puffed-up pillow. A hand rubbed against my wrist. My eyelids fluttered. The light changed at a window. But no more. I lay calm in the knowledge that little details were in focus. Thin five-sixteenth flathead Craftsman screwdriver 41587 K WF. Security in the hand. The fixer who couldn't fix anything before. But now everything was going to be different with a firmer grip on what had made me who I am, with a calmness that came with accepting what I could not change.

I met Chief's eyes. His face was calm. I was afraid to speak. Afraid to break the moment apart with words. I waited and breathed air deep into my chest. Finally, Chief spoke. "It's over."

"It is beginning," I said.

"I know. Tell me about it."

"The children," I said. "We were all children. I wasn't special. Kat and Peter weren't special. We were the children who disappeared. Skye and Iona aren't special. They're two of the many children who've disappeared.

"I brought Kat and Peter back from the forest. I walked below the water with the stone. I drove the hatchet deep into my father's chest. Before I didn't know when I shot Madson. I didn't know. But I'm going to find out everything."

"Jack. We'll have breakfast now," Chief said. "We have work to do."

We walked together from the sweat lodge to Chief's house.

Chief, Tony, and I ate in silence at the kitchen table. When I finished, I wiped my mouth with a paper towel. "What was with the feathers, rattles, and drums?" I asked. "I remember a rooster. Are you sure you guys know what you're doing?"

Tony chuckled his mouth full of eggs.

"Got it all from an internet search," Chief said.

"You're not serious."

"Yep. You white guys need your Little Big Man."

"You're putting me on?"

He smiled.

I smiled, not knowing why. I looked them in the eyes, and they both smiled back at me and broke out laughing. "So, catch me up," I said.

"Murphy's gone," Chief said.

"What?" I started to panic.

"No. Not gone," Chief said. "Suspended without pay. Some prick higher up is in charge. He's kicking butt and you can be sure Murphy's butt has had its share."

"For what?"

"Tony heard from Reilly that rumor has it they didn't like the way things were handled with the attack on Louie's house. Don't like the fact you're mixed up in this. Back on your home turf. Someone's getting flak for the body count."

I didn't say anything but figured this was trumped up to put a lid on investigations that should have been done long ago. "Where is she?"

"I asked her to come past the barricade," Chief said. "It's still up. Been up since the shootout. No one can think they can walk in on us. Not Russians. Not the force. Gonna stay that way until things cool down. She'll be over this afternoon. No telling what mood she'll be in since she might be blaming you, and First Nations aren't exactly getting a free pass." He looked a little worried. "Police can't stand a show of force, so to speak, unless it's theirs," Chief said. "Those fucking Russians got what was coming to them, and they've gone off licking their wounds."

"The force doesn't give a shit about dead Russians," I said, "but they sure don't want someone else standing them up. What happened to Ivan Barsukov?"

"Murphy took him to the clinic in town and put a twenty-four-hour guard on him. He skipped out and left the guard bleeding on the floor."

"Fuck," I said.

"They're looking for him. Figure he's headed north to Campbell River to recover."

"I wouldn't be too sure of that," I said.

"Oh, Jack," Chief said. "There's something else."

I looked at him, and the weight of the beleaguered descended on me. "Stacie?"

"Not a word. Something else."

"Fuck's sake."

Then he unloaded. Tony moved closer like he knew he would need to restrain me.

"The plane didn't arrive on the mainland," Chief said.

I was stunned. My worst nightmare. I'd pleaded with them to stay put. I stood up but I couldn't catch my breath. I stumbled forward, but Tony managed to ease me back into my chair.

"The plane disappeared.' Chief said. "I don't know if it went down over the strait, or someone got to the pilot, and he redirected the flight."

I'd warned Del about the weather. I reassured her that if she stayed until the storm passed, I could keep her safe with police protection. But she wouldn't listen. I'd always had a switch in my head, not a short fuse but a trigger that got squeezed when I was truly angry. Everything became internal, calm as a flatlined monitor when the heart stops. And there was a burning, a concentration, a lit cigarette end inside my brain when the psychic pain blots out my reason, dispenses with fear, discards any caring. And as the burning festers, I become cold, quiet, and lethal. All the eyes in the room were watching me. I couldn't move.

Then Murphy walked through the door. I'd never seen her more reserved, hard-faced with something angry beneath the skin. I saw all that same sorrow in her that was pent up inside my own gut. She looked at me, and I looked at her, and I knew we both looked the same. Our faces were drawn and empty, raging and yet resigned. She sat down on an empty kitchen chair and said, "You look like shit."

"I heard."

"Fuck them."

"Whose butt does everyone have to kiss now?" I said.

"Conner. RCMP brass from the mainland. Big cojones. There's no way he's clean. It's common knowledge over there. Here too. Right on down the line, everyone does the job. Busts their humps for collars, but no one can get anywhere near the pricks who call the big shots."

"This Conner," I said. "Tell me about him." Chief and Tony listened, trading glances.

"The rank and file are scared of him," Murphy said. "They don't know what to expect. But there are suspicions that he's in someone's pocket. He's on the take. Intricately involved at the highest level."

"You think he'll make a move on the barricades?" Chief asked.

"Honestly, I don't think he'll care," Murphy said. "You are contained on the reserve behind your barricades. He can control the land exits to the reserve. He can try to patrol the water. He'll wait you out until things calm down."

"You want some eggs?" Tony said. "I can whip some up."

"Coffee would be great."

He poured her a cup, and I watched her warm her hands and take a sip. My heart raced with panic. "Del and my little girl are missing," I said. "Where do we go from here? The twins haven't yet been found. Stacie's gone. I feel like a total fuck-up."

No one said a word.

"My mind has been opened. Murphy, I know what happened when I was a kid. I know what happened with Madson. I know about the lake. I know who's responsible, but I need to talk it out. Lay it all out and take a deep look at the connections."

There was a boot scrape at the door. I turned and couldn't believe my eyes. Stacie stood in the doorway, her small pack on her back and my duffle over a shoulder. "Jack, it's time to stop fucking around," she said. "Haven't we got work to do?"

"You gave her a gun," I said. "What happened to you? What were you thinking? I thought you were dead. She could have killed herself. She could have blown a hole in my chest." It all spewed out.

Stacie walked into the kitchen. There were no empty chairs, so she hoisted herself onto the countertop, turned her body so she could sit on the surface, and dangled her legs over the edge. She wore the same clothes as the last time I'd seen her, but now they looked like something that should be burned.

"Where have you been?"

"I taught her how to hold it. Pull the trigger without letting it jump in her hand. The same way I taught her to run, to stay fit all that time you left us back at the house. We didn't sit around."

"Why'd you leave her? Where did you go?"

Chief spoke up. "It's a long story. Complicated."

"You knew about where she was? And didn't bother telling me?"

"Hold on," Chief said.

"Hold on nothing. I thought the Russians had her. Thought something worse."

"That's why you drank yourself into oblivion last night?"

I stared hard at Chief. Looked over toward Tony. There was no answer. My teeth dug into my cheeks.

"Chief told me about the plane," Stacie said.

"I don't want it to be true."

"How do you feel now?" Tony said. His voice had a calming effect on me.

My abdomen tightened into a knot. "Watch me. I am not going down that road again. I know where I've been, and I know where I'm going." I held my hand out. It was shaking, but I knew I had control. I decided to calm down. To listen, for a change. "What was that stuff you gave me to drink?"

"We got it from the cooking channel," Chief said. "You're fixed, right? Not broken anymore?"

No long story about traditional remedies. I gave him the thin smile I reserved for a smart-ass but let his attempt to lighten the mood slide. "Seems like we all have stories to tell," I said.

"Let's clear the table," Chief said. "Set up a command center." I thought he was being dramatic with the command center shit, but he was right. It was time for action. We were behind the barricades. Murphy was on suspension. Iona and Skye were still missing. The money was missing. Del and Jessica never made it to the mainland. I couldn't make myself believe they might be dead. I couldn't go there. I remembered where I'd stashed the drugs. I remembered my traumas, and that told everything.

"I'll make some more coffee," Tony said. "There's another storm coming."

Yeah. He didn't know how accurate that was.

CHAPTERS 35

Stacie spread out all the information she found at the library.

I asked her, "You're not going to tell us where you've been?"

"Patience."

We all looked at one glaring front-page headline. "Parents found brutally murdered in homestead kitchen." There were soft news headlines as well, clipped from interior pages. Stories about the orphaned children going to the mainland, and cages found in the McQueen homestead barn. All the stories dated within a one-month period.

Murphy threw down the articles from the Shaplow News. The ones I'd left in her car. We passed the articles around.

"I'd have been three years old," Chief said.

"Me too," Tony added.

Everyone looked at me. "I was nine."

There was a long silence. I couldn't hold out. Couldn't outwait them. My heart pounded. It felt like a rat had crawled down my throat and was gnawing at my lungs. "The children are Kat and Peter and Jack," I said. "Their parents dropped them off in the woods. They survived and returned home to be caged in the barn as they'd always been caged each night with the other kids who came and went. Jack is one of the orphaned children who lived in a group foster center on the mainland, who fooled the psych tests, and made it into the army. He's the kid who buried himself in books and self-defense. Who's trained to kill—Special Forces. He's the kid who watched Mr. Madson and his father in a rowboat dump a long plastic bag into Shaplow Lake.

"Jack is the kid who knew his best friend, Tyler, would try to run away from home. Jack listened to Tyler tell him that he couldn't take it anymore, couldn't take lying in bed upstairs, waiting for his father to come to him. Tyler told Jack the day before he died what he was going to do with the axe hidden behind his pillow, the next time his father came up the stairs. Jack is the boy who saw the rowboat and the plastic bag lowered into the lake. He was the boy who knew that Tyler in the end was unable to escape.

"Jack is the boy who played with Tyler Madson and dug tunnels for their escape. The boy who walked into the lake with a stone fastened to his waist, took his knife, and cut the plastic open, and found his friend Tyler. He's the boy who blocked out these images, these memories when he got to the mainland. He's the boy who sees his mother's broken body under the kitchen table, lying in her own blood and her teeth scattered on the floor."

When I stopped speaking, I was exhausted. No one disturbed the silence. Everyone's head was lowered, and when they raised their eyes, I saw their empathy and concern.

"That homestead double murder is still a cold case," Murphy said. "No one ever found enough evidence to zero in on anyone."

"What's with the cages in the barn?" Stacie asked.

Again, there was a long silence until I spoke. "It wasn't right," I said. "I knew it wasn't right. The cages. Filled with mostly small children, but also young women. No one stayed very long. Some did, but most stayed for a week or so, and then they'd be gone. Others took their place."

"Human trafficking," Murphy said. "You do remember now, Jack, when we worked that case. Remember?"

"Blocked it out," I said.

"Yes, you did. Tell us now?"

"The cages. Some of us weren't always in cages. Kat and Peter and I, we got to go in the house. We got to play in the yard. We water-skied with Tyler. He and I dug the tunnels between our houses. We created rooms beneath the ground, where we could hide. But we were always too afraid to run away. There really wasn't anywhere to go."

I paused and a vivid memory cracked open. "Sometimes they took us up to the big house. Got us all dressed up in costumes. We'd get in fancy cars and go up to the gates, but we wouldn't drive up to the house. They'd let us out inside the gates where the hill began, and the forest sheltered everything so you couldn't see the house. There were iron doors in the hillside, and they opened them and led us through a long tunnel. There were tunnels leading everywhere, but we stuck to the main one where the lights were on."

"Tunnels from when they used to mine the coal," Chief said. "Many people died in those tunnels. First Nations, but mostly Chinese. There was no safety then. I've read about the disasters. Those Chinese didn't even have any names in the books, only numbers."

"At the house?" Stacie asked.

"Kat, Peter, Tyler, some older kids, and good-looking young women. That's who went up to the big house. Once we got there, they scrubbed us up. Dressed us in skimpy costumes, feathers, and sequins, and we were paraded around rooms filled with costumed guests with old-style masks. Looking back on it, we were appetizers."

I paused and took a deep breath. Almost threw up my coffee and eggs. I'd never spoken about this. I'd lost the memories. Or so I thought. I forced myself to go on. "The older kids were put on a stage and made to perform. You know. Carne cruda. Everyone was watching. The night, for us, sank into a darkness full of tears, but we played along because they scared us with a box of severed fingers from the boys and girls who tried to run."

"The big house? The Strang house?" Murphy said.

I looked to Chief and Tony. They were solemn. I tried to read them. Was this a surprise for them, or had I confirmed suspicions they already had.

"Tell us about Tyler Madson," Stacie said.

I looked at Chief. "What was in that drink?" I said. "Don't bullshit me."

"Honest. The cooking channel. Drinks with Cochise and Geronimo."

Everyone laughed. It broke the tension.

"Stop fucking with me."

"You want to know?" Tony said.

Focus, Jack. "My brain's working overtime," I said. "It's all jumping out on me. I want to know if it's me. Yeah, I want to know."

"Shrooms," Tony said. "The magic kind. They've done studies in low doses. We gave you a lot, plus secret sauce."

"What were you thinking? Mixed with alcohol, I could have died."

I saw Tony's eyes meet with Chief's.

"We were watching over you," Tony said. "We took it for a test drive, and no one died."

"That's not the point. Sure, I have the memories back. I am not sure I should thank you."

I looked at Stacie and Murphy. I could see they understood my conflicted emotions. Maybe Chief and Tony tried to help me find the light, to unlock the terror of not knowing what happened to me. Maybe I should be thanking them.

"Tyler was a captive too," I said. "He was my best friend. We dug our tunnels together so we could hide. A safe place when a day turned bad. Tyler's father was like mine. They kept the cages together. Took us to the big house. But Tyler told me his father would visit him at night. That's why he built his tunnels, so he could disappear. They were his obsession. Digging and hiding in the dark earth was his obsession. He was older than me. I remember how he'd drive the motorboat with the Evinrude. I remember summer days on the lake when we didn't think about the dark. Just the sun and the water droplets on our skin. Some days were better than others. We never thought we could really get away.

"Murphy and I were about to ask Madson questions concerning the missing kids before they closed the case on us. He came toward me with an axe. I fired my service gun. One bullet in the chest. Then I couldn't stop. I emptied the clip.

Went up before Internal Affairs. They sent me for tests. Don't know what they found, but I was gone. It makes sense to me now that someone used the incident to force me out of the RCMP."

I paused and felt empty.

"I saw them drop Tyler in the lake from a rowboat. Mr. Madson took the body under the water," I said. "I walked to the bottom of the lake with a stone to hold me down. I cut his body loose from the plastic bag, and he floated to the surface. I brought him to the shore and carried him to the tunnels we dug. I created a space on the side and carved a shelf and laid him there, then I filled it in so he wouldn't be bothered anymore, and he would be safe and at peace. It was shortly after, that Kat and Peter, and I were dropped off in the woods."

Murphy asked, "Do you know who killed your parents?"

"No, I don't know anything,"

CHAPTER 36

I walked outside. I was hyperventilating, gasping. Bent over, heaving. The eggs and coffee lay in the grass at my feet. Stacie followed me out. She was patient. She placed one hand on my shoulder and her palm on my forehead. A few dry heaves and I collected myself. Her palm was warm against my cold sweat. I took deep breaths and stared around me in the harsh morning light. Then Stacie and I walked along the road.

"When I saw the black Escalade," she said, "I thought it belonged to Voice, the guy you talked about, but it was the Russians. The license was 347 AWP. I left Jessica with the Glock because that's the type of gun she used for target practice. Once someone came into the house, I fired. I took a gun from the guy I hit before the fire started."

"There must have been more than one," I said.

"Two more. Pretty confident to send only three. There were two beside the black Escalade. Both men were dead from what looked like gunshot wounds. I had to think fast. I hauled the two bodies onto the floor behind the back seat. They were lean but muscular guys. I tugged and levered them into the SUV. I didn't want anyone suspecting us of murder with the way things had been going. I figured Jessica would be fine once the fire attracted everyone. Then she'd be found. I jumped into the Escalade and drove north on the Island Highway toward Campbell River. I figured the bodies belonged to Tarasov, so why not dump them in his lap. I'm not sure I was thinking straight. On second thought, maybe I should have stayed with Jessica. I don't know."

I let any thought of blaming her slide. In the heat of it, I might have done the same. But I would have gone back for her. No point getting worked up now. "So, the Russians and whoever killed them are at war," I said, "and we're caught in the middle."

"From what I found out from hacking into records on the force, and the odd news article, there's been a fuzzy response to crime on the Island and there's been a turf war here for over a year. You'd think with such a big island, the boys could carve out their own territories. Live and let live."

When I was a kid, it was the big house on the hill, and everyone toed the line. But when I was on the force with Murphy, we knew fresh players had migrated to the action. Now I assumed that Anton Tarasov had emerged as the only competition left for the Strang family on the hill.

"Tarasov is definitely involved," Stacie said. "I drove to Campbell River. It's a quaint North-Island town before the wilderness gets rugged. That's where he's based, apart from a home on the mainland and a few homes in Europe. He's a Soviet breakup survivor. He's a street kid, a child soldier who made it in a free-for-all for power. He's pure brutality. Owns real estate in town, the marina, and has a huge yacht he uses as a mobile base, to run back and forth along the strait and over to the mainland. I scoped it all out, did my research. He's got a small, fortified island in Desolation Sound, where the strait narrows up from Campbell River."

"Where'd you leave the Escalade?"

"I stashed it off-road in the bush, about a mile outside the town. The location is well-hidden until we want someone to find it."

"How did you manage to get back here?"

"I took the bus. I slept all the way."

"So, you have a plan?"

I was amazed she'd done all that on her own. I shouldn't have been because I'd always known how capable she was. But she'd risked her life for this. For me. "When you asked me to take you with me," I said, "I didn't agree to you risking your life. You know Jessica and Del didn't make it back to the mainland?"

"Chief told me. I did some checking. The company had all their planes equipped with real-time tracking. It's got an SOS button for emergencies. No button was pushed. No automatic signal for a sudden drop in altitude. In fact, the whole system disengaged five minutes into the flight over the Georgia Strait. The aircraft dropped off the radar with no distress signal and no verbal communication."

"And you know this how?"

"Do you need to ask me this?"

I saw the calm, patient resolve melted from her face for a moment. The clarity in her features went out of focus. Then she was back watching my expression, maybe thinking how my voice had cracked on the last word in my sentence. "So, what are you saying?" I asked.

"That is state-of-the-art tracking. No way it would stop working. I think the pilot cut the system, then dropped the plane below the radar. Nap-of-the-earth. Low-level fighter planes use that tactic. And we have mountains to block the radar. The plane didn't crash. Someone got to them."

"Who?"

"The plane could be anywhere around here, and we wouldn't know it," she said.

So, who had Jessica and Del? Who had Iona and Skye? I started putting the pieces together. "My family's gone because of me, and whoever's responsible wants me to come for them. They want the drugs. The money. Iona and Skye were shunted from house to house around Vancouver. Captives. Doing whatever they asked. But who had my family? Tarasov? Strang?"

"That's it," Stacie said. "I figure we have to flush one of them out, and right now Anton Tarasov is the ripe one."

"You have something in mind?"

"Just the two of us. We don't want the cavalry. With each group vying for more control, I don't trust the force. There are cops in each pocket, at all levels, and they're warring with each other. There are a few honest cops who can be trusted. But how can we tell who they are? I'll bet Murphy can't tell you that either."

"You're right," I said. "She's watching her back."

We'd walked up the road and approached the barricades on the north side. A front-end loader had brought a rusted car wreck, boulders, timber, and shoveled earthworks in and around the mass of steel, rock, and wood. The fortifications were manned by young, First Nations men with scarves across their mouths, bandanas, and balaclavas. Each warrior was toting an automatic rifle, staying low and vigilant. We watched from a low spot on the road, then turned and walked back to Chief's house. This wasn't our fight, but I could see myself connected to them. I was glad for the sanctuary, and the respite we had right now. I was glad I remembered. I was glad the PTSD memory issues caused by my childhood and my killing of Frederick Madson were behind me. But even though there was calm, I knew a storm was about to explode out of me. No amount of therapy or a magic mushroom spirit journey could erase my inner wiring.

CHAPTER 37

Tony lent me the keys to his truck. He knew where we were going. Said he'd keep it quiet. Gave me a route out of the reserve to avoid the police. I'd put a quarter of the drugs in a plastic bag and stowed the rest back beneath the nets. I drove up to the barricades and took the truck off-road, into the gully across the open field, and back onto the road which got me past the police blockade. I headed for the main highway, north to Campbell River. Stacie brought the 9mm Makarov with an 18-bullet clip she pulled off the guy in the homestead before the fire. I had the Glock in my jacket pocket, as well as the Beretta strapped to my leg. The cocaine was behind the seat.

We drove in silence for a while, each inside our thoughts.

"That bag of stuff back there?" she said. "Where did you get it?"

I told her about the firefight, and how I found the drugs and hid them under the nets outside the cannery. "What do you think?" I said. "Ian Stewart is the shooter who put the bullets into people's hands and feet as a torture method. He tracks down Iona and Skye on the mainland, traces them from the widow's place where the Chief hid them, then to school, and to Anderson, and finally to West 32nd. He smells what they're into. He's not there for them but for the action, something he can steal easily, like money or drugs or both. But he's playing a dangerous game because there are more players than he realizes. When he gets to 3360 West 32nd, the girls aren't there. Maybe he gets surprised, caught in the house, looking for something to steal when the two Russians come home. I don't know what goes down, but I suspect he gets the jump on them, ties them up, and shoots their hands and feet. Then tortures them to find out where the money and the drugs are."

"You don't figure he killed them?"

"No, he was a weasel, a bad father, a wife-beater, and a womanizer, but I don't think he was a cold-blooded executioner. We're looking for someone much more ruthless. Someone on a par with these Russians. Since we know the Strang organization is involved in running drugs on the mainland using Mike Burns and Laura Wells to groom the kids, I figure the Russians were the buyers. The money went missing, and the drugs never stayed at the drop on West 32nd. I think the girls kept the drugs they were transporting and took the money too. Found it in the house and took off scared before anyone showed up to get it. The two Russians bought it because the deal went south."

It dawned on me that the police surveillance photos of me going into the house must have been shared with the Russians, or why else would they have come to the marina looking for me. I didn't mention this to Stacie. Didn't want to get into the Russian-in-the-river thing.

"So, the girls come over to the Island," Stacie said. "Ian figures that's where they'd go and follows them. That video at the ferry with them lugging the expedition packs. They were carrying drugs and money. What were they thinking? How do you figure they thought they could get away, and what were they going to do with all that at their age?"

"Kids. Maybe they simply reacted. Didn't think ahead."

"Well, that's plain stupid and suicidal," Stacie said. "You figure they're dead?"

"I don't know. The money is missing. And no one except you and I know where the drugs are. The girls might be dead."

Stacie nodded. "And when they got in the Civic, Ian Stewart followed them," she said. "And he was the one who shot the two Hanses in the hands and feet. His trademark, right? He takes the drugs and the money and stashes them on the reserve. The drugs in the boat behind Louie's place, the money may be somewhere nearby too."

"But what about the girls?" I said. "Did they finally run off and hide somewhere? And who killed the two guys in the trunk? I figure it was Strang. He lost his drugs, and he never got the money. Someone had to pay. The Lumbar twins, Hans One and Two were cannon fodder as well as loose ends. But Murphy thinks Ian Stewart is capable of murder which creates another line of inquiry."

We stopped talking for a while. The rain hit so hard that the wipers barely removed the water from the windscreen. We crawled along the highway. There was no one else on the road.

"So how are we going to proceed up there?" Stacie asked.

CHAPTER 38

We were parked on a logging spur that led off a smaller logging road that led off a road they called a Main about five miles into the bush, outside of Campbell River.

"I disconnected the GPS," Stacie said.

I'd always thought she was brilliant.

"Well?" she said.

"Right, make me do the dirty work."

The Escalade was parked on a slim trail that petered out into overgrown tire tracks. The car was covered with salal branches and fir boughs that blended into the forest. Stacie had done that and left it to sit unnoticed now for two days. I could smell the decomposing bodies when I opened the rear passenger door. I dumped the cocaine bricks onto the seat beside the dead men. The bricks weighed about twenty pounds; worth on the street, a little over a million dollars. Enough to make someone get excited. The rest of it, still hidden under the nets, was worth about three million. Which could be a very large carrot. A few flies came out the door, but the rest were busy crawling on the bodies. When I got back to Tony's truck I said, "Do we activate the GPS?"

"You mean the factory SuperNav/GPS/Navigation System," Stacie said.

"Smart-ass. Whatever."

"Yeah, we have plenty of time."

"It's all yours," I said.

Stacie left me in the truck and went into the Escalade's driver's side. She was back within a minute.

"That was fast," I said.

"I just plugged it back in. Finding it the first time was the hard part."

"How do you know this stuff?"

"I was always handy. Anyway, if you don't know, go on the Internet. Everything's there."

"Right. I'm too old school here. Do you think I can catch up?"

"Only if you want to invest the time. It's not rocket science." She smiled at me and shook her head. "Let's go. I'll show you the town. Tarasov's town."

We backed up the spur, swung around, and left the Escalade behind.

When we reached Campbell River, I pulled into a grocery store lot, killed the engine, and sank back in the seat. "What now?" I asked.

"Let me orient you before we go to the tea house."

There was a larger parking lot across the street, near a marina and a huge wharf. Stacie looked down toward the water.

"Are we going down there?" I asked.

"You should get a look at the yacht to know how big a deal this guy is."

"Oh," I said and climbed from the truck. Stacie tucked her computer and the Makarov under the seat. I didn't say anything, but I opened the truck door and put my Glock under my seat.

"Something hot about that one, too?" Stacie said.

"No, but the Makarov is the gun you took from the dead Russian at the homestead."

A brisk breeze came off the water from the east, whipping the waves into whitecaps. The sun crept in and out of dark grey clouds—a tease of light before the darkness and heavy rain to come.

We walked down to the wharf. We tried to move like locals who knew what they were doing. Like we had a purpose and somewhere to go. Heads down, fighting the wind. Tarasov's yacht was in the deepest berth at the end of the wharf.

"It's a Hull F 75 – CODECASA 42 Vintage Series," Stacie said.

She could have been describing a bottle of wine for all I knew.

"Not a super yacht, but big enough to impress around here. He's got something bigger in the Mediterranean."

"Are we going to get to see this guy?" I asked.

Yeah. Trust me. I phoned ahead. But not here. All that's here is the captain and the crew. We're going for tea, aren't we Jack?"

"If you say so. It's your plan."

"The Tea House is an interesting cover," Stacie said. "A front for Tarasov's office and an official business. A refined contrast to the brutal side of the man."

I felt desperate, wondering who had Jessica and Del and imagining what could happen to them. Wondering, too, who had the twins—if they were still alive. My stomach was a bag of rats chewing at me to make something happen. To make Jessica safe again.

The Tea House seemed out of place for Campbell River. The space was filled with small tables, fine China settings, linen tablecloths, and doilies on comfortable lounge chairs. Even by mainland standards, the place was too fancy.

A tall, long-legged hostess seated us in a corner by the window. We were not alone. Small groups and a few deuces sipped tea and ate petit-fours and wheaten scones. I glanced at the menu. "Get a load of the prices here," I said.

"Relax," Stacie said. "Let's go through the motions. Enjoy the tea. Don't make a scene." She smiled and shook her head at me.

I fell in line, looked at the menu, and chose 1894 Select Tea, described as a unique blend of Ceylon and Assam black teas, carefully selected to produce a rich flavorful cup. I chose a wheaten scone to go with it. Stacie ordered a Chun Mee green tea with a raspberry petit-four. When the order came, we sipped our tea and munched our confections. I managed to drop part of my butter-lathered scone in mid-bite. It bounced on the table's edge and tumbled to the floor. Great. I kicked the largest piece underneath the table. Stacie looked at me as if to say, "You can dress him up, but you gotta bring him back to apologize."

She laughed. "Jack, you take yourself too seriously."

When we finished, a tall thin man without a single wrinkle in his suit came to stand beside our table. "Please, come with me," he said. "The tea is on the house."

Stacie looked at me. This was it. We followed him down a small corridor that opened into a larger room. We were ushered through another door. We faced two huge men in suits that were slightly tighter than they had to be. They patted us down.

"You'll find one down there," I said pointing to my ankle. Good thing we didn't have the Makarov, I thought. One of the men pointed to the double doors, and the other went to open them. We entered to find Anton Tarasov seated in a high-backed leather chair. He stood. He was over six feet tall and dressed in a tailored grey business suit, the crease in his pants sharp as a razor's edge. We shook hands and he motioned us to a three-seat, matching leather sofa across from the chair. Tarasov took his seat. The big guys stood by the doors, their hands dangling in front. We weren't going anywhere without their permission.

"Would you like some more tea, or something stronger?" Anton Tarasov said.

We both declined and sat forward on the sofa. To our left was a long, carved oak desk. Everything was in order, symmetrical and balanced. Oriental carpets were spread atop the hardwood flooring. A few small windows with frosted glass. An elegant office made from the sow's ear of a business front. I wondered what exactly attracted him to the boonies and drew him away from yachts, Europe, and the French Riviera.

Anton Tarasov sat erect. A man expecting to be feared. He was poised, with intense, blue eyes that didn't blink. "Let's talk, Jack McQueen," he said. "Since your assistant has been so adamant that we have something to discuss."

"You know what I'm going to say. I want my daughter and my wife back unharmed. I want to find two girls who've been missing for far too long."

"What makes you think I can help you?"

"I respect you, Mr. Tarasov. You may be dangerous, but I don't think you randomly hurt innocents. It's not good form for you. Not the way your games are played."

"And why would I want to help you? Why would I risk my business reputation by getting muddled in your problems?"

"You're a businessman," I said, "and I have something of interest to you."

"Really," he said as if he had no idea what was coming next.

I felt I was some park player who sat down with Boris Spassky for a not-so-friendly chess game.

"Really," I said. "I want you to help me with what I can offer you in return."

"And what makes you think I want to be bothered?"

He wanted me to make the first move. Expose a key piece on the board. Enough was enough. Stacie was strangely quiet, and I was glad she was.

"I know not to refer to you as an oligarch. You don't work well with the government. I know you're from a Siberian coal town where your father worked in the mines. I know getting to where you are now was not easy. You don't suffer fools, and you are relentless in pursuit of your dreams. I know you feel privileged to have risen above the rule of law. And I know that no matter how much you have, you hate to spend money and not get something you paid dearly for." I watched his face for a tell. There was nothing. He was cold as ice that burns the skin.

"You've done some research," he said. "I'm impressed."

"You can give the credit to Stacie."

"So, what do you have that I would be interested in?"

"Cocaine worth four million dollars."

Tarasov's voice turned a tad sharp. "Can you give me back more than six lives? Can you give me back my close friends, Yuri Dostonovich and Ivan Barsukov?"

"I do not know these men."

I saw him look for a tell and smile.

"Perhaps Ivan can tell you about how healthy he is and how well he was treated," he said. "Perhaps Yuri can come back from a watery grave and tell you what happened to him."

I was starting to feel this had been a mistake. That we were in over our heads. What was Stacie thinking? What was I thinking?

"Let us stay in the here and now, Mr. Tarasov," I said. "We're both businessmen. You are big business. I am a small business and am concerned for my family and the family of the two girls. Your losses are business. My losses are personal. I have something you want. I have your cocaine. I didn't steal it. I found it where someone else hid it and figured out who should have it. I know who stole it. I can provide it for you, but I want my family safe. If you have my daughter and my wife, we can simply trade. No questions. No follow-up. I don't think you have my family, but I think you know who does. I also know who has the money you spent to buy the cocaine you don't have. Otto Strang took the money and stole the cocaine. Which is why I need your help."

"You want me to help you take on Otto Strang? I am a practical businessman. The odds tell me that your venture has many risks. I am legitimate here. I own this town, literally. I own more than you can research. So why would I risk everything?"

"But you already have, so don't bluff me. Why would you destroy my friend's marina? Why come after me at my farmhouse in Shaplow? Why come on the reserve with hired thugs? Not your friends, but thugs. So, don't kid me."

"I assume you have plan," he said.

"Your Escalade."

"Oh, it has been missing. It is transportation for my boys. Nothing special."

"I'll let you find it, as a down payment on the plan. A show of good faith. A quarter of what you want is inside. But I must tell you, the two men you sent to Shaplow the night my house burned down are there too, and they're not healthy."

"I had nothing to do with burning your house down."

"I know. And I had nothing to do with the deaths of the two men. The third man? The price of doing business, combined with self-defense and the defense of my family."

Tarasov was silent for a long time. The two guys at the door never even twitched. Tarasov got up and walked to a small window behind his desk and stood there for a good five minutes. Finally, he said, "What is to stop me from having you tortured, so you give up what I want?"

"You are an honorable man. My fight is not with you. We have reconnected the GPS on the Escalade. A colleague knows we are here with you. If we don't walk out through your Tea House front door in the next ten minutes, someone in authority is going to find the Escalade, and that will make your life very uncomfortable." It was a huge bluff. I wasn't worried.

"Tell me this plan."

We told him the plan. I got my gun back and we walked out the front door ten minutes later, then drove back to Shaplow Lake.

CHAPTER 39

The next morning, I woke up in a room in The Duke, with Stacie beside me. I recalled tossing and turning in my nightmares until I felt her warm body slide close to my back. That had been enough to calm my mind into a long sleep that lasted until day light woke me.

There was a knock on the door. I opened it. It was the same girl who brought the sandwiches after the fire. This time she had breakfast and a package. I hadn't pre-ordered breakfast, but accepted it anyway, tipped her, and closed the door. I glanced back at Stacie. She was still beneath the covers, but I could see she had the Makarov in her hand.

Breakfast was scrambled eggs, bacon, sausage, and toast with a thermos of coffee. I'd told Tony we'd be staying at The Duke overnight and we had his truck. That might explain the breakfast order, but the package was a different matter. We ate and left the package until we could settle down with our coffee.

The package was an eight-by-ten-inch box, sealed with duct tape and wrapped with orange string. "TO JACK MCQUEEN" was printed on the box, in black marker. The box was light. I shook it. Decided it was safe and opened it by ripping the duct tape and prying up the flaps. There were several items inside. A photograph of an ankle with a tattooed dolphin. A second photo shows two wrists with shell bracelets. Another with a close-up of two faces, Skye, and Iona, streaked with dirt and tears. The dolphin looked like Lobelia's work. The picture of the shell bracelets was like the one Mrs. Milroy had shown me.

A final photo showed Jessica and her mother hugging each other against a dark wood background. They wore the same clothes from the day they boarded the Cessna floatplane.

The last things in the box were a pale green feather, an emerald-green sequin, and two locks of hair. I turned over the Del-and-Jessica photo. There was writing on the back, in block letters: COME ALONE. YOU KNOW. FEATHERS IN YOUR HAIR.

Jessica and Del. Feathers in my hair. Green feathers and sequins on yellow leotards. Cigar smoke. Aftershave.

A shiver ran through me.

> I'm dancing. Bare feet. Puffy sequined shorts. Green feathers in my hair. Lipstick. The smell of tobacco and aftershave swirls around me. I'm dancing on someone's feet. My feet and legs move to the music and the rhythm of the tuxedo man's legs. The notes are calliope. Circus. Something happy without a name, and I know this music leads me, leads us all, the giggling voices in the room. What happened then? That memory came into focus. I am dancing with my father. I am dancing with the tuxedo man.

Back in the present, I couldn't let my thoughts go to what might be happening to my family.

"What's the matter?" Stacie said.

I couldn't speak. Couldn't tell her where I'd just been.

Stacie looked at me. Held me. That was all.

I made two calls, one to Tony and another to Mark on his boat. I arranged for Stacie and me to meet Tony on the reserve. I told Mark about the plan we'd arranged with Tarasov and asked him if he'd be a part of it.

Then I got Stacie to locate Murphy's address, in case she'd moved since I'd been to her place. The address was the same. I called her and asked her if we could come over. She was fine with the idea.

Murphy met us at the main entrance to her townhouse complex. She ushered us inside. Her unit was on the ground floor, with an ocean view. We sat at the kitchen table "Coffee?" she asked.

"No time," I said. Right now, I'm going after Jessica and Del. I'm not waiting anymore."

"Jack, you should know that word on the street is some men went to the underpass where many street people sleep at night. They rousted everyone, and they've all disappeared."

"Jimmy Walker?"

"No. He's the one telling everyone what happened."

I had more than a hunch as to where they were. I told Murphy what Stacie and I had worked out about a run on the Strang estate. Then I asked for her help.

"Count me in," she said.

"Get the largest bolt cutters you can, and two short pieces of rebar," I said to Murphy. "For the razor wire. Rebar to check it's not electrified… Can you get trustworthy cops together to follow you without Conner's permission?"

"I think so," she said, "but I've got to know a little more than what you've told me so far. Do you know what we can expect up there? Numbers? Can we trust the Russians, as you say? This guy Mark, is he reliable? Have you got Chief and the men on the barricades involved? Can you assure me that Conner won't find out in advance and send in corrupt officers whom he trusts?"

"We don't know how many men Otto Strang has working for him on the estate," Stacie said. "But we're planning on twenty to thirty. We just came back from talking to Anton Tarasov. The man's as nice as an eel, but we have something he wants."

"Mark is solid," I said. "I'll get Chief on board this afternoon. Conner's another story. One you might know more about in your position. Is Reilly a guy you'll ask to come out?"

"Yes. He's tough. Rough around the edges. Maybe long-time upset I got promoted before him, but he's unhappy with Conner coming in. I believe he's honest and he's pissed about what's happened to me and feels it could happen to him."

"Maybe he'll know how much Conner knows," I said, "and how deep your commanding officer is in this."

"He's savvy. Knows these days there are direct links between prominent criminals, politicians, and high-ranking police officers. He's kept his nose clean. Followed orders. I think it's time for him to step up."

"Can you form a team of five and take the tunnel with Chief?" I asked.

"Leave it to me. 7:00 pm, right?" Murphy said.

"Right."

Stacie and I headed to the reserve to talk to Chief, thinking dark thoughts about the future. Why would Otto Strang lure me to him all alone? If he wanted to harm me, there had to be easier ways.

I swung down the reserve road toward the barricade. Two cruisers were parked in a V-shape, facing me, about a hundred yards from the boundary line. The force was serious about control, keeping the First Nations on the reserve, and keeping others out. I wondered how long this charade would continue. Maybe until they could get to the reason why the Russians came in the first place and to cool things down. Historically, tensions between First Nations and non-First Nations had been high in communities that bordered the reserves. Mainly over competing land use, rather than drug lord raids to retrieve stolen products and money.

An officer I didn't recognize turned Stacie and me around. The other one covered him as if he were in actual danger. Driving back the other way, we passed numerous cruisers and a small swat truck moving toward the barricade. I pulled over and called Chief.

"Chief. We were turned around at the barricade. RCMP cruisers are coming down the road fast toward the barricade." I clicked off and said to Stacie, "Don't think we need to be trapped in there." I called Chief again and asked him to put Tony on the line. "Tony, I know you're going to be pinned down, but I'm making a move on the Strang estate through the woods. The force is arriving at the barricades right now. I've told Chief. Don't know if they're going to puff out their chests or try to end this, but I need you and Chief and anyone you can spare to get to that main tunnel, the one with the steel door up to the Strang estate. Murphy has put together a team of cops she can trust. She'll have bolt cutters and rebar, but Strang has guards outside the entrance to the tunnel. Maybe the inside too."

"We'll talk about it. Leave it to me."

I heard a commotion in the background then the connection went dead. I looked over to Stacie in the passenger seat. "We might be on our own."

CHAPTER 40

At 7:00 p.m., Stacie and I sat in Tony's truck on the south side of Shaplow Lake, staring at the main gate to the Strang estate. I'd bought a six-foot sawhorse ladder and my own bolt cutters. We both needed an edge to get over the thick stone wall that extended from the ocean on both sides of the property and curved around away from the shoreline to a second gate. The wall enclosed the entire estate. At the water the wall continued into the sea and extended into the strait, curling into a breakwater that protected an inlet. The wall was topped with broken glass and razor wire.

Rifle fire came from the direction of the adjacent reserve. I imagined the force storming the barricades or pinning the defenders down. Toward the strait, all was quiet. If Tarasov kept his word, gunmen would move toward the estate's shoreline while others would make for the government wharf beside the First Nations reserve where Mark would be waiting with the cocaine. If I was wrong, all the Russians would go to meet Mark at the wharf. In which case I worried for Mark's safety, though he had his instructions. With any luck, Tony and Chief had a few band members, and Murphy had Reilly and a few others; all in all, enough to assault the tunnel. This was our two-pronged attack.

Stacie and I planned to take the surgical route by going over the wall and scrambling into the forest that led up to the house. Murphy and Reilly would take the tunnel with the First Nations men and enter the house from underground.

I looked in the rearview mirror. My eyes were red-rimmed and hot-wired. I felt solitary, half-mad. I was fueled by fury and revenge. It was a dangerous state. Nothing to check me, keep me in balance, keep me clear and focused on the quest to save my family. The terror in Stacie's eyes reflected my emotions back at me. "Jack," she said. "Take a deep breath. Count to ten."

"So now you're my therapist?"

"We've got a plan. We've set it in motion. We execute. The tension you're giving off is making this old truck hum. Settle. Settle."

She said the last two words as if she'd disciplined a frenzied dog. But I knew she was right, and I went down the checklist in my mind and breathed in and out until I was calm again.

"Are you ready to get out of the truck?" I asked.

"It's time." She leaned over and kissed me on the side of the neck above my collar.

I rubbed the back of her head and agreed. "It's time." I took the ladder from the truck bed and handed the bolt cutters and rebar to Stacie. We walked into the darkness. I looked along the wall, saw the gate with its guardhouse, and a guard sitting inside. It was raining, and his face was blurred through the water running down the window. Better for us as we moved through the trees toward the water, farther down the wall. The tunnel entrance was beyond the wall to our right. I set the ladder against the wall and climbed high enough to throw a piece of rebar at the razor wire. No spark so, not electrified. I cut the razor wire and used my jacket to cushion the broken glass atop the wall. Stacie had no trouble scraping over the wall. I muddled over after her and we hit the ground on the other side. Stacie landed like an acrobat. I landed like a wrestler.

We'd discussed surveillance cameras and kept an eye out for them. The cameras would matter for Murphy and Reilly at the tunnel, but we might be able to avoid them. If not, Otto Strang would watch us coming like a spider watching its prey step toward the web.

The rain was a steady downpour now. It filled the forest with white noise. A blessing and a curse for anyone listening for unwanted sounds in the dark. We moved together through the old growth; huge Douglas-fir trees, over nine hundred years old, tall, straight, and thick with roots splayed out in all directions, barely beneath the surface. Stacie and I had discussed tripwires and kept our eyes peeled.

We'd worked out head and hand signals. She motioned me forward and to the left, while she advanced to the right and widened the gap between us. But we kept each other in sight. Then we stopped and listened through rain that sounded like sand rushing through a plastic pipe. In the distance, I saw a bare-bulb light to Stacie's right and a covered shelter beside the tunnel entrance and its padlocked steel doors. I heard a click. A face glowed through the rain, and then another. Two guards standing outside were lighting up to smoke. Were Murphy and Chief's teams in place or were we on our own.

I signaled that we should move ahead and to the left, to bypass the tunnel and move uphill toward the house. And so we went, careful to blend into the darkness and the rain. I thought of the guards at the tunnel. There would surely be a camera there. Murphy and Reilly would know that. I could do nothing about it anyway.

We reached the forest's edge without incident. We watched the back of the house, a hundred yards distant; open space, manicured grass. We didn't speak, as planned. I made a motion with my hands like two jaws opening and closing: dogs. I thought if there were dogs, they'd growl first unless they had been trained to remain silent. I wouldn't worry about that. We watched the stone patio for movement. That was a likely station for a guard or a pair of sleeping dogs. Or both. We saw nothing. I watched and waited, getting a sense of the patrol pattern.

Fifteen minutes passed, and then I heard gunfire behind us, by the tunnel entrance. Then silence.

Lights came on in the house. I motioned Stacie to sit tight until I felt it was safe for her to come up to the patio. She shook her head from side to side. I squinted at her, gritted my teeth, and cut my hand across the air. As I left my cover, I glanced back and saw the fiery anger in her eyes. She didn't understand why I was crazy. She didn't understand my fear for her.

CHAPTER 41

The estate was more like a British manor house from another century than a North American home. Instead of wood or brick, it was constructed from huge limestone blocks. Stone patios and balconies. The place looked to be over forty thousand square feet. Large enough to hide anything. I started to think I was alone on a suicide mission. But I knew that if I survived and Stacie didn't, I wouldn't be able to live with myself.

My only thought now was to find Jessica and Del and get them out, even though I knew this was a setup. My prime mission was my family. If we didn't locate the twins inside, I'd have to deal with finding the twins later, that is if I survived. There would be cameras focused on the doors. I'd try to avoid them by staying in the shadows. I knew Strang and his men would be waiting for me, and that seeing me alone on camera wouldn't change anything for them. They might even have infrared cameras; in which case they could have spotted me in the forest.

I crossed the lawn and leaned against the wall beside the raised patio. I stayed low, curled around the stone railing, and crept up the steps. Once on the patio, I crossed its stone surface and pressed myself against the mansion's wall. I waited and listened. I heard gritty footsteps on the patio. Then I saw them. Two guards moved past each other in the rain. How could I have missed them? Once they passed, I watched them move toward the building, one on each side of me, about a hundred feet out. My heart jumped, and my breathing sounded like freight trains shunting back and forth. How could they have been so close and missed me? How could I have missed them? Then I thought they had already seen me and were waiting for movement before they opened fire. I decided to stay put.

Both men lit up their cigarettes. A short time later, the one on my left finished his cigarette and butted it out on the patio floor. He walked across the patio. The one on my right walked a few steps and pulled up a chair, facing out toward the lawn. He had an Uzi placed on his lap. I made a move and slid along the wall of the house until I was directly behind him and in line with the other guy. It was quick. I smashed the Glock across his head. I grabbed the Uzi, and checked it was set for R—repeating. When the other guard turned to fire, I sprayed him, and he dropped. Silence. I ran over and grabbed his Uzi as well, then slung both over my shoulder and moved back to the wall.

I used the Glock handle to smash a patio-level window, cleared the frame with an Uzi barrel, reached in, opened the latch, and stepped over the sill into a large dark room. But something seemed weird—as if I were in a funhouse. The shapes were unexpected for a great room, a library, or a billiard room. There were obstacles and corners, places to hide, and low neon lights. In the center was a traditional carousel. The room was a miniature arena, with banked seating that curled around three sides. I stepped onto the carousel platform beside a white horse, its hooves stretched out in full gallop, its eyes wide and filled with fear. I knew his fear, and saw his nostrils flared with it.

Circus music suddenly blared into the room. "The Entrance of the Gladiators". Red lights came on beneath the carousel canopy. A short wall with multiple entrances ringed the carousel, which was bathed in red and blue light, with neon graffiti tags sprayed on the vertical surfaces. This was a circus war zone, and I flashed back to blocked memories of the nights we were costumed and masked and set loose to ride the wild horses and shoot the laser guns. This was the captured, abused children's playhouse.

The carousel started turning. The lights flashed on and off, so the room was dark and shadowed, then blindingly bright. My senses became disoriented. My eyes had difficulty adjusting. The vast ceiling was a dome painted black and studded with stars. Thunder sounds cracked and strobe lights sliced the ceiling with spears like lightning. I crouched outside the carousel, beside a panicked horse, uncertain of what to do.

I heard the first pock. Plaster from a horse's hoof sliced across my cheek, sharp as a paper cut. Blood dripped to the carousel floor as I spun around surrounded by music and thunder. Another shot, and a burst of automatic fire. Fragments of frantic horses exploded in the air, leaving a cloud of powdery dust suspended all around me. I slid an Uzi from my shoulder and fired in a spray. I crawled facing the carousel's spin. The Uzis were standard, with thirty-two rounds in the magazines, less what I'd used. I regretted that I didn't take the time to search the guards' bodies for extra magazines.

Another burst of fire. A horse's head exploded beside me, while the body kept galloping. I retaliated into the neon darkness and a return bullet buzzed past my ear. A mirrored panel at the carousel's center exploded. I turned and fired, dropping a black shape on its way from one neon obstacle to another. I lay flat and saw a pair of legs among the galloping horses. I fired the Uzi in a concentrated spray that cut the assailant down. I was breathing hard, forcing back vomit from fear and the thought of what I'd done. In combat, in the army, it was always the same. I did what I had to do, but never liked it. Some did, but they were truly lost and crazy. They were the soldiers who never returned or, if they did, could not adjust and remained rudderless in their own dark dead limbo world.

The music stopped and someone turned the strobe lights off.

"Lay it down, Jack. You're not leaving here."

It was Voice, from back on the mainland. From the Escalade.

"Got the money, Jack? Not got the money, well, no one's leaving here."

I'd also heard his voice when I was a boy.

I asked, "You want the money you gave me to stop looking for those teenage girls?"

I slid further along the floor, beneath the next horse. A single shot crashed into the horse's ear. We were still turning 'round and 'round, without the music. I rolled off the carousel, to the bare concrete of the inner circle. The carousel turned around me, and as the horses rushed past, I watched the low walls, the sculpted rocks and barricades set up for laser tag. I saw a shoulder and a green neon reflection on a rifle barrel. I readied the second Uzi and waited for the same galloping horses to come around so the sight line would be identical, then stood up and fired repeatedly. The problem was knowing how many men were in the arena with me. With the next look, I saw the gunman on the floor. I could only see his legs. His upper body was in shadow.

The music started again, and I jumped back on the carousel and walked back through the horses and wild animals galloping and leaping on either side of me. I needed to make the rest of the Uzi clip a leveler. On the carousel now, other men were firing handguns. We lit up the overhead lights' red glare with our muzzle flashes. The sound was deafening. Plaster animal pieces flew in all directions and my blood seeped from multiple wounds. I slumped down with a bullet in my left shoulder and a bullet slash on my calf. That was enough to take me down. I dropped the Uzi, took the Glock from my jacket pocket, and rolled into the center again. I heard a boot scrape on the concrete beside my ear. Looked up at a pistol barrel pointed at my head. I heard a shot.

The pistol dropped from the assailant's hand as his face flew over me in a mess of blood and tissue. His body dropped across me as he fell. Stacie stood in the carousel's center. The Makarov in her hands.

There was no time. The music stopped. The chipped and broken horses slowed to a canter and stopped. Stacie and I stood together. The lights came on in the arena, and someone clapped. Then there was a different voice.

"Well done, Jack McQueen and your delightful friend. You have made a shamble of my sport." The man spoke from the upper levels, in the seating above the arena floor. "You are surrounded. You are outgunned and I unfortunately have lost too many men to continue this charade. Take a close look Jack now that you're in the light."

He had a point. There were six shooters with their weapons trained on us. I looked at Stacie. We both knew we had to give it up. I couldn't raise my left arm which hung limp at my side. And the slash in my calf had me lame.

"So, it's a truce," I said.

"Not exactly. But we can talk."

Voice spoke from the left. "Throw out your weapons."

Stacie threw out her Makarov, and I tossed out my Glock. The air was plaster dust and gun smoke.

"Hands on your heads. Walk out on your knees. Don't try anything on the way through the horses or you're dead."

Once we were out, they patted us down. I recognized Voice in the light. Nicholas Calvino.

"Calvino," I said. "You can do better than this. Working for a pedophile. You get behind bars and you won't last five minutes before you're digesting the sharpened end of a toothbrush."

"Shut up, asshole."

They found the Beretta at my ankle.

"I said all of them," Calvino said.

He smashed me in the face with the pistol butt. I went down and he kicked me in the neck and the shoulders. My vision blurred. The last thing I remembered was the searing pain in my shoulder, ribs, and legs as I was first beaten, then hauled up the stairs to the second level.

CHAPTER 42

Otto Strang's manor house stood up to William Randolph Hearst's modest place on the California coast. It wasn't exactly a castle, but it seemed impregnable. I'd led Stacie into a trap, and if we were doubly unlucky, Murphy and Chief would wind up here too. As for Tarasov's gang, I guessed they were going for the drugs and that was it.

From the top of the stairs, we were carried into a massive assembly room with walnut paneling and vivid tapestries. There was a fireplace with an Italian marble mantel and columns. Plush, hand-woven carpets covered the floor.

Otto Strang sat behind a hand-carved Jacobean oak desk across the room from me. Five other men were in the room. Three stood with their backs to the windows. One stood beside the fireplace. Stacie and I knelt on clear heavy-duty plastic, our hands behind our heads. The last guy stood over us with a Glock 20 pressed against my head. Once he finished with us, we'd be rolled up in the plastic and taken out like trash. My shoulder was raging, and I tried not to faint. Stacie was shaking.

Otto Strang was about seventy. I counted back the years until I was nine. He was forty-two the year I killed my father. The year I lost track of Kat and Peter. He ran things on the hill the year we were shipped off to foster homes. He had us brought up through the large tunnels to parties in this house. Later, when I worked with Murphy, we were closing in on him, then it all fell apart for me, and someone shelved the investigation.

"You have been so accommodating, Jack McQueen," Otto Strang said.

I wasn't sure what he meant at first. Then it dawned on me.

"And look what you have brought me," Strang continued. "A pretty perky gift."

"Fuck off, Strang."

My head was ripped back by a fist holding a gun, and my cheek opened like a soft fruit. My blood dripped on the plastic. The gun's cold barrel again pressed against my temple.

"Now let's stay civilized, shall we? You break into my home, cause damage, and use foul language. Seems you haven't changed much over the years."

"What would you know about it?"

Strang had changed. He was no longer young, handsome, and athletic. He was obese. His face was blotched and pocked. His lips were thick, veined, and blubbery. His excesses had not been kind to him. He was a tooth that's had too much candy over a long time. I wanted so badly to extract that tooth, but my wish seemed unlikely to be granted.

"Jack McQueen. I do remember you. Years ago, dressed up in pantaloons, rouge on your cheeks, and lipstick on your lips. Oh, you made such a delightful bum boy then, like the brother and sister, and that Madson boy."

He chuckled. His eyes glanced to the right as if recalling the graphic details. Here was the man who destroyed my family once and was doing it again. I couldn't speak.

"Where's the money?"

"What money?" I asked.

"I know all about it. You think you're the only one who can follow a trail?"

"I can give you back the money that Calvino gave me since I didn't do what I was told. Neat how you set it up. Teased me off, knowing full well I wouldn't bite. Like it was all a game to you."

"It is a game. It's a game right now, but the clock is running out. I know you've gone to Tarasov with the drugs, so where's the money?"

"If I had it, believe me, if I thought for a moment, you'd let my daughter and my wife go, I'd give it to you. I don't care about your money. Ask the Russians. Maybe they still have it."

I got another crack across the face. This time with a fist. I slumped sideways and spit blood onto the plastic-covered floor. I heard gunshots below us, and outside in the distance. I looked up at Strang. He was enjoying this.

"The Russians are a joke. Little League thugs. Peasants. Want to throw their weight around outside their fucked-up country. They buy my drugs, and traffic human beings. They're like everyone else, looking for something easy. Something they can exploit, use, and then abandon to slavery."

Otto Strang was revoltingly smug. There was something absolute about his confidence.

"Mr. McQueen, I am more selective. Let's say a connoisseur. A jobber with taste who imports and selects individuals for their talents and exports them to the appropriate markets—pretty girls, ugly girls, young boys, strong men, down-and-outs who waste society's resources anyway, addicts. They all have value. They're commodities, and various markets have the right fit."

I wondered why he was telling me this. A confessional, knowing he was going to kill me.

"What's this got to do with me? Why lure me here by trying to keep me away? What's your motivation? Some sick fuck still toying with a child's life?"

"Tanner McQueen, your father? That's a laugh. He worked for me. Frederick Madson worked for me. They had a good thing going, back in the day. You killed them both. You got too close a few years back, but you failed. I could have killed you when you killed Madson, but I thought that discrediting you would work. When I heard you blocked it all out, well, that was perfect."

"So why this charade? You could have grabbed me anytime you liked."

"Call it an old man's whim. I like to play games with my adversaries. You got away before and it has irritated me ever since. Besides, operations were getting messy over on the mainland, and Chief had hired you to find his missing girls. They were delivering drugs for the organization and poof; the drugs and money disappear. You were going to search for them. And I somehow knew that after coming so close two years back, you'd return to the Island and to Otto Strang. So, it was a simple manipulation. I sent you that package and knew by the contents, you'd know who sent it, and where you'd find your precious family, and here you are."

"Your men attacked me outside of my wife's house, right?"

"Only to let you know we were still in the picture. To convince you we wanted you to back off the case, which made you more determined."

"The homestead? My wife and child? Was that necessary?"

"By then the money and the drugs were missing. The Russians came after you, not me. I waited for you to come to me. The fire? Maybe my boys got carried away."

"They killed the Russians too?" I said.

"A business necessity."

"I got away, but what happened to my brother and sister? Did Peter and Kat get away?"

"Jack. They are not your brother and sister, and they're probably dead by now."

"Liar."

"Honestly, it was a loss for me. They were such sweet things. I could have made money with them. They got sent away. Not by me."

"Liar. Kat and Peter are my brother and sister. Why would they not be?"

"Because the people at the homestead, the ones you call father and mother? They brought you to the Island. They're not your parents. They found you and they took you. Did the same for all the kids that were there. You were nothing special, except the old man fancied keeping you three around. I told him many times to sell you off."

Otto Strang laughed. He was enjoying this, the way a boy who tortures small animals finds pleasure in their pain. A numbness crept over me. I couldn't speak.

Calvino wasn't in the room. I assumed he dragged us up here to be toys for Strang's evil sport. I'd had enough of Strang, his self-important righteousness, his candid confessions, his business, and his vices. I wanted to leap across the room and tear him limb from limb.

The gunfire outside became more prominent. The windows were a wash of rain as the wind whipped the deluge into a fury. Sounds of voices and scrambling footsteps filtered in from outside the room.

Otto nodded to the guy holding the Glock 20 to my head and said, "Tell me who has the money. Where can I find it?"

I stared back at him and said nothing. The guy drove the Glock hard into my injured shoulder. The room swirled. I almost passed out. I heard glass smash and wood splinter at a floor-to-ceiling window. The three guys by the windows were killed as three of Tarasov's men shot them through the glass and then hurled themselves through the balcony windows. Murphy and Tony burst through the door at the same time.

I kicked the legs from under my torturer and twisted his gun arm back until it snapped at the elbow. I held the arm and the Glock with both hands, pain vibrating through my trembling body. Stacie dived to the floor. I pressed my tormentor's finger down on the Glock's trigger and shot the guy at the fireplace. Otto stood behind his desk and leveled a pump-action shotgun he'd had on his lap. I fired the Glock again and again while Otto managed to pump twice and fired as he stumbled backward with a ragged hole where his left eye had been. The shotgun's blasts played havoc with the ceiling as Otto hit the floor, stone-cold dead.

I wrestled the Glock from my captor and smashed it into his forehead until he passed out.

Stacie was gone. I rushed from the room and found her kicking in every door in the long hall. She had a gun in her hand which she must have scooped off the floor. I joined her as the last door splintered inward revealing Del and Jessica, both tied and gagged. Calvino had a gun to Jessica's head. Stacie and I pointed guns at Calvino. It was a typical stand-off, almost a cliché—if not for the fact that it was my family on the line.

"I'm walking out of here," Calvino said.

"Not so sure of yourself anymore, Calvino?" I said. "Otto's dead. Head's blown off. You should see the mess."

"Back off. I'll blow her fucking head off, too."

His other hand was shaking, a twitch that told me everything was not all right. Then Stacie said, "Shoelace."

What? Jessica dropped her head and flopped forward. Stacie fired and Calvino was blown back dead against the wall.

I looked at Stacie. "It's the code we had," she said. "We practiced it when we were training with the guns at the homestead. 'Shoelace.' Drop as far as you can to give someone the shot."

I untied Del and Jessica. Jessica fell into Stacie's arms and cried. Del couldn't do more than let me hold her. We were both shaking.

CHAPTER 43

How do you tell a story with so many moving parts set in motion simultaneously? Stacie and I had set the plan and gathered the personnel. Considered all the variables, we thought—but once everything started moving, there were surprises. Strang's manor house was a carnal mess. Not a place we wanted to stay for very long. We needed to get out and fast. I suspected but didn't know for sure that all hell was breaking loose within the force. Tarasov's yacht was to be in the strait for the drugs. From the yacht, his men would be sent out to the Shaplow wharf to pick up the drugs from Mark. I didn't know that Conner had been tipped off by an informant about Tarasov's yacht and that the RCMP would be mobilized with reinforcements from down island specifically to intercept the cocaine transfer to the yacht.

The first thing I did was get Stacie, Jessica, Del, Murphy, Tony, and myself away from the mansion. Murphy had told me nothing about the Strang tunnels. Reilly and the three officers she'd brought were still there, dealing with what they'd found. I decided if the twins were captive in the mansion, the police would find them. If not, then I still had work to do, and I'd worry about that later. Stacie and I broke out the way we came in and went down through the forest to the tunnel opening. We met Chief there, and he came with us over the wall and into town. We gathered up the First Nations men who'd been wounded. I had a bullet wound in my left shoulder, a deep gash in my calf, and a face that resembled hamburger meat. Chief drove with me in his Chevy Nova. An uninjured band member drove a beat-up Plymouth, with many of the injured men bleeding on the seats. The local clinic wouldn't take us, so we ended up staggering into the emergency at Nanaimo General Hospital an hour later. We were met with surprised looks and many questions. They put a guard on us, while Chief and the other driver hung out in the waiting room. Many were critical. I didn't have a choice about leaving the hospital after they'd patched me up, since I needed more recovery time and the police wanted to question me back in Shaplow.

The local newspaper, The Shaplow News, and media from the mainland had already been covering the standoff at the reserve, but now reporters were in a frenzy to get details about the attack on Strang's place. They camped out at the hospital, at the reserve entrance, and outside the police perimeter at the Strang mansion.

Stacie and Murphy took Del and Jessica to Murphy's home to be safe. Tony went with them for added protection. I called Mark while I was recovering at the hospital. We talked. I said, "Tell me what happened." So, he told me what went down. Two Russians came, huge guys. Mark passed the drugs over to them from his boat. They'd come from out in the strait, with a sleek cigarette cedar strip motorboat, and left immediately. He said the force was waiting for them out on the water. He heard a few shots, and the last thing he remembered hearing was the roar of the cedar strip disappearing into the rain and the police boat being left behind. He said he heard later that the police boarded a yacht in the strait. There was a helipad on the top deck, but no helicopter. And no Russians on board. They only found the crew, all non-Russians with nothing much to say and little English with which to say it.

I also called Murphy. I didn't say much but got what happened in the tunnel from her perspective. Outside the steel doors to the tunnel, they subdued the guards. I wasn't sure if that meant killed or disabled. Didn't ask. They used bolt cutters to take off the chains and padlocks. Murphy and Tony figured there'd be guards inside, and played it cautiously, letting the guards fire first. That gave away their position, allowing return fire.

Murphy said the rest was uneventful for a while. She couldn't get over the fact that the tunnel had a poured-concrete floor and sculpted-concrete walls and ceilings. She'd been expecting mud, water, and rotting beams. But she wasn't prepared for what she found closer to the house. Reilly and the three other trusted officers were left down there, and they had a story to tell the force when it arrived. She said I wouldn't believe what she had to say, so I didn't ask.

Smaller passages ran off the main tunnel to warehouse rooms. They found floor-to-ceiling cages holding many people. Some were illegal immigrants, the container types who'd been lucky enough to make it from Asia in search of a better life. Murphy said they were on hold until they could be sold off to massage parlors, brothels, or slave factories to work off their debt for their transportation costs.

There were young girls, some from the Island, some from reserves. Most were drugged and looked sad and used. There were street people, some locals Murphy knew, and Jimmy's recently abducted friends. Murphy and Reilly guessed they were considered expendable and were headed for hard labor away from the public eye.

All the children who'd disappeared showed signs of being used and abused.

Bones were found in one tunnel behind a steel door that concealed a catacomb. All the bones were human, and some were children's bones. They'd been there a while, broken up in pieces. Murphy's description made me think of Shaplow Lake and what I'd found there. And it made me think of Tyler and how I still needed to deal with that.

Murphy said that after we got out, Conner and the force secured the place. The Russians who came in through the window had vanished in the darkness. No Russians had been arrested. The force rounded up the victims in the tunnels, arrested everyone who worked for the estate, and brought in a crime scene forensics team to gather evidence. Officers commandeered Tarasov's yacht but found nothing on it and had to let it go soon after.

Murphy said the news outlets were flying reporters in to cover things. Official RCMP media coverage was, as usual, concise, and limited in detail, but the presence of so many reporters turned the town into a circus. It seemed my name and whereabouts were getting a lot of coverage. Murphy warned me to expect hysteria and turmoil in Shaplow, as well as outside the hospital.

Four days passed before I saw real daylight. They kept me in longer than the rest, so when I walked out from my recovery, Chief was sitting in the waiting room with an officer on each side of him. Chief had been coming to the hospital every day, but the hospital had orders from the police that I was to have no visitors. Chief was there to drive me home. Conner had arranged for the officers to make sure I didn't skip the Island before he questioned me. Suspicious prick. I figured my reputation for getting involved in deep shit would always follow me.

My stomach still felt queasy when I thought about the investigation and how it led me here. I'd called Stacie and talked to her and Jessica to make sure they were still safe. I wanted desperately to get back to Shaplow. I'd heard nothing about the twins. It was obvious now that Strang did not have them.

We came out of the Nanaimo General Hospital to reporters shouting questions at us. The police presence helped us get through the mob to Chief's Chevy Nova. We drove away from the pick-up circle leaving the press frenzied and disappointed.

CHAPTER 44

Chief drove, an officer beside him. I was in the back on the diagonal beside the other constable. Two cruisers, each staffed by one driver, formed an unwanted convoy with us in the middle. Neither Chief nor I spoke. I thought maybe Chief would go directly to the reserve where we could hopefully avoid the third degree. The cops slapped their jaws together, chewing gum.

During my hospital recovery, the storm broke, and northwest winds off the Pacific brought high pressure and blue skies. But as we headed back to Shaplow Lake, the sky turned brown, with deep black crevices more suited to our destination, bringing rain. I wanted this to be over, but I was no closer to Iona and Skye than I had been when Chief sat down beside me in Brogans. The equation had two sides. The money and the drugs. One element was missing.

Tarasov could smell a trap. That or he just had the sense to get what he wanted and get out. Strang took Jessica and Del, knowing I'd come after them. The package was what bothered me. Two shell bracelets, two locks of hair, their photo, the photo of the dolphin tattoo, and the photo of Del and Jessica. I got the picture after I opened the package. Jessica and Del's photograph, the clipped hair, the smell familiar to me had convinced me that Strang had them. But why the photos displaying the bracelets, the photo of the twins, and the photo of the dolphin tattoo if Strang didn't have them? After combing for days through the Strang estate, surely the police would have found them, but to my limited knowledge, they had not been found. Strange that he had those photos related to the twins, photos he used to further convince me to come to him.

Halfway to Shaplow, the cops pulled out sandwiches and started munching in our faces. Chief twitched even more and moved his butt from side to side as he drove.

"Fucking guys," I said. "Didn't your mothers teach you any manners?"

The guy beside me was thick around the neck, and a fold of red skin flopped over a tight collar. He wasn't old, but his nose and ears were out of proportion to the rest of his face. The guy up front was rugby beef, cauliflower ears, with rolls of bristled flesh on a shorn head. He turned to his buddy in the back and said, "You hear something buzzing back there?" His mouth full of chicken, lettuce, and mayonnaise.

I looked out the window and let it slide. The rain turned heavy. The forest flashed by like wallpaper, the same green, same patterns, boring now in the mood I was in. I sank into an impatient silence. Not cowed but determined.

After another half hour passed, we arrived not at the reserve but at the Shaplow Lake Detachment. We were met by more reporters at the public parking lot entrance.

Soon after, I found myself back in an interrogation room. They took Chief somewhere else, and I was left to wait. After a while, Conner stepped in with Reilly and they sat down. I knew it was Conner because of his arrogance. I decided I'd see how he was before raising my hackles. The trauma to my body was not conducive to remaining calm and collected. And the stiff ride up-Island with the two bulls was enough to try the patience of a nun.

Reilly looked sympathetic. Conner's face was scraped rock. Hard granite. Cold as ice.

"We need to clear a few things up," Reilly said.

I nodded and met their eyes.

"Who do you think you are?" Conner said. "What gives you the authority to organize a takedown? Get people shot and killed? Involve my staff without consulting me?"

"I—"

"Shut up. I'm not finished. You were a rebellious asshole back when you were on the force. Screws loose. For what you did last week, I could have you in a cell where the sun doesn't shine, and you'd be someone's private bitch every night. But you know Jack, you're a lucky prick, because your old lady is connected, and you saved her life. Quite the hero."

I could see he was pissed that he wasn't the hero here, only the backup, an appendage to the operation.

"What I want to know is who has the money from the drug transaction with Tarasov? Do you know? Because if I find you're holding back, connected wife or not, I'll find you and you'll wish you were never born."

Reilly added his two cents, "You had the drugs, right? That's how you baited the Russians to help you create an alternate assault. The drugs were the currency you dealt with, right?"

I didn't admit anything. "You guys fucked up out on the water," I said.

Conner waded in with, "You little prick. Think you're so smart. How do I know you didn't tip Tarasov off so he and his men could get away?"

"He's smarter than you think. Those guys don't survive if they're not. If you'd met the man, you'd know." I was pushing it, so I settled back. Let them calm down. They were venting.

"The money?" Conner said.

"Your guess is as good as mine. I figure Ian Stewart buried it somewhere. And he ain't talking."

"We found many bones in those tunnels," Reilly said. "Years and years of bones. Forensics says back almost thirty years. When you were a kid. What's your spin on the bones?"

"It's what happens to human merchandise that gets spoiled," I said. "Hard to get the mind around that."

"There were small bones," Reilly said.

I looked up at Conner. He might be in someone's pocket, but he was not beyond revulsion over the things they'd found in the tunnels.

"There's a closed file here," I said, "from when Murphy and I were investigating missing persons a few years back. As a kid, I discovered something in the lake. There are bodies down there. Chained or wired to the stumps where the Strang property butts up against the public road. I watched my father and Mr. Madson dump something into Shaplow Lake. Madson went underwater with it, then came up and they rowed away. I took a heavy rock and walked in from the shore. There were many small bodies. I found my best friend wrapped in plastic, tied to a stump. I ripped the plastic open and carried Tyler from the lake. I buried him in the tunnel between our homestead and the Madson place, then my mind blocked it out. The day I shot Frederick Madson, he came at me with an axe, and all the bodies and Tyler's face came back to me, and I squeezed the trigger until the clip was empty. I killed the man who killed my best friend."

The room was silent. I heard Reilly's heavy breathing, and even Conner's stony features softened a bit.

"Get divers over to the lake," I said. "I'll show you where I buried Tyler's body. Mrs. Madson, she wants to know."

The room was silent for a long time. Then Conner said, "You're free to go. Don't leave town. We'll come and get you when we go out to the lake, and you can show us."

I got up and walked out the door, past the desk sergeant, and into the light. I might have thought my body would be unburdened. That the bag of stones would tumble open and set me free. But I was still left with Kat and Peter missing from my life. And if Strang had spoken the truth about our origins, I knew my early life was still missing. And after all these weeks, I'd failed to find Iona and Skye. I knew darkness still hovered over the landscape.

When I left, there were only half a dozen reporters on the sidewalk. I buzzed through them with no comment and walked toward The Duke at a fast clip. The bar drew me like a siren toward the rocks. I used my cell to call Becky, my tech-savvy former cop who I paid to hack for information. "Hi Becky, Jack. You must do me one more favor. It'll be the last."

"You expect me to believe that?" Becky said. "What have you been up to? There are stories about a big bust where you are."

"Yeah. That's me. No time to talk. I need someone to go to see Mrs. Milroy." I gave her the address. "Ask her about the photo of the two shell bracelets strung together with nylon fishing line. Does she still have it? If not, what happened to it? If someone came and took the photo, I need an accurate description. Thanks. Call me back as soon as you can."

I hung up and continued toward The Duke. Partway up the hill, Murphy's car pulled alongside. She rolled down the window. "Get in," she said.

There wasn't any argument.

CHAPTER 45

Ten minutes later Murphy pulled off the road, onto a gravel driveway that opened into a slightly rolling meadow. I saw Tony's truck beside a helicopter. He leaned against the driver's door. "Does that helicopter belong to the force?" I asked.

"Not over here it doesn't," Murphy said. "That's higher up the food chain. The Ministry of the Attorney General. Del, Jessica, and Stacie are going home in style."

The three women leaned against Tony's truck. Each had a small carry-on. One scorched bunny slipper protruded from Jessica's pack. She'd gone way past bunny slippers. It was sad. Del wore the same rain gear and hiking boots she wore when she pummeled me after the fire. My heart was racing at what I'd caused them to go through. We stopped beside them and got out. I leaned over to Murphy. I asked, "The missing plane and pilot?"

"Strang got to the pilot. He made him land the plane on the water. Jessica and Del were taken at gunpoint, by boat to the big house. Your ex memorized the tail number on the plane; we're tracking it down."

"You'll get the pilot, then."

"In time."

Murphy turned her attention to Jessica and Del. "Thought I'd bring him to see you off," she said.

I stood like an idiot. Speechless.

Jessica stood beside Stacie, her arms around her waist.

"It's over, Jack," Del said.

I stared down at the grass, noticing the different stalks and blades, the small webs, and the linkages. I looked closely, and long enough that an entire world appeared. A world apathetic to the larger world above it. Spiders, beetles, earwigs. In that microcosm, a drama played out beside my feet.

"I know," I said.

There was nothing else to say. I recalled Del's voice from the stairs in her home. I can't get over you. She could now, and so could Jessica.

"Daddy." She left Stacie's side and ran to me. She buried her face in my chest and sobbed. Her entire body shook with her leaving. I bent down and she reached up and kissed me on the cheek.

"Daddy," she whispered. "I'll take care of mama."

"I'm sure you will," I said softly into her ear. "You've got to let me keep in touch." I pulled out a cleaned version of the satin trim of her child's blank that I'd saved from the fire and handed it to her.

She took it and stepped back and said, "I wouldn't have it any other way."

Del stepped forward. "The house is being sold whether you like it or not," she said. "You'll need to contribute your signature. I've handed in my resignation. I have a line on a new job in Seattle. There are no problems. A brush-up for the state bar exams. Jessica seems all grown up, thanks to you. I don't blame you, Jack. It would be like blaming a dog that's been abused. We don't blame you. There's no solution anymore."

Del held me, and I was the shaking body in her arms. It was beneath the skin. A touch I'll never touch again. Then she turned and gathered up Jessica, and they climbed into the helicopter. Stacie fell into my arms. She looked like a trauma victim. Worn. Hollow-eyed.

"Going back so soon?" I said.

"You're not going to find those girls. I'm too tired now to help you. Got unfinished business to attend to anyway."

I wondered what she meant by that, but let it slide. "You'll keep in touch?" I said.

"Call me when you decide to come back over. We can grab a bite and I'll catch you up." She moved to turn away, then swung back, stepped close, and kissed me on the lips. Once she was in the chopper, the rotors cranked up. A moment later, the bird lifted off and the ladies waved out the window.

I turned to Tony. I wanted so badly to share a drink with him but couldn't go there. "Thanks, Tony." I didn't know what else to say.

"Murphy," Tony said, "can you get him home before I smack him one."

"Will do," she said. It's going to be a while before he's over this."

I drifted to the last touch with Del. In my head, I recited my own words, written after I'd signed the custody agreement.

> "We used to dance naked in the rain, by firelight, stare upon the stars, make love beside the embers and the ash, wake up with the corn whispering in the wind, and listen to small creatures dreaming."

CHAPTER 46

Murphy drove me to her place. I had nowhere else to go except maybe The Duke, but this time booze and solitude were not what I needed.

Her living room was OCD-tidy. A small reed basket rested on a square coffee table. No dust. No dishes in the sink. The refrigerator was almost as pristine as if it were in the appliance store. I sat down on the couch, leaned over the arm, and looked at the baseboard. No scuff marks. No dust bunnies. Two CDs were placed on the end table as decor. I moved them slightly. There was no dust.

Murphy sat down in a chair across from me. "Don't get any ideas," Murphy said. "You're staying here until you've healed a bit. I don't want you wandering around homeless and going on a bender."

"And aren't you Mother Teresa?"

"For once in your life, take some advice. There's nothing more you can do. You need to rest. They only released you from the hospital because they needed the bed. Don't kid yourself. When Chief called me about your discharge, I told them you could stay here. You're sleeping on the couch. That's it."

"Don't fancy yourself, Murphy. It's been a long time." I regretted the words as soon as they were out. I shook my head and looked down at the coffee table. "I'm sorry," I said.

"Things never change, do they? Do you know the number of times I've heard sorry in my life? And not all of them from you." she laughed.

I laughed. Said, "Really. I'm sorry."

"You know Conner lifted my suspension."

"No thanks to me."

"It's bigger than you. Don't kid yourself. As you know I didn't have any reports that said I played well with others. Conner is who his superiors on the force need to protect their interests over here."

"Whose interests?"

"We never know, but there are always those at the trough, and they like a clean house—one they can control while seeming to do justice."

"Conner's not exactly clean," I said.

"No, he's not, but he's someone who can come in and take command of a situation. Tighten a few screws, no pun intended. So, right now, I am cannon fodder. It won't surprise me if they transfer me from this detachment."

"You're telling me they wanted Strang's operation cleaned up all along?"

"It looks that way," Murphy said. "I think this business with the human trafficking's too much to ignore. The drugs, sure. They're everywhere and everyone's involved somewhere along the line to make it all work for the cartels and the local grow-op guys. It's the human trafficking the RCMP wants to crack down on."

"Do you think there will be a follow-up with Tyler's body in the homestead tunnel?" I said. "Will they send divers into the lake?"

"It's happening now."

"And DNA? Will they test the bodies for DNA matches with all those missing kids?"

"That's the plan," she said. "Takes a while. It isn't TV. Do you want a cup of tea?"

She steered me in the right direction. Tea, not Jameson. "Tea's fine. Green?"

"If you like."

She went to the kitchen, and I heard her pouring water into a kettle. Tea was spooned out into a filter in the teapot. Real tea. Not bags of dust swept up from a plantation shed floor. "Is it Japanese or Chinese?" I asked.

"You'll have to wait and taste it. See if you know the difference, mister smart-ass."

Six minutes later, she brought the tea in two glass mugs.

"What kind?" I asked.

Murphy sat back in a chair matching the couch. "Chinese. Dragon Well from Hangzhou."

"What's going to happen to the Strang estate?" I said.

"Everyone they could get their hands on has been charged. Sadly, we got mostly little fish. Otto Strang and Calvino were big enough that we could have levered them into other fish, but we all know where they are now."

"Self-defense and you know it."

"And Conner knows it. And Conner knows that there are friends, not yours but your ex has legal connections with the Attorney General's Office and her friends are very happy Otto Strang and Calvino are gone."

"Strang's sons?"

"Can't touch them. They disappeared so far down a rabbit hole you'd hardly notice they're related. Otto and Calvino were old school. James and John Strang, not so much. They're triple-A. Teflon. Can't touch them because they don't get their hands dirty, and they pay off the right people."

"The property?"

"Once all the trials are over and done with, the tunnels will be filled in. The arena will be cleared. The property right now is evidence, so it will be held along with everything in it. Then the property becomes part of the Strang estate, and the two sons will inherit everything." She sighed and leaned back in her chair.

"Any more questions?" she said. "I'm getting tired now. I have sheets for you and a blanket, and there are towels in the bathroom for a shower when you get up. I'm going to bed. Don't get up if you hear me. I get up early. Two hours before work, so don't get up and bug me before the job. I need that time. You can make your own coffee, and there's breakfast stuff in the cupboard above the fridge. I'll see you in the late afternoon. I want you to stay here and recuperate. Stay here. Got it?"

"I got it." Then I thought of Mark. "What happened to Mark once he dealt with the Russians?"

"It is interesting that you ask," she said. "It appears he and his boat disappeared. Conner is still investigating details on who met with the Russians to pass on the drugs."

I was relieved. I almost asked her about the package involving materials about the twins' stuff. Everyone seemed to have forgotten about them. But I didn't say anything. I'd wait until Becky called. See what she had.

I heard Murphy in the morning. Decided to take her advice and rolled over. Waited for Becky's call, which came that afternoon. "The guy I sent over finally got back to me," she said. "A Mrs. Milroy, right? Well, someone did come over to ask about the twin girls she had boarding with her. Asked if they left anything when they disappeared. Yep, a photograph of their arms displaying the shell bracelets. Mrs. Milroy said she showed the photo to two people. One man she described as handsome and polite. She remembered the name, Jack McQueen."

"Okay. Did you get the other person's description?"

"According to my guy, she's got a good memory. Some of those old broads are sharp. Guess I shouldn't call them that. I'll be there someday, and I hope I'm on the ball, rather than sorting buttons at an old age home."

"Right. Right. Spit it out for me."

"Mrs. Milroy said a tall First Nations guy. Good looking. He was asking about the twins. He asked if he could have the photograph. She gave it to him since he said he was a relative. Also, she said that another guy came by too who said he was their father."

"Did she get a name?"

"No, only that he was their father and needed to get in touch with them."

"Was this before or after she gave the photograph to the tall First Nations guy?

"Just a minute." There was silence on the line, then Becky came back. "Before."

"Anything else?"

"That's it, Jack."

"Thanks," I said. I made a note to send Becky flowers and a gift certificate for Benny's, her favorite restaurant. I made myself a coffee and found some bread for toast. Pulled my pants over my boxers. Same shirt. Strapped the Beretta on my ankle. They'd returned it at the station. They didn't return the Glock since it had been discharged and was classified as evidence. I put my checked lumber jacket on the back of the kitchen chair. Buttered the toast. Figured out the steps. Stayed in the moment.

CHAPTER 47

The afternoon was bright, clear blue skies with white caps blowing in off the strait. The fir and cedar swayed in the wind from the southeast. I could hear the surf against the headland at Raker's Point. The road leading to the reserve was deserted. The remnants of the barricade lay scattered on either side. Sofas with their stuffing in the wind, charred lumber, a broken dining room set, smoking fifty-five-gallon barrels. All the young First Nations men had gone home. There wasn't any police presence anymore.

I walked over to Chief's house. Hammered on the door. No one answered. His truck was gone. I walked back to Louie's house on the chance that she was there. Something in the kids' room had been worrying me. The house looked the same, except that while the door was still broken, plywood had been nailed over the opening. The cardboard boxes I'd seen sprouting up through the grass on my first visit were now composting into the lawn. The rusting tricycle handlebars jutted into the air like antlers to ward off evil.

I went around back and knocked again. I heard shuffling feet, and Louie came to the door. I held up the girls' framed picture, the one I'd borrowed.

Louie's face was tired. Not beaten, but it had that psychic numbness to it. Her face and soul had been broken, repaired, and broken again.

"You remembered." She took the picture frame from my hand. "At least I've got their picture now." She stepped back and said, "Come in." She sat down at the kitchen table and played with the strands of her hair. I sat down on another chair.

"I got nothing to offer you," she said.

"Don't need anything, thanks."

"You found them, didn't you?"

"No, Louie, I did not. They've disappeared and I'm running out of places to look. I figured your husband had them. But then he's dead."

"You killed him, didn't you?"

"I did not. I had a word with him over at Nemo's, as you said. But someone else killed him. Tried to make it look like me."

Louie didn't respond. Didn't make eye contact. Looked down at the tabletop. Then she said, "Don't make much difference. I'm glad he's gone."

"Louie. Listen. Can you tell me what he did when he was here last? Can you close your eyes and run me through it? Anything? Little details?"

"Don't want to talk about him."

I needed her to open a crack. "A little memory, a small detail might help me find them," I said. "I think they're still alive. I'm sure of it, but not for long."

She looked surprised and doubtful. She was close to rock bottom but hadn't given up a mother's hope.

"Well, he came back as usual. He'd been drinking. He still had the bottle with him. He tried to get me drinking too, then as usual you know, he'd be getting after me. I wasn't that interested, so he started getting mean and that. Nothing much else."

"Did he go anywhere in particular in the house?"

"What do you mean, particular?"

"Did he go outside? Did he go into one specific room?"

"What are you getting at?"

"I think he may have hidden something when he was here."

"Like what?" I looked at her face. She was thinking, running her mind through a memory palace, as they say.

"Drugs, maybe money."

"Where would he find drugs or money?"

"I think he was tracking your daughters all along, first on the mainland, and then when they came back to the Island."

"He didn't say anything about the girls. He hardly cared. He did go out to the boat. Spent some time out there."

"Anywhere else he went?"

"I remember after. . . I was lying on the couch. He spent time looking through the kids' stuff in the closet in their bedroom."

"What's in there?"

"I'll show you."

Louie got up and I followed her into the bedroom. She opened the closet door. It was a walk-in closet, but there was no space to walk in.

"Who did this?" I asked.

"I did," Louie said. "I couldn't stand it anymore. After the shooting when I came back and the house was such a mess and the place had been tossed, I couldn't. I couldn't. I stuffed it all back in there. Stuff was missing too. The big bear. I used to sit with them when they were little, and we'd have tea. I made the bear from fur. Put a zipper in the back. I stuffed it with old clothes. Iona and Skye when they were little thought it was store-bought. Why would someone take the bear?"

I closed my eyes. I let the room absorb my thoughts. I waited for past images I'd seen. And there in the corner, all patched together with rabbit and fox fur was a chubby honey bear.

"You say the room was tossed?"

"Yeah. I was pissed. What right do they have?"

"Who?"

"The cops. You guys. It was you, Tony, and some cops who were there. And the men with the guns. And all this. Nothing has brought my babies back."

"Anyone come by the house before you got back in it? Anyone come by after you got settled in?"

Louie started thinking. I felt she was on the edge, and I was losing her, so I said, "Maybe Tony? Chief? Anyone from outside the reserve?"

"No one from outside would get in. The barricades kept them out. Tony brought me back after I identified Ian's body, but that's the last I've seen of Tony. Before I got back, Chief said he'd hang around to look after the place and he came around more than usual when I was settled. He kept asking if I was okay. Once he asked if anything was missing. Seemed a bit weird to me but I think he blames himself for the girls."

"I went looking for him earlier," I said. "Where's he likely to hang out if he's still on the reserve?"

"I don't much know. Maybe he'd be up past the cannery at Raker's Point. I know he likes to go up there."

I got the sense she stumbled on a memory and kept it to herself like maybe she'd been up there with him sometime, but I let it slide.

"Louie, I want you to promise me something. Stay put. I'll be back tonight. Don't go out. Don't talk to anyone."

She didn't get up from the table. She tilted her head toward me and said, "Okay." With no conviction, hope dripped away from her lips.

When I closed the back door, I could hear her muffled crying and imagined she'd put her face down into her arms.

CHAPTER 48

The cannery was on private property, adjacent to First Nations land at the end of a cove that was hedged in by a small headland on the north and Raker's Point on the south. Raker's Point was an imposing, downward-sloping escarpment that overhung the sea, capped by a massive rock layer. The softer layers beneath were continually being eroded, the sediment carried farther north where the sand was laid down in a benign series of beaches that formed the reserve's shoreline.

A narrow path led up from the reserve's main habitat. At the highest point, there was a dry-stone wall where the path passed through from the original reserve to the cannery. Years ago, it was a thriving operation, when the salmon runs were massive, and the waters yielded a sustainable harvest. But that was long gone with greed, overfishing, and factory farms.

Tony's truck sat off the road, near where the path began. It wasn't unusual to see vehicles parked anywhere, since there were no real roads apart from Cougar Creek Road.

The cannery and its wharf bordered the deep water where trawlers once came with their catches. The cannery stretched cold and empty before me. I stood on the wharf for a moment. The waves slapped up from underneath and through the boards with the high tide. This was where I'd stashed the cocaine. Where Murphy had tortured Ivan Barsukov. It might also be an ideal place to keep two girls in storage.

I thought I'd put it all together. The Strang operation using Mike Burns and Laura Wells had the girls involved in moving drugs across the city. Ian Stewart followed them, figuring he'd make a score when the opportunity arose. Chief, I believed, was looking out for his nieces. He'd set them up at Mrs. Milroy's house, but when he found out Ian Stewart was tailing them, he started following Stewart. Then things must have started to get out of Chief's control. I got on to Chief when Louie mentioned that he came back, searched the boat, rummaged in the kid's room, and asked about stuff going missing.

I pulled my Beretta from the ankle holster and entered the cannery. The light outside was dropping quickly with the autumn sun. It would be dark within half an hour. I searched the rooms, looking for concealed doors or hatches in the floor. I raced the dying light.

In one room, a door led to a smaller room that led to a storage closet. The room grabbed my interest because there were sheets of new plastic laid out on the floor. Nylon rope, duct tape, and a box cutter on a side table. The storage closet was dark and bare. My duffle bag with my basic investigative stuff had burned when the Westie Van caught fire the night the homestead burned to the ground, or I'd have my flashlight.

I remembered I still had the matches from the bar, where I'd bought cigarettes for Jimmy. I struck one and let it burn until the nerves in my fingers made me drop it on the floor. Unlike the rest of the cannery, the floor here wasn't dusty. I struck another match and checked the closet walls. I saw hinges, but no door handle or latch. I struck another match and felt with my fingers. I felt an edge, but nothing moved when I pulled on it. I backed into the larger room, where there was still some light. I saw a nail hammered into the wall as if used for a hook at one time. It was loose enough to wiggle out. I used the box cutter to hammer the nail into the base of the hinges, pushing out the bolts that held them together. It took a while, but eventually, I was able to pry the door off the wall from the hinge side. It was pitch black on the other side of the door.

I knew I was on the right track because I could smell urine and feces, and when I struck a few more matches, the shape of the room became clear. There was a mattress in the corner. Some soiled blankets and sheets. Chains were attached to the wall with two padlocks and on the floor was a pail filled with human waste. But no girls. I lit one more match and swung it around the entire room. Then I left the room and started searching other areas in the cannery.

In one room I broke through thin wood planks nailed over a door. I lit another match and saw that the door was sealed by a rusty hasp latch with a padlock. I took careful aim with the Beretta and blew the latch free. I swung the door open. A figure loomed in the shadows at the back of a small room. My heart raced and, in an instant, I saw the enemy coming through the morning mist at our position in Afghanistan. I saw Mr. Madson with his axe. I saw by candlelight the glowing eyes of a man I thought was my father, the blood, and the broken teeth. I held the Beretta in both hands.

"Don't fucking move or I'll shoot," I said, and waited. The figure didn't move. His huge shape stood there. Still holding the gun, I lit a match and stepped closer. Then I lit another. And another. Until I realized why the figure didn't move. It was the honey bear. Five feet tall and two feet wide. I felt its shape, the stuffing inside. Something wasn't right. I reached behind the bear, opened the zipper, and reached in. The honey bear wasn't stuffed with old clothes; it was stuffed with money. I stood back and he stared me down.

CHAPTER 49

A few minutes later I scrambled through salal, six feet high on either side on a path that led up from the cannery in switchbacks, ending at Raker's Point. It was a long hike that opened onto grassy crags with Garry oaks and Arbutus eking out footholds in the shallow soil between the rocks. The point sloped down in a jut of rock toward the strait.

On top, a small fire fluttered, and behind the flames was a smudge of movement. The darkness made this place alien to me. I got close enough to make out Chief and the twins. The girls were tied together back-to-back, duct-taped, and sitting by the fire. I saw a metallic glint in the firelight. Chief had a rifle, and he pointed the barrel at me.

"Don't come any farther, Jack," Chief said. "You don't want to be here."

"And why is that?"

"This is not your business now."

"You don't have to do this," I said. "It doesn't have to end this way." The Beretta was still in my hand. "Tell me you're a good man, Chief. Say it's so."

The silent tension hummed like a snare drum.

"It's not so. Where the money goes, you find the ugliness."

"Let the girls go. I can take them down the path. Louie will want to see them."

Chief waved his rifle around. "It's way past that now," he said. "Can't you see there's no turning back?"

"Talk to me then. Tell me how we got to be here. We've come a long way from searching for two missing girls. Back then I believed you wanted me to find them."

"I did. Believe me, I did."

There was a pleading quality to his voice. I sensed that he no longer thought that he was the Chief, the man who pleaded with me in Brogans. He'd been a noble man, deserving respect, but he had fallen prey to a trap both set for him and made by himself.

"Something's been bothering me," I said. "How'd you happen to come into Brogans to ask me to find these girls, when you knew all along? Was it more about me than them?"

"You always were too smart. Thought you bought into it."

"I did. You had me until I got back over here. That was it, wasn't it?"

"It started out that way. I wanted you to find the girls. I wanted you back on the Island. I needed you to stir it up to make a takedown happen with Otto Strang. He's had me under his thumb all my life. He's had everyone here under his thumb. You were the answer. It worked, didn't it? It worked. And the Russians? I figured you'd deal with them too. The force has done bugger all over the years. I watched these guys with money and connections come in and set up any operation they wanted. Strang was the worst. He preyed on the vulnerable."

"Tell me where it all went wrong." I took a step forward and leaned against a rocky ridge. I was partly in shadow, with intermittent light from the fire flickering across me.

"Don't move any closer."

"So, tell me. We've got all night here."

Chief was silent for a long beat. "I had tabs on them when they were at the boarding house and going to school," he said. "But over the summer, they got mixed up delivering drugs. I got a hunch the vice-principal gave them the connection. That's when they moved out to 394 Anderson and stayed with that young couple. I still had a guy watching the kids and the couple. I found out their names are Mike Burns and Laura Wells. The woman drove them to exchange drugs for money. I wondered why she sent the kids to make the exchange. That couple worked for Strang, and they were grooming them to be couriers and something more than that. Then Ian Stewart, their father, showed up and started following them. Most of the time, the girls were supervised, but even so, I thought it strange that drug dealers would trust kids they picked up on the street. They didn't since they watched them. Like it was a test. I couldn't get too close. Neither could Ian Stewart. But I knew if I waited long enough, I'd get a chance. I knew Ian was thinking that too."

"The two dead guys at 3360 West 32nd?" I asked. "That was you?"

"That was Ian Stewart. He went in for torture."

"Torture? So, Ian Stewart didn't kill them?" I asked.

"That's what I originally thought, but now I know he killed them. He wasn't the sharpest knife in the drawer, but he realized he couldn't leave those Russians alive after they'd seen his face."

"Are you lying to me? It's you who killed those two Russians?"

"I swear it, Jack. I didn't. I never set foot in that house."

"So how is it we're sitting here talking with this mess around us?"

"It started with the kids when they moved from Mrs. Milroy's home and were manipulated by this couple Burns and Wells. It was then Ian Stewart showed up and started following them. The guy I had on following the kids, also started following Stewart. But he fucked up. He lost track of the kids when they made their regular delivery. That day the kids did not come back to Laura Wells' car. They disappeared. I worried that something horrible had happened to them involving the drugs and money. My thoughts ran crazy. Did they take the drugs instead of delivering them, or did they take the money and not return to Laura Well's car? I knew they were in trouble then. That's when I hired you to find them. I knew they were running scared and hoped they'd go back to the Island."

"You are not telling me the whole truth," I said.

"Ian Stewart was in the wind and the girls were gone. I figured the girls would run to the Island, so I kept a watch on both ferry routes. Sure enough, they showed up, and so did Stewart. I followed Stewart. I knew he'd lead me to the girls. I didn't know for sure they had the money and the drugs. I was guessing since no one else seemed to have it. The girls got picked up by a Blue Civic in Nanaimo. Stewart followed the Civic and I followed Stewart."

"Now let me guess. Ian Stewart tortured the two guys in the Civic. And you found them."

I could see Chief getting more agitated. The twins were squirming in their ropes and duct tape.

"Not exactly," he said.

"You killed them?"

"No, I lost Stewart on the way up the Island Highway."

"You're kidding me? Do you expect me to believe you? When you hired me, why didn't you tell me the whole story—the kids being groomed as couriers, how much danger they must have been in, Ian Stewart showing up and following them."

"I told you what I knew at the time," he said.

I didn't believe him.

"Did you find the Honda Civic?"

"No but like everyone else I heard about it," he said.

"So, who killed the two men in the Civic?" The police have not released the details, but I know those two men were shot in the feet and hands and then bludgeoned to death."

"Ian Stewart killed them. He took the drugs, the money, and Iona and Skye."

"That's an assumption that Ian Stewart caught up to the Honda Civic."

"When the murders were reported in the community," he said, "I started to look for Ian Stewart and like he always does, he showed up at Louie's place. From there I followed him around. Something switched in me. I started thinking about the money and how much those drugs were worth on the street. I know I wasn't thinking straight. I got so angry. It was as if everything going on in my whole life boiled over."

"What is it that kept you from thinking straight? Finding your nieces alive and returning them to their mother, or finding the drugs and money?"

"I lost it outside Nemo's when you saved those drugged-up women. I needed to find out where the girls were and where the drugs and money were hidden. That prick deserved to die."

"Well, how did that work out for you? Hell of a thing to do, Chief, clocking an old friend with a sap."

"I had to get him to talk. He needed to tell me where the girls were and where he'd hidden the drugs, so I dragged him into the shoreline undergrowth, took the butt of the pool cue, and threatened him."

"And he told you where the twins were being held. But he didn't tell you about the drugs or the money, did he?"

"Bastard. He'd give up the girls but not what I really wanted."

"But you had a sense of where the drugs and the money were, didn't you? You found the girls in the cannery, and you kept them there until you could find the drugs and money. But you never found the drugs or the money, did you?"

"Someone beat me to the drugs on the night of the firefight with the Russians."

"I did, Chief. I found the drugs in the derelict boat behind Louie's house. I used those drugs to convince the Russians to be involved in Otto Strang's takedown."

I kept quiet about the honey bear and let him think the money was still out there.

"You know you're not a killer, really, don't you, Chief? So, the girls? They are a problem, aren't they? Think about it. You could have been a hero. You found the girls. You could have returned them to their mother."

Chief couldn't answer. He stared across at me with the fire and his tied-up nieces between us.

"Chief, you know what I think? You're a good guy who made a wrong turn. You went down a dark alley and can't find your way back. After you killed Stewart, you could have taken me out to sea and let me die, but you didn't. You put me soaking wet on a beach at the high tide line, with only my feet in the water, and you didn't leave me too long, did you?"

"I couldn't, could I?"

"You're not a bad guy. You're not a guy who kills people on a regular basis. You're not a guy who kills kids, are you?"

"You don't see. I needed money. Trust me, I needed it, badly. I was hanging on. Don't you see the temptation that money is?"

"The money you gave me back at Brogans," I said. "Where'd that come from?"

"It belonged to the band."

"For fuck's sake, why do you need Russian money so badly? It wasn't just money you needed to pay back the band, was it?"

"I owed Strang money. Loans for gambling debts. And I'd built up more debts gambling on the mainland. Once the claws are in you, it's like a cougar on your back and you can't shake it off."

"The bracelets from the girls? The photos?"

"I took a chance that you could help me get out of this. Strang knew I'd hired you. He saw this as an opportunity to get you back on the Island so he could get back at you. I gave that stuff to Strang so he could use it to get you to go to the big house. I prayed you'd find a way to kill him. I was sinking."

"Did you give him a photo of my daughter and her mother?"

"No. That wasn't me."

"You don't think I know what happens when the bottom drops off quickly," I said, "and you find yourself in over your head?"

"But Jack. I need the money. That's why I am up here. I've threatened the girls to tell me where the money is, but they won't tell me. They say they do not know where their father hid it."

"How is being up here going to convince them?"

"They're afraid of heights like their mother. If they won't tell me, they know they're going over the cliff."

I looked over at the twins who were terrified.

"It's not too late," I said. "You can be a hero. I know where the money is. We can all walk down from here."

"It is too late. I'm not a hero now. These girls know what kind of man I am. My sister will know who her brother really is. The band will know. I can't go back."

A twig snapped to our right and Chief fired the rifle. I saw the butt of a black-tail deer hop over a mossy crag and disappear in a hollow beneath an Arbutus tree's warped trunk. It provided a distraction. I leaped forward, drove my legs toward Chief, saw him turn toward where I'd been, and felt our bodies collide.

I took him across the chest with my shoulder. My pain was like a spike in my arm. I caught his wrist and pinned his arm back, so the rifle barrel was pointing at the stars. I heard the girls' muffled struggle. As Chief tumbled backward toward the edge where the escarpment dropped into the sea below, I saw the rope tied around his other wrist. Iona and Skye were on the other end and were being pulled along the sloping surface toward where the point dropped into the sea. Chief dug in with his heels as we both slid closer to the lip. I smashed the arm holding the rifle against the ground and the gun flew into the darkness.

Chief's fist came back at me and caught my wounded shoulder. My eyes watered. My teeth ground against each other and my scream was pure adrenaline. I kicked him in the face and grabbed at his leg as he slid down the slope, with the twins trapped in the tangled rope he held. I let go of Chief and held onto the girls to keep them from going over the edge. What strength I had in my shoulder was fading. With my knee jammed between the rocks, I wedged my leg into a crevice.

The rope attached to Chief played out as he neared the cliff's edge and caught in one last cleft in the eroded surface. I held tight to the girls, and Chief slid off the edge. But the taut rope in the cleft held him in the air dangling just below me. I pulled the box cutter from a pocket and cut the rope near the girls freeing them from their connection to their uncle.

I gripped the taut rope locked in the cleft. In the near-total darkness of passing out from the pain in my shoulder and calf, I leaned over the edge. I dropped the loose end and gripped the taut rope that held Chief as he dangled above the crashing surf below. I pulled hand over hand, and his body rose in the air. "Stay with me," I said.

I tried one more hand over hand, but gravity was against me. A knife flashed in Chief's free hand. Then he severed the rope and dropped like a stone into the dark and raging sea.

Iona and Skye shimmied away from the edge with their hands still tied together. I pulled myself from the crevice, back to where the land was solid and the wind less intense. I toppled backward onto a bed of moss.

The box cutter lay open on the ground. I got up and walked toward the twins who were still too close to the drop-off to be safe. They huddled together, tied, gagged, and afraid to move.

I cut the duct tape from their wrists and ankles and removed their gags.

"Let's take you to your mother," I said. "She's been worried about you for a long time."

They followed me down the path to the cannery. They shied back as if thinking I might lock them in again. I left them outside. "I need to get something," I said.

I went into the room grabbed the bear and hoisted it over my good shoulder.

"That thing. Where did that come from?" Iona said. "We always hated that bear. Couldn't tell mom that since she made it for us."

"It scared us really," Skye said. "What are you going to do with it?"

"I think I know someone who can use this old bear."

When we passed Tony's truck, I put the bear in the passenger seat. The bear filled it up, and I could imagine Tony and the bear stuffed in the cab as they went for a ride together.

Before I took them home, I sat the girls down on the ground beside Tony's truck.

"You've heard what your uncle said up on the point. But I want to hear your story. The police will want to talk to you. Your mom and I can help you with that later, but I need to know how you got mixed up in this."

I sat beside them, my arms wrapped around my knees, and waited for them to speak.

The girls were silent for a few beats, then Iona spoke. "We had to leave the reserve. We weren't safe."

Skye nodded.

"I understand," I said. "What happened in Vancouver?"

"Our uncle found us," Skye said. "That was a good thing. He found a safe place for us to live at Mrs. Milroy's. We finished grade nine in the spring, but when summer came, we started hanging out at night, going to Stanley Park, and one day we met these two guys, Sammy, and Frankie. We hung out getting a suntan, smoking weed, and drinking beer, then one thing led to another." She fell silent.

I didn't interrupt and waited.

"At first it was fun," Iona said. "They gave us money to meet people and sell drugs for them. They watched us and people would come up to us in the park and we would sell these packets for cash. And we got to keep some money. But then they had us take larger amounts to houses at night and by the end of summer we had more money than we ever had in our lives."

"Was that all you had to do?" This was a difficult question that I thought they wouldn't answer.

They looked at each other with the sad faces.

Skye nodded and Iona said. "Yes. We did what most men want."

"I understand," I didn't press for details. The police would do that. "Was that at the end of the summer before you returned to school?"

"Yes, but we only stayed in school in September for three weeks," Iona said, "before Sammy and Frankie took us to meet Mike and Laura. That's when we left Mrs. Milroy's house."

"Can you tell me about the day you left Vancouver to come back to the Island?"

"One day Laura was taking us in her car as she did once a week to this house where we'd take a backpack into the house and the guys in the house would give us a backpack back. We took in drugs and left with the money. We did this for a few weeks. Each time the backpacks were heavier.

"That day in October when we went into the house, we found the two guys dead on the floor."

"You went in the front door of the house," I asked.

"No. We always used the lane and entered by the back door. That's what the guys told us to do."

"Why did they have you do that?" I thought of Reynold's surveillance operation.

"That's what the guys did to make sure no one saw us."

"And what was it like in the house that day?" I said.

"The place was trashed. Skye and I were in a panic, but she went to where the guys hid their money, and it was in a compartment beneath a kitchen cupboard as usual in the backpack. We saw an opportunity and took both backpacks. We didn't go back to Laura's car but instead took the buses to the ferry."

"You didn't stop to see anyone?" I said.

"We saw a school friend, but we were in a hurry," Skye said. And I thought I'd get a tat at this tattoo parlor. We went in there, but decided we needed to get going."

"Your father?" I said.

"If it wasn't for him," Iona said, "we'd never have left the Island, and all this wouldn't have happened."

"I know about Sammy and Frankie and that they picked you up in Nanaimo," I said. "I am aware of what happened to them."

Both started to cry. They held each other.

"Your father killed them, didn't he?"

Through their tears, they both nodded.

"You saw him put them in the trunk? And your father kept you captive in the cannery and took the backpacks."

"Yes. He made us do things with him. He threatened to kill us." Iona said. "Then our uncle found us, but he didn't let us go. He wanted to know where the drugs and money were hidden, but we didn't know. He didn't believe us. That is why he was going to throw us off Raker's Point."

They cried some more. They didn't need to know about the shovels Sammy and Frankie had in the trunk of the Honda Civic and what they might have been planning for them at the end of that logging spur.

"Let's get you home to your mom," I said.

When we went inside the house, Louie was sleeping on the couch. The two girls woke her up. They acted more like the kids they were than whoever they thought they were. I left them, walked out into the night, felt in my pocket, and switched off my recorder that I'd set in motion before I approached Chief on the point, and during the questioning of the twins, then I phoned Tony and left a message for him about the bear.

CHAPTER 50

Over the next few weeks, I needed to finish a few things. I was pleased to hear from Murphy that the force found a gun beneath the trash in the alley behind Nemo's. The ballistics matched with the bullets in the Russian's foreheads found at West 32nd Street and in the hands of Hans One and Two. Murphy told me that Reilly asked Conner to inquire about the surveillance team of Reynolds and his partner with a focus on why there were no photographs showing the twins or the dead Russians entering the house. Nothing came from that inquiry. But the Combined Forces Special Enforcement Unit – British Columbia investigated the 394 Anderson address. Initially, Mike Burns and Laura Wells were nowhere to be found. However, a week later their bodies were found floating in the Burrard Inlet near the Vancouver shipping docks. Their deaths remain unsolved. An APB was issued for Ivan Barsukov but he'd disappeared.

The force found Tyler's bones buried in the tunnel leading from the homestead to his mother's property. With that discovery, the memories came back more clearly than before. Also, I turned over to Murphy the digital card from my recorder that had contained the conversation with the Chief and my interview with the twins.

Tyler was buried in the Shaplow Cemetery. Tony paid for all of it, and I stood weeping with Mrs. Madson as they lowered the tiny coffin into the ground. The divers found more skeletal remains in Shaplow Lake.

After the forensics teams on the mainland analyzed the bones from the Strang tunnels, they were returned to the town for burial in a mass grave in the Shaplow Cemetery. Tony found the money for a monument.

The people who were found in the cages had been taken into custody and physically assessed. Police and social services documented their stories. Canadian Immigration Services integrated the victims into society.

Tony became the band leader on the reserve. He was determined to make right whatever he could. There was a lot of cash. He set up a few safety deposit box accounts in various cities on the Island for when it might be needed. But for the bulk of the money, he decided to deposit it offshore in shell companies, so it would not be traced back to him or the band. Louie got enough to repair her home and get the girls settled in. Tony gave me some cash for all my trouble, along with cash for anyone I knew who'd been involved.

He bought the cannery and turned it into a small business incubator where band members could start businesses, learn about business plans, and have a decent chance of success. Already, there were a few businesses starting to thrive. A fishing company focused on guided sport fishing. A courier company picked up and delivered on the Island and between Vancouver Island and the mainland. Louie and a few partners began knitting traditional sweaters again, and Iona and Skye were involved as well. Computer-savvy First Nations teenagers started a consulting company and built in an educational component so anyone could learn computer skills at any level. Seemed too good to be true that so much light was shining now, considering it was spawned from darkness.

I was anxious to know the DNA results from the bones that came back over but I was left without closure. Kat and Peter's bones were not among those found. Now all I could do was tell myself there was still hope. I set up a file and planned to research foster homes they might have been sent to. I was hopeful.

Two months passed by, taking us through the winter rain and into a slow protracted spring. Mark who had disappeared on his Ranger Tug, called, and offered to take me across the strait to Vancouver.

First, I visited Lobelia's Lair. She remembered me from the fall. I told her the good news about the twins because I sensed she cared. She tattooed a small blue butterfly on my right pectoral. It was a whim.

I drove a rental to the marina on the delta and stared at the carnage that was left. I couldn't blame Mark for wanting to distance himself.

I phoned Geena, the twin's high-school friend. I told her that Iona and Skye were safe and back on the reserve. Didn't get into any details but hooked her up with a number she could phone or text to contact them. Figured it couldn't hurt to keep them in touch. Finally, I dropped by Mrs. Milroy's house and let her know the kids were safe at home. She was delighted to hear the news. Said she'd worried quite a lot over the winter.

Then I arranged to meet Stacie.

I came early and sat in a back booth at Brogans in West End Vancouver, facing the door with my back against the wall. I nursed a Coke Classic and tried not to think about the sugar in each can. There was more danger of certain death in one can than in any Jameson-and-Guinness combination. But I stayed with my program to be clean, at least for now. I'd done what I'd come over for and tied up all the loose ends.

I took a sip of the Coke Classic. I'd tried the Zero and the Diet, but neither cut it for me. I was on the edge, even with the sugar in soft drinks.

Stacie walked in wearing hiking boots, black Levi's, and a blue-and-white plaid shirt over a Tee.

I stood up and then sat down. She slid around beside me, leaned over, and kissed me on the lips. A kiss I couldn't quite interpret. But it got me interested.

"Drink?" I said.

"The usual. Single malt." She nodded to the bartender, and her drink arrived a moment later.

"Good to see you," I said. "Busy?"

"I helped Jessica and Del settle in Seattle. For Jessica."

"Thanks," I said.

"Del's done the state bar refresher. She started a practice. You should think about visiting them, seeing the Pacific Northwest, or Cascadia as they call it now."

"Don't bother. I can't risk getting back into their lives. That's the point, isn't it?"

"Neither wants to shut you out," she said. "What have you been doing with yourself for the last two months?"

I told her all the stuff. Showed her my tattoo.

"You're such a kid." Then she leaned toward me. "Girl investigator brings brass knuckles for both hands, walks into an office, breezes past reception into the target's office. Says, "Remember me?" Hits her twice with her fists, kick-boxes her in the neck, and knees her between the legs. Gets a flash of recognition back. The target isn't going to be cruising anymore, but if she does, she'll be a bottom feeder."

I blew out the long draft of air I'd been holding in my chest. "I'd stay away from that investigator," I said. "Nobody's going to mess with her again."

"That's what I figured when I heard the story," Stacie said.

"You still playing for the other team?"

"I'm a free agent now."

"Good to know."

"What are you going to do?" Stacie asked.

"I need a rest. I need to sort out how to heal. Mark has a line on a float cabin on the West coast of Vancouver Island. I'm going to hole up there. Not tell anyone."

"You told me."

"You're welcome to come and visit anytime. It's not much, and there's no room for privacy."

"I can handle that. You might see me one day." Stacie took a beat. "Come back to the security gig with me. I always have work for occasional bodyguards."

I gulped down more Coke Classic.

Stacie continued. "You know how I said you didn't look at all like your parents, and Strang said you were picked up by them and they weren't related to you? You might want to think about your real name."

"Real name? Like whom I am?"

She saw me fiddling with the recorder in my jacket pocket.

"Have you done any more recording?" she asked.

"Back on the Island did you listen to everything I recorded?"

"No. I started, but you know, then I couldn't. Too personal. Listening further would have been an invasion. But I did wonder what's been driving you."

"You want that in words?"

"I think I do?" she said.

"I'll let you know when I figure it out. I got issues."

"Right."

She got up to leave, and I passed her a few packages from Tony. "You might be needing these. I owe you a lot more."

She put the money in her purse.

"You sure do, Jack McQueen. I plan to collect one day."

She swirled around with her purse on her shoulder and walked out with all the swagger of the toughest girl in town.

"Goodbye, Stacie," I said to myself, and I could hear her whisper in my ear. "You're not getting off that easy, Jack." And then she was gone

I clicked on the recorder.

"Caught on her words, a broken bird can fly."

A few minutes later, I left Brogans and started down Denman toward Georgia, not really knowing what might be coming around the corner. A track from Bad Man's Blood by Ray Bonneville started up inside my head and was dueling it out with the best of Roy Buchanan's Guitar on Fire. It was a good mix.

Sort of like a shot of J and G.

Acknowledgements

Patricia Carroll for inspiring me and for beta-reading early drafts. She has been a keen developmental and line editor.

Bette Armstrong and family for being there for me during my childhood and beyond.

Margaret Hudson who also has been a supporter in beginning and final stages of reading.

Renni Browne, founder of The Editorial Department, former senior editor at William Morrow and coauthor of the bestselling Self-Editing for Fiction Writers, for her help with this manuscript through developmental and copy edits. Her encouragement and advice have been invaluable.

Ross Browne, President and Director of Author Services for the Editorial Department for his guidance.

John Robert Marlow, author, editor and screenwriter for his assistance with line-editing.

Heather Scott, Brett Scott, Jillian Scott and Isabella Scott for their encouragement and inspiration.

About the Author

David P. Fraser has lived in the UK, Canada, the US and Mexico, but now he lives on an island in the Pacific. His poetry and short stories have appeared in many journals and anthologies. Also, he has published six collections of poetry.

Now he focuses on writing mystery thrillers. When he is not writing he likes to hike in the mountains and along the coastline trails, as well as ski and play tennis.

Dead or Disappeared is his first Jack McQueen novel.
His second McQueen thriller in the series,
Dead by the Hands of Other Men,
will be available in 2024.

Contact: ascentaspirations@gmail.com